Dr Kristin Melina is a forensic consultant for the VFSC. On a hot night she finds herself at a crime scene where a man has been decapitated and his wife almost beaten to death. Clues indicate that the assault is the work of Walter Dunn, a closer friend of the couple. But as Dr Melina and her partner Frank Moore track down the killer, someone gets to him before they do, and they now have a double homicide on their hands. Caught in a strange triangle between those left behind and those who are forced to move on, Dr Melina finds her life turned upside down as she relentlessly tracks down the real murderer before she becomes the next victim.

LAURENT BOULANGER is the author of the critically acclaimed novel 'The Girl From France', winner of the 2014 Paris Book Festival awards, and 'Better Dead Than Never', 2014 eLit Bronze Winner for Best Multicultural Fiction. 'First Kill' won a Tom Howard Mystery contest Honorable Mention for Best Crime Fiction.

FIRST KILL

FIRST KILL

Laurent Boulanger

SNIPER BOOKS

Sniper Books

Copyright © 2018 Laurent Boulanger

First published in Australia by Sniper Books
Sniper Books is an imprint of Lake Ozark Press

Typeset in Garamond

Cover design © 2018 Lake Ozark Press

FOR
Jennifer Dabbs

CHAPTER ONE

The call came at 2.15 a.m. on Thursday the 20th of February.

No one ever called me in the middle of the night, unless it was murder.

The hottest February for over a hundred years had swept over the city. I remember the day clearly, not only because of the middle-of-the-night telephone call, but also because of the *Herald-Sun*'s headline 'Sizzler of the Century', which would be splattered over its a.m. edition in a few hours.

Lying naked in bed, soaked from head to toe, still feeling the full effect of the forty-one degree temperature from the previous day, I longed for some sleep. Somehow, in the middle of this heat, I managed a sore throat, which glued me to bed for the entire previous weekend.

Melbourne was one of the worst cities in the world for meteorologists and citizens alike. Days, which promised to be filled with sunshine, ended in a downpour.

Whenever Melburnians decided to wear jumpers and winter woollies, because of a cold morning snap, they ended up swimming in perspiration for the rest of the day.

On the floor, next to my bed, were my panties, bra, and a half-filled, plastic bottle of purified water. I'd been drinking since I got to bed to combat loss of fluid from the heat.

A street light outside illuminated the bedroom brightly enough to be annoying

The sheets on my back were soaked with sweat. Flipping from one side of the bed to the other, I was desperately seeking a dry spot. I turned my blue pillow over every fifteen minutes. Perspiration had given the pillow an unpleasant bittersweet smell.

My clammy, swollen fingers kept brushing my auburn hair behind my ears.

A car outside drove past while I reached for the telephone on my side-table.

My throat was still tight when I answered the call.

'This better be good,' I said to the voice on the other end of the line.

'Oh, it's good all right,' the voice answered, unable to hide the excitement in its tone.

If I hadn't known better, I would have thought Frank Moore's voice was that of a serial killer, or some journalist, who got off every time he heard someone got butchered in the middle of the night.

But Senior Sergeant Frank Moore was not a serial killer, nor a journalist.

He was head of the Crime Scene Division at the Victorian Forensic Science Centre (VFSC) on Forensic Drive, Macleod. He thrived on really bad cases. It gave him the chance to play cat and mouse with human vile, be it serial killers, child molesters or rapists.

Six months ago, I became the first unsworn civilian authorised to conduct both crime-scene examination and homicidal investigation whenever it suited the VFSC and the Criminal Investigation Branch (CIB). The Deputy Commissioner of Police had been opposed to this project since the beginning of my appointment. Prior to that day, I worked as an academic consultant for whoever was willing to pay for my opinion.

In ten minutes I was showered, making as little noise as possible. Michael, my twelve-year-old son, was sleeping in the room next to mine, and I hated to think I'd woken him up.

By the time Frank Moore parked his white Ford Falcon with government plates in the driveway, I was already downstairs from my second-floor apartment on Chapel Street.

Wearing navy slacks with a white blouse, I would have

2

rather worn a dress with this heat. But I knew better than going to a crime scene and looking too pretty. Men lusted after me more often than I cared to satisfy them even though I never considered myself to be Vogue material.

The air outside was dense and warm. It was hard to believe it was the middle of the night.

'You're still using Velvet soap,' Frank said, sniffing the air as I jumped in the passenger seat.

'And this Homebrand shampoo is killing your hair,' I laughed while gazing at his thinning hair. The air conditioning caused a tightening sensation in my throat, but the rest of my body was shivering in delight.

'Ha, ha,' he answered dryly. 'Very funny, Ms Malina'.

'Dr Kristin Malina, if you don't mind.' Kritina Oliveira Dos Malina was my birth name, but I dropped the middle names of my Brazilian ancestors when I turned eighteen. And I only insisted on the Dr in front of my name to remind others, especially men, I was up to their level.

'Oh, for Christ's sake. I don't tag my friggin' B.A. behind my name every time I need to be announced. What is it, you've got an inferiority complex or something? I know you're a woman, and that's fine with me. You're better than all the guys I know out there. I wouldn't be driving at two-thirty in the morning to your place if it wasn't true.'

I sighed, but laughed on the inside. I found it funny that he took it so seriously. 'All right, made your point. But I'm a thirty-nine year-old single mother, and you're forty-seven, in bad need of a hair transplant, never-married and horny as a cat on heat. I think I've got the right to be cautious.'

He threw his indicator to the left, turned onto Alma Road and said, 'Jesus, Malina, you sound like I'm trying to come on to you. What do you think? I've got nothing better to do all day than think about sex? You've really got some twisted, preconceived ideas about what men are like.'

'I never said anything about your sex life.'

'You just compared me to a horny cat.'

'You're misinterpreting everything. I said nothing about your sex life.'

'You just did.'

'No I didn't.'

3

'Yes, you did.'

I gave up. 'Oh, what does it matter, anyway? Are you going to tell me what's going down, or are we going to argue all night like a couple of teenagers?'

He shook his head slowly, and I knew he was hurt.

I liked Frank Moore very much, but receding hairlines and thick, dark moustaches didn't turn me on. He was far from being ugly, but then, there was nothing physically attractive about him either. If I'd met him in the street, I'd have never looked twice. A prominent nose, a strong jaw line, and two beady green eyes. He stood at around one hundred and eighty centimetres, tall enough to stare down at me, and weighed a reasonable eighty-something kilos. He reminded me of a crocodile, as if he was ready to bite someone's head off. Like most men of his age, his belly could have done with toning-up.

Frank always wore the same pair of cream-coloured slacks and a white shirt two-sizes too small, causing his underarms to produce two horrible yellow stains. Maybe it made him feel muscular or something. And his car stunk like an ashtray. He made an effort not to smoke when I was around because he knew how much I hated it.

I opened my window fully despite the fact that he had turned on the air conditioning.

He cleared his throat, a signal to ask me if I was ready to hear the story.

When I nodded, he went on, 'Some old man called up and said he heard a terrible scream from the apartment next door. They sent someone to check it out. And then I got called.'

'Where?'

'Port Melbourne. Five minutes from here.'

'And?'

'The place is covered in blood. One person is down, the other in a state of shock.'

'Murder?'

'Think so, otherwise you wouldn't be here.'

'That's all you've got?'

'That's all I was given.'

'How did the person die? Did they get to tell you that?'

'That's what we're about to find out.'

4

Uniformed Officers were at the scene in Port Melbourne when we got there. They had requested the presence of Frank Moore and myself.

Frank and I worked as a team on many previous homicides, and although we could get on each other's nerves, we always managed to put a good case together.

Frank had been involved in many important cases around the State, including the Russell Street Bombing, the Hoddle Street Massacre, and the recent bushfire in the Dandenong Ranges.

My reputation rested on a fourteen-month training stint at the FBI Academy in Quantico, USA, in conjunction with programs at the University of Virginia and the Armed Forces Institute of Pathology.

When the white Ford Falcon entered Kensington Street in Port Melbourne, beaming blue and red emergency lights were flashing like the entrance of the Crown Casino. An ambulance was already at the scene.

Kensington Street was filled with units and flats mainly occupied by young professionals who could not yet afford a house of their own.

Dark trees lined both sides of the pedestrian walks, making it difficult to observe our surroundings.

Frank parked the car on the other side of the street. I shook my head at the circus of lights and on-lookers parading in their nightgowns and pyjamas in front of a three-storey, Georgian-style, grey building.

We stepped out of the white Ford without a word and attached our photo identification to our breast pockets.

Frank's credentials confirmed he was a sworn member of the Victoria Police.

'Christ, I hope no one's touched anything,' Frank muttered as we approached the multitude of curious on-lookers. He was carrying a Physical Evidence Recovery Kit (PERK) in two dark briefcases, which he'd just removed from the trunk of the Ford.

The PERK was filled with scissors, probes, tweezers, brushes of various sizes and shape, an eye glass, scalpel handles, rulers, a compass, a number of writing tools, assorted packaging and stick-on labels. The purpose of the PERK was to help us gather physical evidence at the crime scene, including semen and other bodily fluids from victims, and trace evidence of all sorts.

I carried a green, army-style, soft bag filled with two sets of overalls, a complete first-aid kit, soft-hats, hard-hats, footwear, eye wear, gloves and various other crime-scene protective wear. I also had my log book with me, where I would write down in detail everything I was going to say and do.

'Check this out,' I said, pointing at a 4WD equipped with a circular, white satellite dish. Its blue and yellow round logo looked uncomfortably familiar. I could almost hear the television station jingle.

'Media. Fucking Media,' Frank muttered.

The Channel 10 news crew was already shooting footage galore.

Frankly, I didn't have any hang-ups about the media. They did their job, and we did ours, and as long as we respected that, everything was fine.

In fact, many difficult homicides had been solved with the help of the media. The only way to get public participation was to use the media to our advantage. In the past, I found making deals and maintaining a good relationship with a particular journalist was what worked best. But if promises were not kept, all hell broke loose on both sides.

What I failed to understand was how journalists always managed to get to a crime scene before we did. And why they couldn't wait until after we had a chance to inspect the area before bombarding us with questions.

Rumour was spreading that some journalists were equipped with police radios, something they'd strongly denied. However, no other explanation rationalised their premature arrival at a crime scene.

As soon as we approached the apartment blocks, someone shoved a large, grey microphone under our noses. The light from a two-thousand watt flash turned me blind.

'Do you know what's going on in here?' asked a journalist, whom I couldn't even make out.

'No,' I answered, trying my best to remain calm. But the heat from the light was killing me, and I could feel my temper snapping. The air felt like the inside of an oven, and I didn't need the additional heat from an artificial sun. 'If there's anything to report, you'll be the first one to know. Promise. Now, could you please let us go through?'

'We've heard someone's been murdered,' the journalist went on.

'No comments at this stage. Could you please get out of the way and let us do our job.' I struggled to move forward. Right at that moment, I sympathised with politicians and celebrities who sometimes lost their cool when constantly harassed by the media.

Frank Moore was posing for the cameras. He was always bad-mouthing the media, but he loved the attention. It made him feel important, just in case he forgot he was.

Too many people were hanging around the block of apartments. No doubt most of them were from the same building. They'd have a story to tell friends at work the next day, a slice of the action worth missing out on sleep for.

One uniformed officer was talking to an attractive, dark-haired, young woman in a white nightgown. Another seemed preoccupied with the lawn in the front yard of the apartment block.

I approached the first officer and noticed immediately he was barely twenty-five. He wore a neatly-trimmed moustache, an obvious attempt to look older in order to be treated with respect by his peers. Perspiration covered his forehead. His name tag read, 'Constable Gus Patterson'.

'What situation have we got here?' I asked without identifying myself.

The young woman in the nightgown, obviously aware she was losing the officer's interest, walked away.

'Dr Kristin Malina?' He glanced at my photo-ID and recognised me straight away, probably from one of the many lectures I gave at the University of Melbourne, Swinburne University of Technology, or the Police Academy in Glen Waverley. 'My partner and I were the first to arrive at the scene. The investigator in charge of the crime scene hasn't turned up yet.'

Did he just forget why he requested my services in the middle of the night?

'That's fine,' I replied, 'I'll be acting as investigator for the time being.' I pointed to the other uniformed officer. 'What's he looking for in the grass? He's not supposed to collect evidence. That's our job.'

'He's not collecting anything. He got sick like a dog when he went inside, so he's chucking his guts out.'

'All right, all right. Where's your log book?'

He gave me a blank look.

'Log book?' I asked again, feeling a stream of sweat trickling down the small of my back.

'Euh, I thought—'

'Jesus, how long have you been here?'

'Twelve months or so.'

'At the *scene*!'

'Fifteen minutes.'

'And who the fuck is co-ordinating the crime-scene?'

'Well...'

'All right, all right, forget it.' The blood was drained from his face. Amazing, I thought, These guys have been here for fifteen minutes, and neither of them have bothered keeping a log. For all we knew, the killer could have walked out right under their noses.

I shifted from one foot to the other and went on. 'Any suspects arrested?'

'No.'

'Has anyone entered the apartment?'

'Constable Williams has.' He said, pointing at his partner, who was now on his hands and knees, on the front lawn, receiving attention from a first-aid attendant.

'Has anyone else, apart from Constable Williams, entered the building?'

'Nope. Just him, that's it, Dr Malina.'

'Good,' I noted the information in my log book.

I looked to where Constable Williams was and realised there was no point asking him details of what he'd seen inside the apartment, although that would have been my first requirement. It looked as if he was still trying to cope with reality.

I turned back to young Patterson 'Did he touch anything?'

'Nothing...well, apart from the girl who was there.'

'What girl?'

'There's someone in there covered in blood, cuts and bruises. That's what he said when he came out. I didn't see anything. I didn't go in the building. He said it was really weird in there, like something from another world.'

'And he touched her?'

'He said she was alive. She seemed dead, he said, but she's alive. So that's why I called an ambulance, and they're just about to go in now. I didn't want to touch anything until you guys got here. I told him you'd be here in a minute, but he said he knew what he was doing and then he went in.'

I spun around, and sure enough two paramedics were rolling a stretcher to the front of the apartment. One was a redneck with tattoos on his forearms, the other looked Italian or Greek.

'Hey, hold on a sec,' I yelled across to them.

All eyes were on me.

It was critical that no one entered the crime scene until I had a chance to look around and preserve the largest amount of evidence possible. Once a person who was not authorised to enter the crime-scene area began tempering with objects and bodies, contamination of the exhibits could make the evidence useless in a court of law. I had witnessed hundreds of cases where police officers and paramedics, through their own ignorance, contaminated a crime scene with fingerprints, footprints, gun residues and fibres. Whatever evidence was collected after that was challenged by the defence in a court of law and rendered impermissible because of its unreliability through contamination.

I paced towards the male paramedics. 'Don't go in there,' I yelled. 'I've got jurisdiction over this crime scene. Nobody goes in there until I say so.'

They looked at each other puzzled. Not all men had got used to the idea of being ordered around by a woman. I was glad I was wearing my pants, in spite of the unbearable heat. It forced them to talk to my face, not my legs.

'But there's someone injured in there,' the first paramedic objected.

'I know.'

9

'Look babe,' the redneck paramedic said, 'we're here to save lives, not to play who's in charge. So, we're going in.'

I wanted to kick him in the shin for calling me *babe*. 'Like hell you are. I'll have you both arrested for knowingly tampering with evidence.'

The redneck made a fist with his right hand and raised his voice. 'There's someone in there who needs medical attention. That officer down there,' he pointed at Constable Williams, 'told us so. I'm here to save lives!'

I gave him a cold stare and shouted louder than him, 'I *know* and so am I.' I held one hand up in the air, as if I was stopping invisible traffic. 'Now, stand-by and wait for my signal.'

He shrugged and muttered under his breath, 'Fuckin' bitch!'

Just at that moment, Frank Moore came and joined me, so I chose to ignore the redneck's comment.

'Nasty shit in there, I heard,' he whispered in my ear. 'You don't have to go in if you don't want to.'

'Give me a break, Frank. I'm not a little girl out of prep.'

In 1991, Frank and I worked on the murder of Sheree Beasley, a gorgeous little six-year old who'd been snatched on her way to a convenience store, near her Rosebud home. After that, I thought I'd be ready for anything.

Violent crimes against children were the worst ones I ever came across. Knowing an innocent young life had been wasted made me angry and bitter. Every other type of crime, I more or less knew I could handle. But brutality against children burned the core of my soul.

Not getting personally involved with the victim's family was impossible. No matter how tough investigators and police officers might appear to be on the outside, deep down, we're all human beings. It took me a long time to get over the horrific sight of the young girl when we found her lifeless body in a drain in Red Hill, three months after she disappeared. Years later, I kept going back to visit the parents, hoping they were coping well. I became their self-appointed psychological counsellor. But they weren't coping well at all. The best we could do was stick together through the ordeal and make sure the victim's family were not forgotten. And long after the killer was in jail, long after the media hype was over, long after everyone had forgotten the torturous ordeal this family had gone through, the agony remained with everyone who was ever involved with this crime. It wasn't just a crime against one person, but a crime against an entire family, an entire community.

After all the horrific homicides I'd attended, I thought I'd be ready for anything.

But nothing had prepared me for what I was about to see.

I'd always had a belief in basic human goodness. I believed that even in someone really bad, something good was there. Just a matter of tapping into it, getting rid of the demons, getting into the heart of the matter. But I was always surprised by the extent of cruelty humans could inflict on each other, making it extremely difficult to sympathise towards criminals.

Normally, Frank and I would have begun by making a general survey of the area by means of photography, video recording, sketches and notes. We would do that prior to examining the critical area of the crime scene. But because we were informed an injured person was inside the apartment, we decided to change the order of things.

I noted in my log book the reason why we decided to enter the apartment prior to making preliminary notes for a plan of action.

I opened the green, soft bag I had with me and emptied the contents.

Frank and I put on disposable surgical gloves, white cotton overalls, and non-slip steel-plated boots. It was so hot, I thought I was going to pass out.

We headed towards the entrance of the building.

The apartment where the alleged murder took place was the first one to our left on the ground floor.

When I entered the foyer of the apartment, the smell of blood was so strong, I felt my insides churning. My survival instincts told me to get out of this place now.

At this stage I wasn't concerned about recording anything. This could wait until we managed to rescue whoever was alive. I knew one person was dead already. How the person died, I never had the chance to ask Constable Williams. And now that he was being treated for shock inside the ambulance, the only thing left to do was to find out for myself.

I stood in front of the dark entrance of the apartment and hesitated for a few seconds.

Frank gave me a stare as if to say, 'you don't have to go in if you don't want to'.

That made me even more determined to proceed.

CHAPTER TWO

The front door of the ground-floor apartment had been left ajar. Straight away, I noticed that the lock had been damaged, and this had obviously been the point of entry for the intruder.

I moved forward.

The hallway was filled with darkness.

I reached for the light switch on my left and flicked it on.

Nothing.

Frank Moore wanted to get in front, but I managed to push him out of the way to get in first.

'Is everything a competition to you?' he whispered.

I ignored his comment and removed a torch from the leg pocket of my overalls. After I flicked it on, I noticed how warm it was in the apartment. And the smell of blood was starting to make me feel uncomfortable. Perhaps not so much the smell, but the apprehension of what I was about to find. For a spilt second, I pictured Constable Williams outside, vomiting on the lawn. I hoped to God he was the sensitive type. And I also wished he had been in shape to take us through the crime scene to soften the blow from any nasty surprises.

I clenched my teeth as I moved two steps forward into the narrow hallway.

I don't know why, but I thought of my son Michael back at home. He'd been in trouble at school lately, and his grades were rather border-line. I shook my head slightly, realising this was really an odd time to think about him. Maybe I was somehow trying to avoid what was coming up.

Frank was following closely behind.

Our field of vision was small and circular, the size allowed by the torch beam.

I could feel my heart drilling through my chest. No one had seen the killer, but maybe he was still hiding somewhere in the house.

The first thing I noticed was two picture frames on my left hanging at an odd angle. They were prints of famous paintings which I couldn't place.

I pointed the torch to the wall on my right side. A small, wooden telephone table was overturned. There seemed to have been some kind of struggle in the hallway. Maybe the owner had intercepted the intruder at the door.

Apart from the disturbed telephone table and the crooked pictures on the wall, the hallway was clean and well-maintained. Although I was uncertain in the semi-darkness, the salmon-coloured carpet seemed brand new. I circled the floor with the torch and noticed dark footprints.

'Hold on a sec,' I commanded Frank.

He froze behind me, obviously not in a hurry to find out what was lurking beyond the hallway.

I kneeled down, passed two fingers over one of the footprints, and brought the fingers to my nose. The smell of blood filled my nostrils. I wiped the gloved fingers over my overalls.

'Fresh blood,' I said.

I knew it could have been footprints left behind by Constable Williams, since he had entered the apartment. And that was what I had been afraid of. Contamination of the crime scene. Constable Williams had no gloves on when he entered the apartment. He'd almost certainly left his fingerprints all over the place. I hope he hadn't tampered with the body of the person who had been killed. I made mental note that Constable Williams fingerprints would have to be taken as a reference sample against all the fingerprints found in the apartment.

While still on my knees, I noticed a telephone cable ripped from the edge of the wall. I followed the telephone cable to its

14

end with the torch. It had been pulled from its connection.

My mind was racing with possibilities.

Whoever broke into the apartment knew what they were doing. This was premeditated otherwise they wouldn't have bothered with the telephone.

'Okay,' I said and stood back on my feet.

Frank didn't say a word. He just followed like somebody's pet.

Halfway up the hallway, there was a room to my left. I would have gone straight past it if it wasn't for the moaning of a woman coming from the direction of the room.

A chill rippled down my spine. 'There's someone in there,' I said.

And I remembered the girl Constable Williams's partner mentioned.

Frank nodded with a grunt.

I pushed the door open.

Immediately, Frank came up behind me and, without warning, reached for the light switch.

When the light came on, we both stared, unable to comprehend what was in front of us. Everything in the room had been overturned.

I circled the room with my eyes. A dressing table, two tallboys, a linen chest, bedside cabinets, a chair. The doors of the wardrobe were wide open and clothes thrown everywhere in the room.

The smell of blood was strongest now, entering my lungs, filtering itself through every cell in my body.

After the initial shock, I realised this was the bedroom of the apartment. At one time, it must have looked warm and inviting. Even though the furniture was overturned, I could tell it was good quality solid timber.

'Jesus Christ,' Frank whispered behind my back. 'What the hell happened here?'

'A burglary gone wrong?' I suggested, because it seemed obvious to me someone had been looking for something.

I could still hear the woman moaning, but couldn't figure out where it was coming from.

And then I noticed a cylindrical shape in the centre of the room.

A blue and grey rug covered in what looked like red paint. So much was splattered on the rug, I wished it was red paint. But it didn't smell like red paint. Now I knew where the smell of blood came from. I made sure my surgical gloves were properly fitted. The last thing I wanted was to catch AIDS or some other blood-transmitted disease.

I jabbed Frank with my elbow gently and pointed towards the blood-soaked carpet. It was very dense in colour. I looked up to see his reaction. His eyes expressed surprise more than anything else.

'You okay?' I asked, knowing he wouldn't tell me even if he wasn't.

'Yeah, yeah.' His eyes wouldn't leave the rolled up rug.

I walked up to the bloody rug, still trying to figure out why it was covered in so much blood. As I stood inches from it, I saw a man lying behind it. He was naked, his body stretched in full, half turned from the waist. It took me seconds to register the other half of what I was seeing.

Next to the body was the man's head lying upside down.

'There's a guy there who's been decapitated,' I informed Frank who was still two feet behind me.

He moved in to inspect the damage. 'Holy shit,' he muttered. 'That's quite a find.'

I couldn't disagree with him, but I didn't find the discovery half as exciting as shocking.

The woman moaned again.

We both looked at each other and then towards the bed.

Frank moved in first.

I kneeled down next to the decapitated man and took down some mental notes. *Neck cut close to shoulders. Severed larynx cartilage flapped out on hollow in collarbone. Victim mid-thirties, brown hair, medium build.* I had never come across a beheaded person before and was kind of intrigued by what I was observing. At the top of his shoulder, where his neck had been cut off, blood was streaming out like a small mountain spring. I looked down the body. He was still wearing his socks, which must have been a colour other than red at some stage.

'She's under the bed,' Frank said, kneeling down, his head tilted at a forty-five degree angle.

I stopped my observation of the severed head and joined

16

him.

The woman was naked and curled up like an embryo. I aimed the beam from my torch towards her. Her entire body was smeared with blood. Her face was covered in cuts and bruises. Her hair looked wet, limp and greasy. It fell half way across her face, concealing her eyes. She looked like a baby seal who had just been bludgeoned to death. She was humming erratically and fidgeting with her hands.

'Let's get her out of here,' I ordered.

We eased her from under the bed and covered her with a blanket.

'Go and tell the paramedics to get in here quickly,' I went on.

Frank gave me a sour look. He loved working with me, but he hated when I started giving him orders. He seemed to forget I was the investigator in charge of the crime scene.

'For Christ's sake, Frank,' I snapped, 'not now. Just get the goddamn paramedics!'

He raced out of the room without further notice.

After the paramedics whisked the girl outside the apartment, I was left alone with Frank.

'What do you think?' he asked, although he probably knew as much as I did.

'Murder, of course. If it was suicide, the guy is rather skillful.' I glanced around the room. 'I'm going to get the cameras from the car. Why don't you begin a general survey so we can work on a plan of action.'

'Yes, *sir*,' he grunted.

I walked back to the hallway, and wondered why we had gotten on each others' nerves since the beginning of this investigation.

What I had just seen hadn't sunk in yet. But I knew it wouldn't take long. I had always been good at accepting reality face on, for better or worse.

Before I reached the front door of the apartment, I realised this was one of the worst jobs I had been involved in. Most homicides in Melbourne were pretty straight forward. A bullet in the head. A knife in the back. Drowned in the bathtub. Only in the USA had I read about cases which could turn a level-headed forensic investigator into a raving lunatic within days. But I had never dealt in real life with anything as bloody as what was in that apartment. After all decapitation was not a common way of killing someone.

Surprisingly enough, in spite of my sensitive reaction to the bloody find, I remained level-headed and believed I would have no problem coping with the investigation. The evidence I had seen began forming in my mind a scenario of what might have happened.

When I stepped outside the apartment, the air felt cool. I knew it was only an illusion, because the temperature had remained above thirty for the last few days. It's just that it had been so hot in the apartment, anywhere else felt cool in comparison.

The paramedics had already left the scene, but a crowd of on-lookers were still hanging around like flies over a decomposing body.

Before the Channel 10 media crew launched its attack on me, I managed to get to the Constable I had spoken to when I arrived at the scene of the crime.

'Why isn't there any crime-scene tape around the area?' I asked. Before he had time to answer and rationalise his lack of experience at a crime scene, I went on, 'I want the area sealed off. I also want anyone who's not a potential witness out of the perimeter immediately. I don't want you or anyone else to speak to the media. That's my job. Is that clear?'

'I'll get on to it.' He took my orders well, and as a result, I liked him straight away.

'What's your name?' I asked, realising I had forgotten since I last spoke to him.

'Constable Gus Patterson,' he said, extending his hand while I checked his name tag.

I gave him a quick but firm handshake and said, 'All right, Gus, you're in charge out here. I'm counting on you to keep everything in order. I want you to prevent any unnecessary walking about in and out of this building, control people moving items anywhere within the crime-scene perimeter, anyone touching surfaces of any type, or removing items from the scene. You think you can handle it?'

'Yes, Dr Malina.'

'And make sure you keep everyone on the other side of the crime-scene tape.'

He nodded.

I managed to get to Frank's Ford without the media hassling me, but I wasn't so lucky on my way back. I carried a large silver hard case filled with camera equipment when they blocked my path. I hadn't noticed straight away, but there were more media 4WDs and vans than when I first went inside the apartment. Journalists from the *Age*, the *Herald-Sun*, Radio National and 3JJJ were also present.

In the distance, I recognised Tim Simons, my personal media-liaison contact at the *Herald-Sun*. We had a mutual respect for each other. Tim Simons, dark-haired, blue-eyed and with a hint of a British accent, had worked with Frank and I on many homicides. He helped us with press releases and fed only enough details to the public for an investigation to proceed with a greater chance of success. In return, whenever an investigation was over, I gave him exclusive rights to a story. For the past two years, Tim Simons won the prestigious Gold Walkley Award for outstanding contribution to journalism.

'Dr Kristin Malina,' yelled a broad-shouldered, blond male journalist. 'You promised you would keep us informed.' That must have been the journalist who'd been hiding behind the two-thousand watt light when I arrived at the scene.

I knew I'd promised to comment later on, but there was no time for a long chit-chat.

'Okay, but this will only take a few seconds, I said. 'We've got one person down and another seriously injured.'

'Do you speculate murder at this stage?'

'We believe it is. Burglary might have been the motive.'

'Any idea who did this?'

'It's too premature to comment at this stage.'

'Any relation with this case and any others? Is this the work of a serial killer?'

This journalist had been watching too much television. 'Like I said, it's a bit premature to give details at this stage. All I can confirm is that yes, it is murder, a probable burglary gone wrong. No, we have not established a link between this crime and any others. And no, it certainly isn't the work of a serial killer. You must be thinking about Seattle or something.

19

That's all I've got for you.'

I began pushing my way towards the apartment.

'How did the victim die?' The journalist went on. 'You didn't tell us how he was murdered.'

'Decapitated,' I answered dryly and entered the building.

Frank Moore and I spent the next five hours going over the Port Melbourne apartment, where the murder of Jeremy Wilson and the battering of his wife Teresa took place. One of their neighbours had informed us of their identities.

We called the State Emergency Services (SES) to provide us with adequate lighting of the area, inside and outside of the building.

Prior to collecting evidence, we proceeded with a preliminary examination, which entailed observation only. The last thing we needed was to risk contaminating the crime scene any more than we already had. Collection of evidence would be done after we'd made a thorough assessment of the crime scene.

The preliminary examination was a walk-through evaluation of the crime scene. This stage was one of the most critical phases of searching the crime scene for evidence. The impressions we gained from this walk-through were going to formulate how the scene would be processed.

During the walk-through, Frank and I kept our hands deep inside the pockets of our overalls, just to stop ourselves from touching anything.

We moved through the apartment by walking in areas which did not appear to contain any potential evidence. I took extra care when walking through the hallway, doorways or any areas where potential footprint or footwear impressions, fingerprints, and other trace evidence could have been left behind.

The only rooms which seemed to have been disturbed were the bedroom and the hallway. A small window in a room adjacent to the bathroom had been left ajar.

I made mental notes of any sign of forced entry, the location of potential items of evidence, and the presence or absence of blood in various areas of the scene.

Following the preliminary examination, we videotaped the

entire area.

Since the introduction of the video camera nearly two decades ago, forensic investigators had additional means to accurately record information. This method of recording information at a crime scene was better than photography at times, because it gave us a three-dimensional view of our surroundings. It also provided us or anyone working on the investigation with a powerful tool to help re-construct a chain of events. Videotaping was also being introduced more and more in courts of law, making a strong visual impact on the jury. This proved very effective when shock and disgust was the reaction the prosecution was aiming at.

We divided other tasks to avoid stepping on each others' toes and to minimise risk of contamination of the exhibits collected. At no time should two pieces of evidence come into contact with one another.

Frank was outside taking the overall and mid-range photographs of the location, including the street sign with the name clearly identified, the front the apartment, and close-ups of any points of interest. Later, if this homicide ever ended up in court, we would have to prove not only how we collected the exhibits, but also where we collected them from.

I took the initial photographs of the immediate crime scene. This had to be done before the removal of Mr Wilson's body. I recalled that pictures of Mrs Wilson should have been taken before she was sent to hospital, but in the condition we found her, I felt at the time photographing her could wait.

I circled Mr Wilson's body and took as many pictures as humanly possible, including close-ups of all visible wounds, bruises, cuts, hands and fingernails. More shots would be taken at the mortuary. For every photograph taken, I used an identifying scale or ruler whenever possible, and made appropriate notes whenever I deemed it necessary.

I noticed that the open wound above the chest where Mr Wilson's head had been severed had stabilised. Although the body was drenched in a pool of blood, making it very difficult to take photographs without causing a mess, little blood was now running from the neck wound. I took shots at various angles and under different light conditions with the help of a portable flash.

I then proceeded with the photography of the entire

bedroom.

Photography was vital for the recording of the crime scene in its original state.

I took hundreds of shots, including detailed photographs of foot marks, blood stains, tool marks, or anything I felt would help with the investigation and, ultimately, the jury in a trial. Nothing could be touched until photography had been completed. Later I would be able to collect exhibits, knowing exactly where I collected them from with the help of photography and painstaking note taking.

Half way through my task, I felt light-headed. I looked around me. Everything seemed surreal, like a still from a horror movie. My tongue was dry like a piece of cardboard. I needed a drink, but knew I shouldn't use any utilities in the apartment. I swallowed and went on with my task.

In addition to photography, I recorded the scene with a sketch. Photographs were two dimensional, and only sketching would give a more accurate idea of measurements. I began with the rough crime scene sketch as soon as I removed and stored the last roll from my Minolta.

I did the sketch on a blank pad. Not exactly a work of art, but it contained enough information which would allow me to work on a final sketch with the help of Sirchie Fingerprint Labs, a computer program designed to accurately create a final sketch from the rough sketch made at a crime scene. The software included crime-scene template libraries with a variety of computer clip-art images, such as positions of victims, weapons, furnishings and bloodstains.

The scene sketch provided me with accurate spatial relationships of every item within the scene. I wrote down every essential piece of information, including the case number, descriptions, the date and time, measurements and scale, and a compass (north) indicator.

One hour into the crime scene evaluation, the coroner arrived. Since I had already finished with the photography, Mr Wilson's body was ready to be removed from the scene. The coroner placed protective paper bags over Mr Wilson's hands prior to carrying the body into the mortuary's van. This procedure protected evidence which might have been present under the fingernails and would be collected later at the mortuary.

The coroner evaluated wounds, post mortem interval, and whatever indicators could have suggested the body may have been moved.

He then proceeded with the help of an assistant to whisk the body away to the mortuary.

I finished my sketch and sighed. Here I was in the middle of the night, bathing in a blood bath, collecting relics from the dead. How did my life turn out so intriguingly complicated?

I proceeded with the collection of major evidence items. This required a great deal of care since any items could have contained trace evidence and fingerprints. Most items were packaged in paper rather than plastic to avoid mould growth from a wet or moist exhibit. I took down details of any stains or damage observed on every item. When packaging was completed, I attached an appropriate label which identified the case number, the item number and a brief description of what the item was.

The collecting of trace evidence would need more time and care. Nothing could be rushed when collecting and recording information at a crime scene. This proved next to impossible since everyone who felt they had some kind of jurisdiction at a crime scene wanted everything done perfectly yesterday.

Trace evidence was the cornerstone of forensic science. Such evidence was normally invisible to the naked eye and included hair, fibres and paint particles. When collecting trace evidence I always kept at the back of my mind a famous observation by Dr Edmond Locard, the father of forensic science: *The microscopic dusts which cover our clothes and our bodies are silent, yet certain and reliable witnesses of each of our actions and contacts.*

I proceeded with adhesive lifts and vacuum-sweepings of areas of particular interest, especially those which were covered in dust, fibres and other foreign objects. I took great care while collecting vacuum sweepings. I made sure the vacuumed areas were specific, not a general "house cleaning" of the crime scene. I'd been made aware a thousand times by laboratory personnel at the VFSC that a large container of dust, hair and fibre was extremely difficult and time consuming to sift through. The last thing I needed was to be known as the monster who gave them boxes filled with common household dust.

Hair and fibres were a pain to collect. Vacuuming or tape-lifting was out of the question since it may have damaged the tiny exhibits before examination.

Blood stains on clothes were collected by using clean scissors and placing the item into a piece of folded paper and then into a labelled plastic-bag. Blood stains on the ground or furniture were scraped using a clean scalpel, or sponged up with a wet piece of cloth, and also stored in paper and plastic-bags.

I'd nearly finished collecting most of the trace evidence in the bedroom when Frank walked in. I was kneeling down with a scalpel in one hand and a folded paper in the other.

'Found some interesting stuff,' he announced while looking at his notepad.

I twisted my lips and looked up. He knew he shouldn't have been in the room at the same time as me, but I let him speak before telling him off.

'You remember the back window?'

'Which one?'

'The one in the room adjacent to the bathroom.'

I nodded. When we did the preliminary examination, I'd made a mental note of the open window and wondered if it was the point of exit.

Frank lifted a labelled transparent vinyl bag and went on, 'A piece of dark fabric got caught in the rotted outer woodwork of the window frame. Looks like the fucker escaped through the back.'

Frank had just confirmed the point of exit.

I raised my eyebrows for him to go on.

'The front door's been forced from the outside by what looks like some kind of leverage tool. Definitely the point of entry.'

I had already noticed that when we first entered the apartment, and when we did the walk-through.

Frank took a deep breath and continued, 'And now for the mother of all evidence.' He opened a Postpack. 'A cook's knife with a twelve-inch blade covered in blood. Found it in the back alley.'

Okay, I had to admit, things were starting to look good. 'I want this whole damn place fingerprinted as soon as I finish with the collection of evidence. Call the fingerprinting unit when we're done,' I said with excitement. 'We're gonna nail the sucker who did this. He's such an amateur, he's left a trail of evidence all over the place.'

I took the Postpack from Frank's hands, and examined the cook's knife up-close. It was covered in blood, but I could still read the serial number on the handle, *G-66923*. Although Frank had already done that, I wrote the number down in my log book. I liked to keep a record of vital exhibits for myself.

'Hey, I've already recorded the details,' Frank protested. His face was flushed.

'I know, I know.'

'So what are you doing?'

'Just go and finish what you're doing.'

'We're supposed to keep separate logs. You're gonna get us confused.'

'We're also supposed to keep investigating in separate rooms to avoid contamination of evidence. Now, go and finish what you're doing.'

'Jesus,' he muttered and walked off.

I removed a small stainless steel ruler from my right pocket and measured the length and width of the knife. A large 30 x 3cm piece. I wrote down the information and took a photo. This precaution was vital in case the knife went missing in the future due to mishandling of forensic evidence by one of the many people who were not authorised to touch evidence, but who would anyway. I filled in my name on the label attached to the Postpack to preserve continuity.

Just as I placed the knife back in the Postpack, Frank walked back in the room.

'I thought I told you not to come here,' I snapped.

'The Deputy Commissioner is here,' he said in a tone that meant trouble.

The Deputy Commissioner of Police was a short, fat guy by the name of Frank Goosh. I never figured out how the hell he ended up with a name like Goosh. It sounded like something out a comic book.

Frank Goosh couldn't stand the sight of me, and I cared little for his opinion. Right from the beginning, he had opposed any restructuring which involved the contracting of civilians to conduct forensic and investigative work. And although he never admitted it openly, I knew he had a hard time accepting that the first person who had been contracted as an unsworn crime-scene examiner and investigator happened to be a woman.

I stood on my feet, my body fully erect. 'Where is he now?' I asked, feeling blood rushing to my head.

'He's just outside the front door. Just about to walk in here' Frank said.

'Jesus Christ!'

I stormed out of the bedroom and down the hallway. My duty as crime-scene examiner was to insure no one entered the crime scene, not even the Prime Minister or the Queen of England. The Deputy Commissioner of Police was well aware of that, but for some reason he obviously believed himself to be an exception.

I intercepted Frank Goosh in front of the apartment, inside the perimeter of the crime-scene, which Constable Gus Patterson had so obediently sealed off with blue and white police tape.

The Deputy Commissioner of Police came towards me, his pot-belly almost bursting out of his blue shirt. His black hair was parted in the middle, his beady dark eyes had virtually no white in them, and his complexion looked like raw hamburger.

'Have you got the situation under control?' he inquired in a tone which reminded me of my school principal a long time ago.

'Mr Goosh, glad you could make it, but I don't recall requesting your presence at this crime scene. Now, if you care to step outside the crime-scene perimeter and stand behind the police tape like everyone else, I'd very much appreciate it.'

'I'm the Deputy Commissioner of Police, Miss Malina. I have a right to be here.'

'It's Dr Malina. I've earned a degree in criminal justice through diligent and hard work, and would appreciate if you would address me as Dr Malina.'

He shifted uncomfortably from one foot to the other. '*Dr* Malina, you're only here because of me. I can have your contract terminated anytime.'

'I appreciate your need to exert your power, Mr Goosh, but

right now you're going to step on the other side of the police line.'

He crossed his arms over his chest, making his stomach protrude even further. 'And who says? You're going to make me? What the hell is your problem, anyway?'

'Mr Goosh, I have legal jurisdiction over this crime scene. If you can't understand that, maybe you should consult the Police Operations Manual and familiarise yourself with its content. In the meantime, either you step on the other side of the police tape, or I'll have you escorted by force.'

He gave me a cold stare. 'Bitch!'

I moved two steps forward. 'What did you call me?'

'You heard. You think you can just walk in and take over everything. I've been doing this longer than you have. I have years of experience. You were still sucking on your mother's nipples when I was chasing criminals. So don't lecture me on what I can or cannot do.'

I felt like running my scalpel right across his throat.

'Mr Goosh, I'm not going to ask you again.'

'You don't know who you're dealing with.—'

I interrupted him before he had time to insult me once more. 'Constable Patterson,' I shouted towards the young officer, who was standing close to the Channel 10 news crew, 'Could you please escort Mr Goosh out of the crime scene?'

'Yes, Dr Malina,' Constable Patterson said, already pacing towards me.

Frank Goosh glanced over his shoulder, towards the constable and turned back to me. 'I'm going to get you for this. You can kiss your job goodbye, you little tart.'

He walked off before Constable Patterson got to him.

I stepped back in the hallway, feeling myself shaking all over.

Goddamn sonofabitch managed to get me frustrated.

I clenched my teeth and proceded with my task.

By the time we closed the place up, we had collected clumps of hair, slivers of broken fingernails from the most unreachable places, a multitude of various fibres, and enough fingerprints to jail the killer twenty times over.

The beheaded body of Jeremy Wilson was now resting in

peace somewhere at the mortuary in Southgate, for a little while anyway, until an autopsy would be performed.

When I climbed back into Frank's Ford Falcon, it was 8.21 a.m.

Daylight had set in a few hours ago. Towards the first hours of daylight, collection of evidence had become much easier. I saw fibres and marks I hadn't been able to see at 3.00 a.m. in spite of additional lighting provided by the SES. I hated collecting evidence at night time, and usually I would wait until the next day. But since we knew we had a killer on the run, we didn't want to waste any more time than necessary.

Frank took a turn into Princes Highway, where the traffic moving towards the city was becoming rather congested. Another working day for normal people.

Drivers were aggressive, as if they actually wanted to get to work more than anything else in the world. Had it been me, I would have taken my time.

Passing one hand over the length of my oval face, I sighed. I was tired and angry. Tired from not getting the sleep I deserved, and damn angry men could commit such atrocities as the one I had seen at the Wilson's place. Over ninety percent of violent crimes were committed by men. Whoever had masterminded this little set-up had the brain of a monkey.

I tightened my seat-belt and turned to Frank. 'Men are a real hazard to the community. This world is in the shape it's in because of men. Without them, there'd be virtually no crime in society. Imagine that, a world without crime.

He shifted uncomfortably.

I made my hands into fists and went on, 'I read once that men should pay extra tax just because they're wasting tax payers' money.'

'And how's that?' he asked, pursing his lips, obviously unwilling to get into a major debate. He had heard it a thousand times before, but when I was frustrated, I couldn't help singing the same tune over and over again.

'Well, to begin with, over ninety percent of crimes are committed by men. To keep one of these men in jail cost thousands of dollars. Take Martin Bryant, the loony who shot all those people in Tasmania. It costs the government over $100,000 a year to keep him alive. For what? Think what this

28

money could be used for instead of being spent on people like him.'

'So you want to re-introduce the death penalty?'

'I didn't say that. All I'm saying is men are the cause of all this shit.'

Frank sighed as he took a left turn. 'So what are you getting at?'

'Nothing. Just observation. I mean just look at the idiot who killed Jeremy Wilson and bashed his wife. He couldn't have made it any easier for us. By the time we've combed through all the evidence, he'll have the entire Federal Police on his trail.'

'You're assuming it's a *he*.'

'I'm assuming?' I shook my head in disbelief. 'Well, what else would it be? An *it*? Men are a soup of androgens. They're conditioned from birth to kill and destroy. The only thing you can do with these types of offenders is to cut off their amygdala.'

He gave me a strange look, and it was obvious he didn't know the amygdala was that part of the brain which is active in the production of aggressive behaviour. In the seventies, when psychosurgery was hip, many aggressors became passive when their amygdala was removed, at the cost of destroying their interest in life by terminating their ability to feel emotions.

Frank pressed his foot flat on the accelerator and overtook a truck with a sticker *you are passing another Fox*. 'I don't know, Malina. Sometimes you come up with the most sexist comments. If I had said the same thing about women, you would have slapped me with a sexual harassment lawsuit.'

I felt my face reddening. 'Hey, come on. I'm only stating the facts here. Studies have clearly indicated that male hormones have a direct correlation with aggressive behaviour. You're not going to refute that as well?'

'I know, I know. And that's what scares me.'

I didn't know what he meant by that, but somehow it upset me.

I felt a lump in my throat as the morning sun glittered on the dirty windscreen.

CHAPTER THREE

On Sunday the 23rd of February, there was a cool change. The sky was covered in grey clouds, and I could have sworn it was going to rain. I opened all the windows of my apartment and went back to bed.

I loved St Kilda. The coastal town was ripped with an arty atmosphere and wacky residents. Not far from my home was a long pier where I often walked in the evening to watch the sunset and unwind. On the weekends, I strolled around the hundreds of craft-market stalls on the Esplanade. Someone said once Melbourne is divided in two. St Kilda and the rest of Melbourne. I agreed.

I moved into an apartment complex when I came back from the USA eight years ago, after graduating from the FBI's National Academy. The real estate agent advertised it as New York living, with its graffiti on the walls and its nine parking spaces for eighteen apartments. But the inside of my apartment was filled with imaginative furniture and items. Although the rooms were small, I'd made the most of the space.

In the main bedroom, a pine-bed-platform was built at cupboard floor level. The mezzanine had been lowered to give enough height for standing. Away from the wall, a flight of stairs created a screen for the bathroom entrance and extra storage space. Additional storage space nested beside the bed. Next to the bathroom was my study with a magnificent panoramic view of Chapel Street through a corner bay window.

Michael's room was next to mine and was kept shut most of the time. I never knew what he was doing in there, and I hated to ask. Teenagers nowadays were a complete mystery to me. They spent more time in front of a computer than living life.

Michael was away for the day, but he never told me where he went. By the time I got up, he was already gone. His independence was beginning to frighten me. I felt redundant. For years, he counted on me for everything. Now, I didn't feel like his mother any longer. We were two strangers living under the same roof. I blamed myself often for the situation we'd found ourselves in. If I had a normal job, I told myself, maybe I would be closer to Michael.

I waited patiently for the hospital to call me so I could interrogate Teresa Wilson over her husband's death. If she had seen the killer, finding him would be easier than we thought. The last we heard of her, she was in some sort of semi-coma. She could wake up at any time.

The Fingerprint Branch on the seventeenth floor of the Police Complex on St Kilda Road failed to find any prints on the cook's knife found at the crime scene.

All the different prints lifted from the Wilson's apartment were entered into the fingerprint database terminal and cross-checked against a hundred-thousands others. Not a single match, not even with the thousand fingerprint cards kept on the seventeenth floor, in a neat little classification known as the Henry System. This was a major set back. It meant whoever killed Jeremy Wilson had no fingerprints on record, and thus had never been convicted of any serious criminal offense. It also meant that at this stage we had no idea who killed Jeremy Wilson, and it would take us a little while longer to figure it out. And time, we all knew, was not a luxury we could afford with a case such as this. The media was on our back, and the general public expected us to perform miracles. What they didn't realise is that it sometimes took months, years to find a criminal. But because of those damn movies and television shows, people made an unrealistic assumption that we could find a killer within a week, no questions about it, full stop.

It's like this and that on television, so why can't you do it this way?

Why is it taking so long? With all this sophisticated equipment and the millions of dollars poured into law-enforcement, why is it taking so long?

And local and state politicians would join in, reminding us how the delay in catching a criminal was tarnishing their images, making the whole process even more of a pain.

I stayed in bed until eleven o'clock that morning. Instead of having breakfast, I went straight to the Balaclava Hotel for a Sunday Special - soup of the day, a roast dinner and a three-dollar coin card for the pokies next door. I ate my Sunday Special all by myself, washed it down with a dollar-ninety Coke, and went straight to the pokies. I cashed in my three-dollar voucher, pocketed the gold coins and walked out of the place. I wasn't a gambler and never would be.

The rest of the day drifted slowly into nothingness.

I stayed home with a forensic medicine book by David Ranson and let the answering machine take the calls. Someone from the *Age*, the *Herald-Sun* and *Time* magazine called. I didn't call back. Instead I called Frank to discuss what we had so far, so that I could write up a preliminary report.

I had been thinking a lot in the last few days, and some kind of scenario had conjured in my mind. I felt like I had a better idea of whom the killer might have been.

'A few things are unclear,' I said, my feet up on the desk of my study, overlooking the tramways on Chapel Street. 'To begin with, everything at the apartment in Port Melbourne was turned upside-down, a clear indication the killer was looking for something. And since the picture frames in the hallway were shifted, whatever the intruder was looking for had to be small, small enough to be concealed behind a picture frame.'

'A burglary. You've got your motive.'

That's what I'd also thought when I first entered the apartment, even when I left it. Crimes were never committed without motive. No one went around breaking into a house or killing someone for no reason. And because items in the apartment had been shifted around, we believed we had established a motive.

'True,' I said. 'At first glance, I'd thought it was burglary too. But what about the telephone cable pulled from its connection?'

'He didn't want the owners to call for help. What's so odd

about that?'

'Okay, so he knew they were in the house from the moment he came through the front door. The telephone cable was in the hallway. He had to rip it off the wall before he got to see anyone. He was ready for a confrontation.'

'Possible. On the other hand, he might have seen the telephone when he walked in the house on that night.'

'Too dark.'

'He could have had a torch.'

'Didn't find one at the crime scene.'

'True.'

I shifted from my chair and rested my feet on the floor. 'And the knife,' I said. 'Criminals don't carry twelve-inch knives when committing a burglary. It's big, inconvenient and hard to dispose of, which explains why he dumped the weapon in the alley way.'

'Malina, so far this is only speculation. A burglar could have easily carried a big knife because he had no other weapons in his possession. There is also the chance that he wanted to scare the living daylight out of his victims. A big knife would have contributed to the overall effect better than a small weapon.'

'I don't think so. I'm certain the reason the intruder came to this house was to hurt and kill.'

'Malina...'

'I can explain.'

'Go on.'

'If all the killer wanted to do was commit a burglary, he didn't have to butcher the occupants. The guy had his head cut off. Have you come across many burglaries where a victim is decapitated? The first thing a burglar would want to do is neutralise the occupants by killing then as quick as possible. Then he can proceed and steal anything he wants. And decapitation might be a sure way to kill someone, but it's not a quick process.'

'Maybe he was a sadist.'

'I agree there, but not a burglar. The way this man had been decapitated and his wife battered, this was a personal thing. Also, no other room in the house, apart from the bedroom and the hallway, have been disturbed. A burglar would have looked everywhere. Even the video recorder was still in the lounge room. What kind of burglar leaves everything behind? This was not a burglary, Frank, this was premeditated murder. No ifs or buts about it.'

'A rape-kill scenario?'

'Maybe, but to begin, we don't know if she's been raped. But even if she had, why would the killer spend so much time decapitating the husband? If he wanted to rape the woman, surely he would have got rid of the husband el pronto, and then spend more time on her. This is overkill Frank. The husband played a major part in this. Whoever did this wanted revenge. Someone burned with the desire to punish both Mr and Mrs Wilson.'

'Who would do something like that?'

'I don't know, but I know for a fact it was someone who knew them. The amount of anger and frenzy that went into the decapitation clearly indicates the killer had built up a lot of frustration, and his cup was overfilled. This was the last straw. Very few people kill for pleasure, in spite of what we read in the press. Revenge and anger are the strongest motivating factors.'

'It doesn't mean he knew them.'

'Oh, yes, it does. He knew where the telephone cable was, even though it was dark in the hallway. He'd been in the apartment before. It had to be a friend, a family member, someone who was jealous. Maybe he didn't even put up a fight when he first walked in the apartment, which explains why I never saw any bruising on Jeremy's body or head.'

'A lover?'

'Possible, but if it was a lover, he'd been in the house before, and probably not when the husband was around.'

We talked a bit more, but ended up with the same conclusion. The motive was revenge or punishment, not burglary like we had first assumed. This meant I would focus my investigation on someone close to the Wilsons.

Before Frank hung up, he promised to call me as soon as he heard anything from Teresa Wilson.

Somehow, my thoughts kept drifting back to the conversation I had with Frank in the car when we left the crime scene in Port Melbourne. I wasn't angry at him, but at myself. Why did I get so upset when the conversation ended? Was I wrong? Didn't he think the killer of Mr Wilson was a complete bastard who didn't deserve to live on taxpayers' money? Didn't he have any compassion for Mrs Wilson? The woman had not only been beaten to a pulp but lost her husband as well. Wasn't he angry like I was towards the man who could do such a thing?

For the rest of the day, my mind was preoccupied with philosophical thoughts. I wasn't sure why this case was affecting me so much in so little time. Maybe it was because the victim was a woman. Maybe it was because she seemed to be my age. Maybe because it could have been me, and the killer could have been someone I knew and trusted.

Michael came home at 7.00 p.m., without acknowledging my presence.

'Where have you been?' I shouted from the kitchen when I heard someone open the front door of the apartment. I was slicing up some tomatoes and green peppers to make a tomato sauce for some Diavolini on the boil.

'Out.'

Goddamn it, I hated it when he treated me like a typical grown up. I put the cooking knife down on the bench. 'Michael, come here and talk to me.'

He walked in the kitchen, his blond fringe half concealing his blue eyes. He reminded me so much of his father, and that made me feel uneasy. He was tall for a twelve-year-old, probably 172 or 173cm. His Michael Jordan T-shirt was two sizes two large and hung lose over a pair of dirty, worn-out Levis, which hung over a pair of Nike running shoes. He held a skate-board under his arm.

'Did you take that thing into the city?' I asked, glaring at the skateboard.

'So what?' His voice was mellow, almost inaudible.

'It's illegal in the CBD area.'

'So what?'

'So what? So what is that there are so many crazy drivers out there, one day I'm gonna get a phone call, and I'll have to see you in hospital and tell you I told you so.'

'Mum, give me a break.'

'All right, all right. But you didn't tell me where you were. I was worried sick. Jesus, you think I like worrying? Why are you doing this to me?'

He gave me a blank look to remind me how pathetic I was when I carried on about nothing.

'Mum,' he added, 'my life doesn't revolve around making it difficult for you. I'm twelve years old. I'm not a baby. And if you bought me a mobile phone, you wouldn't have to worry in the first place.'

You are a baby, I thought, and you'll always be. 'You don't need a mobile phone,' I retorted. 'You can ring from a phone booth to tell me where you are.'

'Chris's got a mobile.'

'Well, you're not Chris.'

He shook his head. 'Forget it.' His body language told me he was ready to walk off.

'Did you have dinner?' I asked.

'I ate out.'

'What?'

'McDonald's.'

'Again. You must have it running in your bloodstream.'

He twisted his mouth. 'Can I go now?' he asked, already walking towards his bedroom.

'Go, it's your life, so you keep reminding me.'

He turned his back on me.

Frustrated, I slammed the palm of my hand on the counter.

Just when he was about to reach the door of his room, he glanced back, hesitated, and finally asked, 'Are you all right?'

I felt myself blush, surprised by his sudden concern. 'I'm fine,' I said, not wanting to cause him any anxiety with my problems. 'It's just work.'

'I read about this bloke who got his head chopped off in the paper. You're working on this thing, aren't you?'

'Yes, Michael, I'm working on the case.'

'Did you see it?'

'See what?'

'The head, you know. Did it look gross?'

'Yes, Michael, it was pretty awful.'

'Any blood?'

'Lots of blood.'

36

'Wow, cool. I want to do what you do when I finish school.'

By 10.00 p.m., Michael was watching television in his room. I was restless and needed to burn some energy. I rolled up by myself to Terry Bennetts' Gymnasium on High Street. No one was there at that time of the night. The radio was locked on Gold FM playing five hours of non-stop seventies music. 'Lost in the seventies' said the D.J.

The gym had this male atmosphere about it. The equipment was kind of old, none of this ultra-chrome stuff, which was just the way I liked it. I wasn't into pretty sport-bras and Hug-A-Figure tracksuit pants. A gymnasium was made for a workout, and this gym looked as if it meant business.

A life-size black-and-white photograph of the now-deceased Terry Bennett hung on one of the walls, next to a leg extension machine. He apparently held the world record for sit-ups at somewhere around 2600. When I first learnt this trivia, I made a quick mental calculation and worked that he would have had to do around eight hours non-stop of sit-ups to accomplish the task. I barely managed sixty sit-ups without a break. I had no intention of beating the world record.

Half an hour into my work out, Ken turned up. Ken worked at the State Library and did around four hours of workout a day. Oddly enough, he looked more like a short labourer than a fifty-year-old librarian. He wore grey hair of a reasonable length and a wild kind of beard. But the most amazing thing was that he could work out for two hours in a row and still look the same. He wasn't particularly muscular, but he did one-hundred-and-twenty pound deadlifts without twitching an eye. And he could hold an interesting conversation between exercise sets.

We talked about blues music and the collapse of the Berlin Wall for a while. It kept my mind off the Wilson's murder. He asked me about what I was working on, but I said the case wasn't over yet so I couldn't discuss anything with him. He took it well like he always did.

I worked my shoulders, biceps, back and abs. During my workout, I drank almost a litre of water from a red Coca-Cola sports-drink bottle I bought from a bicycle shop on Chapel Street. If I had nothing to drink while exercising, I'd die of dehydration. How Ken could workout for two hours without a drop of water was incomprehensible.

It took me an hour and a half to be exhausted enough to decide to get back home.

When I said goodbye to Ken and left the gym, the air was chilled. I felt my throat tightening, a reminder that my chest cold wasn't over yet. I still had to be careful.

Just as I stepped inside my blue Lancer, my mobile phone rang.

'Dr Malina.'

'It's Frank. We've got a meeting first thing in the morning at the VFSC with the Deputy Commissioner of Police.'

I felt blood rushing to my head.

I knew what this was going to be about.

Monday morning, I showered and dressed in my best attire - navy Country Road pants with matching jacket and white blouse. I was ready to face three men in business suits who would challenge me with their bureaucratic maze and chauvinistic attitude. Of course, I never believed Frank was one of *them*, but when he was with the boys, he acted like them. Or he said nothing, and pretended I was invisible.

The traffic was chaotic at 8.20 a.m., and it took me a good hour and a half to get to Macleod where the VFSC was located.

I had the radio tuned to Radio National. I heard my own voice commenting on the Wilson's homicide. People called the program host straight after the news to debate if Melbourne was becoming too dangerous, if there was too much violence on television, and if one day we would end up killing each other off the way Americans did.

I turned the radio off.

It made me angry to realise everyone was so ignorant. I knew for a fact that murder rates had dropped dramatically in Australia for the past three or four years. I also knew New York's murder rate had dropped by sixty percent in the past two years.

And then they tell you about the murder rate in America, but no one mentions other countries, like China, where crime figures were probably tampered, where people disappeared and no one said a word. Places like Bosnia where one year of war killed more people than ten years of homicides in the entire United States. Third world countries where thousands of children died everyday from malnutrition and diseases; children who were literally *murdered* by their government too busy playing war games.

I shrugged, concluding that even in heaven, people would have something to complain about.

The VFSC was located close to Macleod Secondary Technical College.

I turned left into Forensic Drive. A large blue sign with 'Victorian Forensic Science Centre' by the side of the road told me I was at the right place. A truck was parked on the right hand side of the road. I passed school kids dressed in yellow school uniforms who waved at me. I waved back. The centre was surrounded with grass and bushland.

I drove past a blue, high steel gate and noticed two Australian flags and a security camera. My speedometer said 40km per hour, 30km over the 10km per hour speed limit. I went right past the car park and towards the main entrance of the building where I was told by another sign to 'Report to Reception'.

The main building was a brown-creamy colour. Gum trees, mostly eucalyptus, lined the car park. More security cameras were staring at me, reflecting the level of paranoia around when this place was first built in the late 1970s.

I parked next to two police cars, in front of the main entrance. Five motorcycles were aligned next to each other, in spite of the no-parking sign. A 3WE chemical hazard sign next to the main entrance caught my attention, reminding me how little I knew about chemical hazard warnings.

I stepped out of the car, went past the entrance's glass sliding doors and entered the main foyer.

I nearly lost balance on the highly polished floor. Pictures, awards and trophies on my left made me turn my head, despite the fact that I'd already seen them hundreds of times.

Without stopping, I entered room C47, the front desk at the centre, also known as Liaison Office.

A computer and dot matrix printer to the left of the door were doing overtime, chucking out continuity labels for evidence collected by various police officers across the State.

I glanced over my shoulder, where a clock on the wall told me I was an hour late.

I stated my purpose to the bearded Liaison Officer and was told to proceed.

After going through a maze of corridors, which I had lost myself in several times when I first visited the centre, I stepped inside the conference room without knocking.

Frank Goosh was slouched in the only black, leather-bound executive chair in the room. He had an arrogant look on his face. His beady black eyes tried to destroy the little confidence I had left. My nerves were raw from the aggressiveness of other drivers out there. We spent time and energy chasing killers, but most killers were on the road.

The other men in the room were Frank Moore and Trevor Mitchell, the Director of the VFSC.

I glanced at Trevor Mitchell's dark suit and white shirt. Not very imaginative, I thought, but considering his position at the VFSC, did he need to be? Trevor Mitchell was in his mid-fifties, grey cropped hair, and had a permanent, severe look on his face.

Empty mugs confirmed each man had already helped himself to a cup of coffee and assorted cream cookies. They were injected with high-octane caffeine, ready to bulldoze through the working day and toss anyone aside who would get in their way. And frankly, I could have done with a cup as well.

Frank Goosh began, 'I guess you don't know, Miss Malina, why we're here.'

'It's *Dr* Malina,' I retorted. I felt edgy and on the defensive.

He turned to Frank and Trevor. 'See what I mean,' he said as if I had lost all my marbles. 'This is the kind of shit I have to put up with.'

And I realised these three men already had a little morning debate about my so-called attitude before I even stepped in the room.

I felt my face changing colour. 'Jesus Christ, Mr Goosh,' I shouted, leaning forward, my arms crossed over my chest. 'I don't address you as Frank. Is it so hard for you to remember the DR in front of my name? I do have a PhD in Criminal Justice, which I worked damn hard to earn.'

He rolled his eyes as the sound of my voice echoed from one corner of the room to the other.

Trevor Mitchell was unimpressed. He pursed his lips and said, 'I'd like to get this over and done with as soon as possible. I've got some other meetings to attend to, and if you two have nothing better to do than fight over trivial matters, I don't mind leaving you alone to sort them out.'

'Everything's fine,' Frank Goosh said, then turning to me, 'Isn't it, *Dr* Kristin Malina?'

I moved back in my chair. 'I guess it is.'

'Good,' Trevor Mitchell said. 'Deputy Commissioner?'

'Ah, yes,'. Frank Goosh fidgeted with his fingers as if he had forgotten what this meeting was all about. 'Dr Malina, it's been decided to pull you out of the Wilson's investigation.'

'What?' I said, absolutely stunned.

'We have an investigator at the CIB who has more experience with these types of murders. We feel that this case has too much of a high-profile. We can't afford mistakes to be made. The media is watching our every move.'

I stood mouth-agape for a few seconds. 'Mistakes? Did I do anything wrong?' I was under a tight contract, which bound me to strict ethical standards of conduct. But as I recalled, I hadn't done anything wrong to date.

'I didn't say that,' he said, addressing me as if I was unfamiliar with the English language. 'You've only been on the job six months, and well, let's just say we would feel more comfortable if someone else, someone who has more experience with these types of homicides, would lead the investigation.'

'I'm the most knowledgeable person in the field. What on earth are you talking about?'

'We're not doubting your knowledge in criminology. We're only concerned with your lack of experience with the media.'

That had to be the worst excuse I'd ever heard. And the fact that he kept referring to himself as *we*, as if everything he told me was a collective decision, made my blood boil.

'Does that have anything to do with the other night?' I snapped.

'What do you mean?' he asked as if he'd suddenly grew a pair of wings, and an aureole floated gently above his cranium.

The sonofabitch was playing games with me.

Eyes crossed the table.

'You're taking this case away from me because I didn't let you in the crime-scene area. Isn't that right?'

He shook his head. 'I don't know what you're talking about?'

You don't know what I'm talking about? You called me a bitch and a little tart, you asshole. I bet you remember that!

I turned to Frank. 'Isn't that right Frank? You were there, remember?' And then I recalled he wasn't there when I had the argument with the Deputy Commissioner of Police.

Frank shook his head, looking as embarrassed as I'd ever seen.

'Goddamn it!' I said. 'I don't believe it. What is this? The Men's Gallery? What do you want me to do next? Table-dance for you?'

'All right, Malina, that's enough,' Trevor Mitchell ordered. 'Frank Goosh *is* the Deputy Commissioner of Police, and if the investigation has been passed on to the CIB, then that's the way it's going to be. The VFSC is a service provider, not an authority.'

'Fine,' I said, trying to regain my composure. He was right on that point. The VFSC didn't serve the police only, but anyone who requested forensic tests to be done. This included defense lawyers, the general public and private companies. Tests, other than those used to help a investigator prepare a case, were subject to a fee.

Frank Goosh smiled a sadistic smile that only I could see. 'I want the entire Wilson's file transferred to the CIB's headquarters by the end of the week.'

Like hell I was going to pass over the Wilson's file. If he wanted it, he'd have to come to my place and beg like a dog. I'll make him do hand-stands, lick my shoes and kiss my arse.

I left the VFSC with a tight throat. The men's club was alive and kicking. I wanted to tell them where to go, and how far to stick it.

But a better idea crossed my mind.

CHAPTER FOUR

At 11.32 p.m. I was in bed. Frank called me to say Teresa Wilson was awake and willing to talk to us. She was staying at St Patrick's Hospital on Barry Street, in South Melbourne.

Frank Moore and I arrived at the hospital in my car. I was still furious from our morning meeting with the Deputy Commissioner of Police and the Director of the VFSC. But I didn't want to give Frank a hard time over it. He'd been nice enough to call me when Mrs Wilson woke up. He knew perfectly well I had nothing more to do with the investigation. He made me promise not to say a word to Trevor Mitchell or anyone, as he was only doing me a favour. I guess it was Frank's way of making it look like he was doing something about my unfair dismissal from the investigation.

'How long has she been awake?' I asked as we pulled into the hospital's car park.

'Half an hour from the time I got the call.'

I parked between an old, green Ford Cortina and a brand new Jeep.

St Patrick's Hospital had been built over a hundred years ago from brownstone blocks. It stood five storeys tall, was cramped with dirty windows and covered with a flat roof. Like most public hospitals in Melbourne, it was big outside, but inconveniently small on the inside, with wards half the size of the original design.

Without a word, Frank and I climbed stairs leading to the main entrance of the hospital. I noticed Frank checking his

Sony tape recorder for batteries. He placed it back in his jacket pocket after flicking it on and off, obviously satisfied it was in working order.

On arrival at the front desk, we introduced ourselves.

In less than a minute, Dr Frank Larousse came to greet us.

'I didn't know you would be coming so fast,' he said while re-adjusting his rimless glasses on the bridge of his nose. The doctor's eyes were red from the stress of double-shifts. His hair was thinning on top, but he didn't look a day over forty. He was not slim, nor bulky, just a comfortable in-between. His white lab coat was opened in the middle, showing a cheap-looking crocodile imitation leather belt, a yellow shirt and a pastel green tie. The doctor was a fashion statement, a walking billboard for all that went wrong with eighties fashion.

Dr Frank Larousse led us down a maze of corridors on the first floor of the building. Finally, he invited us into his office, which was so secluded, I wondered if I'd ever be capable of finding it again by myself. Posters of Gray's Anatomy hung on the walls. A bookshelf, filled with everything from pharmaceutical references to doctors' ethical procedures, stood on his right. I noticed a hardcover novel, wrapped in a bright orange jacket, titled *Contagious*. The writer was Robin Cook, a world-wide bestselling author and a doctor who wrote medical thrillers.

Behind Dr Larousse's back was a grey, four-drawer filing cabinet with no labels indicating the contents of the drawers.

His desk top was arranged with files and notebooks, all neatly and clinically stacked together.

He spoke to us as if we were two of his patients. 'I just want to run through the preliminary report before you go and meet Mrs Wilson. In fact, it would be better if you came back to see her tomorrow. But since you're here, and she's willing to talk to you, I guess now is as good a time as ever.'

We nodded in silence, waiting as the doctor shuffled some paper on his desk. He lifted a yellow manilla folder and pulled a page from its content.

'Here we go. Her name is Teresa Vivienne Wilson, age 34, Caucasian with no superficial deformities.' He glanced in our direction to see that he hadn't lost us, and went on, 'We've found bruising all over her body, including the legs, buttocks, arms and face.'

'Someone beat her up?' Frank asked, raising his brow.

'That's what I would conclude. We've also found numerous abrasions and small cuts on her face, abdomen and arms. Intermittent haemorrhaging was present from both nostrils. Her scalp was covered with small wounds, and hair at the crown was matted with blood.'

I swallowed as I pictured in my mind's eye what Teresa Wilson had gone through.

Dr Larousse continued his monologue, 'Three of her fingernails were broken, and both hands swollen. When she arrived at the hospital, she was in hypovolemic shock. Her skin was cold and pale with blueness at the lips and fingers. She was restless and confused, something normal after the ordeal she went through.'

'And where did you take her after the initial examination?' I asked, speaking up for the first time since we'd been in the doctor's office.

'I've had her transferred to a supportive environment and administered a saline solution. Within hours her temperature rose, her skin tone improved, and her mental orientation was more or less restored. Two hours later she slipped into a semi-coma, most likely due to post-traumatic shock.'

'What about rape?' Frank asked for both of us.

'Ah, I was going to get to that. We found bruising, scratching and localised swelling around the external genitals. Dried blood was located in the anus. Examination of the vagina with a speculum resulted in the discovery of a copious amount of a substance consistent with appearance and viscosity of semen. The substance was removed from around the neck of the cervix. Severe scratches were found in the anterior wall of the vagina.'

'So she was raped?' Frank asked again impatiently.

'I'm getting there. The opening of her anus appeared patulous and cut in several places. I examined the interior of the anus with a speculum and came up with a squash ball lying in the cavity of the rectum.'

'A what?' I muttered, wondering if I had heard correctly.

'A squash ball. You know, a hard rubber ball, the type used to play that game where the players hit the ball against a wall.'

I knew what a squash ball was. I just couldn't understand what it was doing inside Teresa Wilson.

Dr Larousse seemed somehow satisfied that he had shocked us. A slight grin on his face made me wonder if he was a touch sadistic.

'The high-friction surface of the squash ball,' he continued, 'caused considerable tissue damage to the anus and the walls of the lower tract of the large bowel. We'll have to remove the ball by surgery under general anaesthetic.'

'Okay, Doctor,' Frank said, 'by-passing any more technical details, what is your opinion on what happened to Mrs Wilson?'

Dr Larousse looked straight at us. 'The preliminary assessment of Mrs Wilson clearly indicates to me that she's been beaten and subjected to an unusual level of physical abuse, and it would appear rape has taken place.'

Both Frank and I scribbled notes in our pad books.

'You don't mind if we get a copy of the preliminary report?' I asked without lifting my eyes from my notes.

'I'll have two sets photocopied by the time you finish interrogating Mrs Wilson.'

We thanked Dr Larousse for his time as he escorted us out of his office.

When Frank Moore and I arrived in Teresa Wilson's room, at the Intensive Care Unit Ward, on the third floor of the building, we brought in a bunch of pink carnations from a shop downstairs, next to the main entrance of the hospital.

Coming face to face with a victim was never easy, no matter how many times we went through the process. Repetition was supposed to make you stronger, but some things were never easy, no matter how many times you dealt with them.

Every time I encountered a crime victim, I was conscious I was dealing with a human being. Ironically, people who caused the damage in the first place usually never saw other people as anything more than objects. This was probably the main difference between them and us. They had lost touch with their inner feelings. They were incapable of sympathy for anyone but themselves. Men who committed atrocities, like the savage beating and raping of Teresa Wilson, were very often self-centred and beyond redemption.

After years of studying the criminal mind, years of interrogating hundreds of criminals and repeat offenders, I was convinced some men could never be rehabilitated, no matter how many years they had been institutionalised, how much medical and psychological therapy they'd received, or how willing they were to better themselves. Their sociopathic attributes were eternally entwined in their general make-up. Recent US research even suggested that their DNA structure could in fact have been altered over a time-period, supporting the long-time hypothesis that everything is mind over matter.

As soon as I walked into Teresa Wilson's room, my heart sank. Her face was puffed up and covered with cuts and bruises. Her complexion was bluish-green, making it difficult to see the person behind the mask. Monitors were used to watch heart and lung function, that is ECG, blood pressure, pulse and respiratory rate. Tubing was attached to various parts of her body, helping to control her urine production and drain output. Her head was maintained high with the help of three pillows. I couldn't help feeling Teresa Wilson was in no condition to answer our questions.

My stomach churned as I tried to comprehend why someone would hurt another person so badly. I surprised myself with that question, especially since I have dealt with hundreds of homicides in the past fifteen years and had already come to some hard-edged conclusions.

Evil bred in and invaded the minds of desperate souls.

We introduced ourselves briefly, and Frank and I promised we'd take little of her time.

'It's all right,' she said, her bruised lower lip quivering. 'I don't mind helping out. There's so much I need to tell you. It's happened so suddenly.'

'We're going to be taping this,' Frank said matter-of-factly, as he removed the Sony recorder from his jacket. 'It's easier if we do. It means we don't have to ask you the same questions over and over again. Is that all right with you?'

Teresa nodded, and Frank switched the tape on.

'Also,' he added, 'I have to inform you that you don't have talk to us if you don't want to. Anything you tell us from now on can be used as evidence in court.'

47

'It's okay,' she said, 'I've got nothing to hide.'

I would be asking all the questions since Frank was a crime-scene examiner and not an investigator. In fact, he wasn't even supposed to be in this room, and since I was told to stop working on the Wilson's case, neither was I. Both of us would be in serious trouble if this thing leaked out.

'You're also allowed to have a lawyer present,' I said, doubting she would need one. But her rights were covered under the *Crimes Act*, and I had a legal obligation to tell her that.

'I don't need a lawyer,' she said.

I agreed by nodding.

Frank placed the small Sony recorder, which had been running for about a minute, in front of Teresa Wilson.

The humming of the tape was all we heard for the next ten seconds.

I sat next to Teresa and tried hard not to hold her hand, even though I had the urge to do so. I wanted to give her a hug and let her know I understood how difficult this was for her. I wanted to tell her she was not alone, that we would do anything to help her get through this. I wanted her to know that if she ever needed a friend, I would be there for her. But I felt it was a bit early to move in so fast. I couldn't help it. Part of me was nothing but raw emotions. Maybe I would wait until the end of the interrogation.

'So, can you tell us what happened?' I began.

'It's all confusing in my head, but I'll do the best I can.'

'It's okay. Take your time. If you need to rest or compose yourself, let us know. If you want to do this tomorrow morning or another day, we can do that. Sergeant Frank Moore will turn the tape recorder off, and we'll start again later.'

'We might as well get it over and done with,' she said, before hesitating for a few seconds. 'I'm not sure where to start. I haven't done this kind of thing before.'

'Tell us what you remember,' I said, finding Teresa amazingly courageous to be willing to go through the entire ordeal again.

'My husband Jeremy is an electronics engineer.' She used the present tense as if he was still alive. It would probably take her a while to realise she would never see him again. 'He works from home, which is great, because we see each other all the time. He is under contract with lots of companies.'

'How long have you been together?' I asked.

'We tied the knot five years ago and moved to Port Melbourne eighteen months ago because of his work. It's much closer to the city and easy for him to find work. He hates wasting time driving.'

'Can you tell us about the night of the attack?'

'I'll try.' She glanced at Frank and then at myself. 'It was late, and Jeremy was finishing a plan he had been working on all day for a company. His deadline was coming up soon, and the project had taken him more time than he'd first anticipated. I was watching television, waiting patiently for him to finish so we could go to bed. When he finally did, I made two cups of hot chocolate, and we had them in the kitchen. A nightly ritual. Warm milk made us sleep better. Really, it was an excuse because we are both chocoholics.'

I smiled at her comment.

She smiled back and went on, 'We made small talk while drinking our chocolate, working out what was ahead of us for the following day. Bedtime was the only time we really got to talk, to spend some quality time together. We were both very busy. After the hot chocolate, we went straight to bed.'

'And?'

'I was almost asleep, and I think Jeremy was too because he was snoring when I heard some kind of noise in the hallway. At first I didn't know what the hell it was, but after listening attentively, I thought it sounded like someone trying to break into the apartment. I woke up Jeremy, and he heard the noise too. It sounded like cracking wood, and Jeremy said someone was breaking in through the front door. I'd never been so scared in my life. Jeremy jumped out of bed completely naked. He raced down the hallway without bothering with his dressing gown. I panicked and reached for the telephone. The line was dead.'

I remembered the telephone cable in the hallway of the Port Melbourne apartment had been ripped from the wall.

Teresa went on, 'Then I heard Jeremy scream his head off, so I jumped out of bed, put on my dressing gown, and grabbed a stout metal ruler from Jeremy's drawing tools. He always kept some tools in the bedroom in case he came up with an idea overnight and wanted to do a quick sketch. Always had work on his mind.

'I rushed into the hallway, and this tall man came crashing on me. He lifted me from the floor and threw me back in the bedroom. I knocked my head against the lower edge of the dressing table and passed out.'

'How long were you unconscious for?' I asked, now totally absorbed by Teresa's story.

'I don't know. I can't remember. Ten minutes. Maybe half an hour. It's hard to say.'

'What happened when you regained consciousness?'

'The overhead light of the bedroom was turned on. The man who attacked me was kneeling on the floor in front of the bed, making broad sweep movements with one hand while holding something down with the other. I looked up from the bed and felt this terrible pain at the back of my neck. I thought I was going to pass out, but I forced myself to stay awake. I looked down my body and saw the same man who attacked me in the hallway. He was bent over and cutting something. It took me at least fifteen seconds to realise the thing he was cutting was Jeremy.'

She stopped for a few seconds, waiting for our reaction. But we said nothing, so she went on, 'He had this huge knife, and the noise was dreadful, like chalk hissing on a blackboard. It sent a jolt through my entire body. A hissing and squelching sound filled my ears. The weird thing was that Jeremy wasn't trying to fight back, as if he was already dead.

'I managed to get on my feet, but the pain at the back of my head was unbearable. I felt dizzy, and I thought I was going to pass out once more.

'I moved closer to the man, and then I saw Jeremy's neck opened like a horrible red mouth. I swear to God, it was the most horrid thing I had ever seen in my life. Less than half an hour ago, he was this person that I knew, and now he had become this bloody mess. I still can't believe it was him. I don't know if I want to remember...'

Teresa lost her composure as tears began cascading down her face.

50

'It's all right. It's over now,' I said, finally holding on to Teresa's hand. 'Nothing's going to happen any more. You're safe now.' I made a gesture for Frank to stop the tape recorder.

'No wait,' Teresa sobbed, 'the worst thing is that I knew him. I knew the man.'

My whole body went on red alert as my eyes met Frank's.

He too had been taken by surprise. He kept the tape recorder going.

'Who was it?' I prompted.

'Walter Dunn. He used to work with Jeremy once. But then, as soon as Jeremy's business began to pick up, he sort of disappeared from our lives.'

I wrote the name down in my notebook.

'Do you know where he lives?'

'No, no, we lost track of him a while ago. In fact, we didn't want to see him any more. So, I was kind of surprised when I saw him that night. He was the last person I'd expected to see.'

'What did he do to you?' I asked, knowing I should let her rest, but she was on a roll, and it was better to get it over and done with in one go while the story was still fresh in her mind.

She locked her eyes into mine and said, 'He turned around with the knife in his hand. It was covered in blood, and I couldn't keep my eyes off it. I thought, oh, my God, he's going to cut my neck like he did to Jeremy. I was so scared. I'd never been so scared in my life, like you know, you're going to die, and there's nothing you can do about it. But he didn't. Instead he threw the knife away. For a moment, I felt relieved knowing he wasn't going to use the knife, but my relief was short-lived. He threw himself on top of me, grinning all the time, in a horrible kind of way, his eyes filled with anger, as if he was evil or something.'

I pressed her hand to encourage her to go on.

And she did. 'I'd never seen Walter this way before. He grabbed me with one hand between my legs and the other at my nightgown and threw me on top of the bed. I knocked the back of my head on the edge of the bed, exactly at the spot where I hit the dressing table earlier on. I thought I was going to pass out again. But I didn't because of the pain.'

I wanted to tell her to take a break if she felt like it, but she seemed too engaged in her story, so I didn't bother.

51

She was moving her free hand as she continued, 'He was muttering something like, "You sonofabitch, motherfucker, two-timing piece of shit", and then he went for me. I tried hard to fight back, but he was much stronger than me. I had not a hope in hell. He tore my underwear and opened me up with his fingers before pumping himself into me. I swear to God, I never thought I was going to come out of this alive. All along, he was groaning in anger and pleasure, beating me across the face with the back of his hand.

'When it was over, he tossed me around and shoved something in my backside. The pain was horrific, like something I'd never felt before. I thought I was going to die. I found it so hard to understand what was going on. So hard to understand why...'

Teresa broke down in tears.

I retrieved my hand from hers and wiped her tears with my thumb. 'All right, that's enough,' I said, 'You've done well.'

I nodded to Frank, and he turned the tape recorder off.

I took Teresa's hand again and added, 'You've been very brave.'

'But maybe I could have saved him,' she said with a coarse voice. 'If only I didn't let him leave the bedroom. Maybe he'd still be alive. Maybe everything would have turned out fine. ' With the tears, the bruising and the cuts, Teresa Wilson was not a pretty sight.

A rage built up inside me. I had never been so angry in my life.

'It's not your fault Teresa,' I said. 'It never was your fault. Don't you dare think for a minute that this had anything to do with you. You couldn't have done anything. You did the best you could. You couldn't have known what he was going to do to Jeremy.'

She nodded in silence, but I could tell my comments didn't make her feel better. She'd been the victim, but also the survivor. She was experiencing a normal post-traumatic reaction. Survivors of an ordeal who'd lost a partner always blamed themselves for not having done enough, even though there was absolutely nothing they could have done.

Sometimes the blame hung around for days.

Sometimes for weeks, months, years.

Sometimes forever.

'What if he comes back to get me?' she sobbed. 'What if he knows I'm not dead and decides to finish me off?'

'We're going to catch him, Teresa,' I said, determined to do what I had just promised. 'We're going to get the sucker and make him pay for everything he's done to you.'

She looked into my eyes and my heart sank, like it had when I first walked in the room.

CHAPTER FIVE

Walter Dunn didn't have a prior criminal record, but his name was listed with Vic Roads, and as a result we had no problem tracking down his address.

Of course, neither Frank Moore, nor myself expected to find Walter Dunn sitting comfortably in front of his television, watching re-runs of old American television series at two o'clock in the morning. For all we knew, he was already half way across Australia or on a 747 flight to America or Europe.

The proper thing to do would have been to inform the detective in charge of the investigation about the current situation. But as it was, both Frank and I were too enraged to wait for someone else to catch the bastard. We could always argue later with the detective that Teresa Wilson was in danger, and there was an urgency in stopping the killer of her husband.

Walter Dunn's residence was listed in Caulfield, not far from Monash University, just off Grange Road.

We drove straight there from the hospital.

I checked the time on the dashboard: 2.16 a.m. This was the second time in a week I'd be up all night. But my mind was clear and alert. The rage inside me fuelled me as if I'd just swallowed ten cups of black coffee.

When we left the hospital, Teresa slipped into a state of shock. She stared at the empty space in front of her, and for a moment I worried that she'd might have slipped back into some sort of coma. I expected her behaviour to become

54

hysterical in the next few days unless she somehow accepted the reality of what had happened. What was strange was that it was all clear in her mind. Some victims of violent crimes sometimes chose not to remember on a conscious level. But Teresa Wilson remembered everything. She had trouble accepting the truth, but she remembered it clearly.

I passed Monash University's Caulfield campus. Streets were dark and empty, except for the odd taxi driver desperately working all night for less than a hundred dollars.

'What do you think the chances are that he'll be home?' Frank asked as he passed a hand over his thinning hair. I glanced at him quietly, trying to keep my eyes on the road. He seemed slightly concerned about our actions.

'Your guess is as good as mine,' I said, giving my full attention back to the road. 'I don't know why he didn't kill the girl. Don't you find him silly, leaving someone behind as a witness?'

Frank shifted on his seat. 'Yeah, but when you consider he's left virtually every imaginable piece of evidence behind, it would have only been a matter of time before we tracked him down, even if he did kill the girl.'

Frank was right of course. We found a piece of fabric that was probably from his wardrobe; a knife with no fingerprints but covered in blood; and hair specimens all over the place.

As I left Princes Highway and took a right turn into Grange Road, I realised this was not only one of the most heart-wrenching cases I had been involved in, but also the easiest one to solve.

And yet something at the back of my mind disturbed me.

If Walter Dunn had premeditated the attack, then why had he been so careless? Could he have been so enraged that he never paid attention to what he was doing? Did he really think he could carry out what he did without getting caught? Most murderers left enough evidence behind for us to work with. But it looked as if Walter Dunn hadn't even tried to conceal his presence at the scene, as if he really wanted to get caught. I wished I knew what was going on in his mind before proceeding. We had no idea what we were up against. And if Teresa's testimony was anything to go by, we were about to deal with a raging lunatic.

The only way we were going to find out why he snapped

was by asking him.

I stopped the car in front of Walter Dunn's Victorian house. Suburbia gave me the creeps, mostly because I grew up there. I kept associating suburbia with normal, everyday, boring life, which was probably an accurate description of the majority of people's lives who lived there.

For as long as I can remember, I've always had a fear of blending in too much with the rest of the world. I feared if too plain and common, I would drown in a sea of ordinary people living monotonous lives.

Back at high school, I tried hard to look different. An easy task, since my parents were of Brazilian origin, and my birth name was Petera Oliveira Dos Malina. My hair was down to my buttocks and darker than charcoal. My bronze skin gave the impression that I was tanned all year round. I wasn't tall, but slim enough to get lustful stares from boys and hatred looks from girls.

My friends were far and few, so I concentrated on working hard. The only thing I had full control over. I knew I could become whatever I wanted to become by using my head. And yet, in spite of my love for studying, I hated school, and the way most teachers taught us without care or compassion. A hidden agenda fuelled my craving to be different. Like most people who have a built-in desire to succeed, I kept secret the details of my dysfunctional family until I turned sixteen, when it became impossible to hide the truth any longer.

The lights at Walter Dunn's home were turned off.

A greyish Honda Prelude occupied the driveway. Because of the darkness, I couldn't quite make out the colour. Everything seemed to be in shades of grey.

'We better watch ourselves,' Frank said as he checked the nine-shot clip of his 9mm semiautomatic pistol, a gift I bought him from one of my visits to the USA. To get it past customs had been a nightmare. I had to apply for a special license, and they grilled me with every question in the book. I remained cooperative because I was aware of the increasing number of concealed weapons finding their way outside the USA.

Frank loved the gun, but he wasn't happy with the fact that he had to release and re-depress the trigger every time he used it, a standard feature of semiautomatic weapons. The pistol was also fitted with a safety mechanism to prevent accidental discharge.

'You stand behind me,' he ordered, as if I had a choice.

I wasn't licensed to carry a weapon, which was the most ridiculous situation to be in when you're an investigator. But the paperwork was in someone's tray, and soon, I was told, even though I'd been waiting nearly a year, I would be authorised to carry my own killing machine.

As we sat in the Lancer, darkness surrounding us, I began to have a really bad feeling about our situation. I knew it was wrong. I shouldn't have been here at all since I'd been barred from the Wilson's homicide. Nor should Frank. His job description as a crime-scene examiner did not entail making arrests. But he could always argue later that he was operating under section 459A of the Victorian *Crimes Act*. As a sworn member, the act gave him the power to enter any premises and arrest a person who had committed a serious indictable offence in the State of Victoria. And Walter definitely fitted the description of such a person. I would have to defend my actions as exercising my rights of citizen's arrest. We had already talked it over on the way from the hospital. We were both willing to cop flack if anything went wrong.

We stepped out of the car and eased ourselves into the front yard. The grass was in bad need of attention. A cool wind sent a shiver down my spine as I illogically wondered why in the world we never called for backup. It was pretty obvious why. We weren't meant to be there, full stop.

'Do you think this is wise?' I whispered, now doubting our reckless move.

'Tssss.. this is not the time to change your mind.'

Frank's bald spot was shining in the street light. Although he was probably the best crime-scene examiner in this country, I felt completely unsafe. We were out of bounds. Frank wasn't trained to jump in on criminals in the middle of the night, especially those who took a delight in cutting your head off or inserting a squash ball up your arse.

'Shit,' I muttered, 'Maybe we should get some help. What if he's got a gun?'

'If he had a gun, he would have blown Jeremy Wilson's head off, not cut it off.'

That was as convincing an answer as I wanted to hear.

'So we're doing the right thing?' I was beginning to lose my cool, which surprised me, and probably Frank because I had always been self-assured in previous homicides.

Frank turned around and breathed right down my neck, 'If you don't want to come, you don't have to. Frankly, I don't care either way. I'm gonna get that sonofabitch with or without you.'

I was taken back by the intensity of his anger. I never noticed at the hospital, but Teresa Wilson's injuries must have affected him deeper than I first realised. My main motivation for trapping Walter Dunn was Teresa's safety. Frank seemed to be fuelled by hate and revenge for the person who had committed such a disturbing crime.

'All right, let's do it,' I said, not feeling I had a choice in the matter.

Frank stood in front of the door, knocked loudly twice, and stepped aside. He pulled the slide on his 9mm semiautomatic to bring the first bullet into firing position. He was ready to perform.

I listened attentively.

Nothing.

'Maybe he's not home,' I whispered, wanting to get back into the safety of my car, call for back up, and let a Special Operations Group do its job.

'His car's here.'

Frank knocked again, this time louder.

Nothing.

'Fuck,' Frank said, 'let's go through the back. He could be asleep.'

We circled the house and landed in a big yard with washing on the line. It smelled like grass and dog droppings. And yet, there were no dogs around. Maybe it was the neighbours.

'He's house-trained,' Frank joked, pointing to the clothes-line with his pistol.

Under the circumstances, I found his joke rather lame.

Perspiration was dripping down the small of my back as we closed in on the back door.

The flyscreen creaked when Frank pulled it towards him.

We both froze like statues, waiting for someone to burst out of the house with a cook's knife, chase us around the backyard, and have the time of his life separating our heads from our bodies.

Nothing.

Frank placed one hand on the knob of the back door, turned it, and pushed the door open.

A wosh of foul air smacked me in the face, sending me two steps backwards.

Frank turned his head, grimaced, looked straight at me and said, 'Shit, this smells awfully familiar.'

We found Walter Dunn with a gunshot wound to the head. He'd shot himself in the temple with a Smith & Wesson .38 service revolver.

Insects were crawling around and inside the body, and fluid was leaking from the nostrils and mouth of the dead man. A putrid odour of decomposition filled my lungs.

Walter's face was almost unrecognisable and had turned greenish-red. I found it horrid, but I had the stomach for it, making it easy for me to do the job I did.

Looking back at the way I felt before we entered the house, I realised I was more at ease coming face to face with a dead Walter Dunn than one who was still alive.

We went back to the car to collect our overalls, boots and other protective equipment. Frank carried the PERK in two separate dark briefcases, while I carried a metal briefcase with two SLRs and enough film to shoot an entire issue of Vogue. Frank had called for backup, not that we really needed it at that point in time.

Prior to collecting evidence, we videotaped the entire crime scene and its vicinity. Videotaping was now the norms for any crime scene where murder or suicide had occurred.

Passing the front yard, video camera rolling, I suddenly realised why the lawn was so overgrown. While Walter Dunn had been busy fermenting his body and turning it into a haven for maggots and insects, nobody bothered maintaining his surroundings.

As I began taking a photographic record of the body, I asked Frank, 'And how the hell are we going to write this one up in the report?'

He shifted uncomfortably from one foot to the other while making a sketch of the room. 'It's all right,' he said, 'I'll take care of it.'

I took two shots of Walter Dunn's temple with a colour film, and two with a black & white infra-red film.

'You'll take care of it. I'm involved in this as much as you are, and I'd like to know how it's going to come out. You knew we weren't supposed to be here in the first place. We should have got backup.'

'I'll take care of it, I said.'

'I know you will. But people are going to ask questions. This is no small investigation. The damn thing's been all over the papers for the last few days. The media is going to ask how we got to the killer, and why we decided to move in on him without following the proper procedures.'

Frank threw his pen on the bloody carpet. 'Jesus, Malina, give me a break. You seem to forget that we decided to come here together. We both made the decision. You're the friggin' crime-scene investigator. I'm only a crime-scene examiner. Why is it that suddenly this whole thing falls on my back? I'm no more responsible than you are.'

Heat rose to my face. Frank was right, and I felt foolish. I'd been working with him for years now, and I should have known better than questioning his every move.

I reloaded a new film in the Minolta and muttered, 'I'm sorry. It's just that it's been a difficult week, and I wasn't expecting this.'

Frank bent down and grabbed his pencil. 'Well, at least we got the bastard. Nothing more is going to happen now. It's black and white. There won't be any prosecution or manhunt. There's no need to rush. This is going straight on file as soon as we're through.'

I felt a sense of relief that this investigation was over in less than a week. The Sheree Beasley homicide dragged on for months before we got the killer. It drained us, especially when we had so little to go on with.

With Jeremy Wilson's murder, there was enough trace evidence and even a witness. It would have been only a matter of time before we would had caught up with Walter Dunn.

But we got lucky, and things went our way in less than a week.

It took us a couple of hours to record everything at the crime scene and collect as much physical evidence as possible. A waste of time, if you asked me. Nobody was going to bother with forensic tests since the case would be classified solved and filed away in the next forty-eight hours.

Nevertheless, we took our time and did our job properly.

The detective in charge of the investigation was not going to be impressed by our procedures. We'd just cost him an additional notch on his resume.

When I tried to collect firearm discharge residue from Walter Dunn's hands with scanning electron microscope (SEM) adhesive stubs, I was unsuccessful because of the level of decomposition on Walter's skin, and the damage done by maggots and insects. This was a bit of a setback since the firearm discharge residue collected from Walter's hands would have confirmed the Smith & Wesson .38 service revolver had been discharged by him.

I reassured myself this incident was a tiny problem since other evidence collected so far at the Wilson's apartment would clearly indicate Walter Dunn was the killer.

I found no firearm discharge residue on Walter's clothing.

Half way through the collection of evidence, we called the SES to provide us with additional lighting. Working in the dark, even with all the house lights turned on, was difficult.

When it came to the wound on Walter's temple, I cut his skin beyond the blackened area surrounding the bullet hole and identified the '12 o'clock position' with a suture. I placed the sample in a glass jar filled with a ten percent formalin mixture. This would help us determine an accurate firing distance and angle for the crime-scene report.

I also took various hair samples from Walter's body to be used against reference samples, that is known samples collected at the Wilson's apartment, and compared with those of the suspect.

I plucked thirty hairs from the pubic area, and thirty hairs from his scalp. All hair samples were stored in folded paper and inserted in clearly labelled plastic bags. The hair samples would confirm the colour, sex and race of the person, as well as the areas of the body from which the evidence came from.

Although we knew where the samples from Walter Dunn's house came from, comparison tests would confirm those samples matched those found at the Wilson's apartment.

Sixty to eighty insects were collected from and under the body, and 90 to 150cm away from the body. I stored them in 70 percent ethyl alcohol per volume in distilled water. They would be forwarded to an entomologist for identification.

I also collected two samples of maggots containing sixty to seventy individuals, and placed one of the samples in a phial with flesh to ensure their survival. The second sample was stored in a glass bottle filled with formalin.

Meanwhile, Frank was busy collecting saliva, soil, tools, tool marks, vegetation, fibres and blood samples. He also found the jacket which matched the piece of cloth found on the window frame of the Wilson's apartment.

The paramedics came ten minutes after I called them, just when we finished taking the final details of the crime scene.

They placed the corpse in a body bag and whisked it to the mortuary in Southgate.

Frank and I drove back to my place since it was less than fifteen minutes away.

'You know,' I said, as we were climbing the stairs to my apartment. 'It's hard for me to believe this is all over. I'm not used to solving homicides in four days.'

'I have to admit this is the easiest case I've been involved in for quite a few years,' Frank replied, his voice strained from lack of sleep.

Normally, homicides took months, sometimes years to solve.

I opened the door to my apartment and turned to Frank. 'You don't have to go home. If you're tired, you can sleep on the couch. It's big, comfortable, and frankly I could do with someone in the house tonight.'

'What about Michael?'

'What *about* Michael?'

Frank had a oblong smile on his face.

'And no, it's not what you think,' I said defensively before he had time to utter a syllable.

'I didn't say anything,' he protested, his hands up in the air. 'You're the one who's invited me in.'

'Just making sure we understand each other.'

I made him a cup of tea while he showered.

At 5.23 a.m., he was snoring on the couch, and I got to bed.

I was restless. My mind was turning endlessly. Flashes of what I had seen in the last few days haunted me. I kept thinking about Teresa and saw myself in her place.

Thank God I was no longer married. If someone had decapitated my husband, they would have had to send me to an asylum and throw away the keys.

I tried hard to close my eyes and escape reality, but when I heard the first tram travelling down Chapel Street, I knew daylight was just around the corner.

And then someone knocked gently on my bedroom door.

'What?'

'Mum?'

'Yes, Michael.'

He poked his head in the room. 'There's a man sleeping in the lounge room.'

'I know. Don't wake him up. He's on our side.'

'Okay, then,' he said, as if we were the dynamic duo.

When he closed the door, I felt like a rotten mother. I didn't spend enough time with Michael.

At around six a.m., I closed my eyes and slept for twenty hours straight.

CHAPTER SIX

On Tuesday the 25th of February, the weather was kind of strange. The day began with a cool wind sweeping in from the ocean. After lunch, it was too hot to even wear a jacket. And that's what I loved about Melbourne weather. Totally unpredictable. This was also why I kept nursing a chest cold which had been close to an end for almost two weeks now. I was seriously wondering if my chest cold wasn't some form of asthma. I knew Australia held one of the world's highest number of asthmatics, and nobody knew why. After all, Australia was one of the least polluted countries on the planet.

I made a mental note to see a specialist, but I knew I would put it off forever. I seldom went to a doctor, and it would take more than a cough to get me there.

Straight after lunch, I got a call from the telephone company asking me how I was going with a case involving a person who was stealing coins from telephone booths in the City of Port Phillip. I told them I'd been busy with a homicide and had little chance to look into it. After hanging up, I decided to do some research in the afternoon. They'd given me the job two weeks ago, and I hadn't done a thing.

Because of the small amount of serious homicides in this state, I supplemented my income by doing private investigative work for financial institutions, large corporations and various government departments.

I spent most of the day shopping on Chapel Street,

indulging at Black Whale and Checkerboard, two second-hand book shops, two hundred metres apart, on the same side of the street. Both owners of the bookshops knew me well since I purchased a ton of books from them at least three times a week. They often gave me a discount on multiple purchases. But I found no information in either shop on stealing money from telephone booths.

I ate a vegetarian souvlaki for lunch and washed it down with a Dr Pepper.

By the time the evening came, I was still restless. I had a vague idea of visiting Teresa Wilson in hospital, but it didn't feel right. She wasn't a relative of mine, nor a friend. And yet, not acknowledging what she had gone through seemed cruel.

I sat on my balcony with *The Rainmaker*, a second-hand hardcover legal thriller by John Grisham. Although the story was well-written and captivated my interest, my thoughts kept drifting back to the Wilson investigation, making it impossible for me to fully emerge myself in the adventure. The past week kept trotting in my mind, and I wasn't going to deny I was now sightly anxious about my future after the Deputy Commissioner of Police would find out I'd deliberately disobeyed a direct order and persisted with the Wilson case.

When Michael came back from god-knows-where, I asked him if he knew anything about people stealing coins from telephone booths.

'Sure, it's on the Internet,' he replied, as if this should have been the first place to look. He was wearing the same Michael Jordan T-shirt he had on all week. I was seriously considering going shopping with him for some new clothes. 'You can get anything from the Internet,' he added, flipping his blond fringe away from his face.

'The Internet?'

'Yeah, some guy name Jolly Roger wrote an entire manual on how to do illegal stuff. You know, basically everything wrong you can do. Fraud, murder, absolutely anything.'

'Jolly Roger? Is that his real name?'

He gave me a look that implied I had no brain left. 'Do you really think someone is going to write all this stuff on the Internet under his real name?'

'Show me.'

I took him to my study, flicked on the computer and logged into the Internet.

Michael accessed one of the most popular Internet search engines.

In less than thirty seconds, Michael located a web-page on how to torture, how to kill with your bare hands, how to make dynamite, how to make bombs, how to break into a house, and how to do another one hundred and one illegal things.

My eyes were open wide in front of the screen. I was astounded at how fast Michael got there. He was better than me on the damn thing. I knew how to trace people, break into government and company databases, but I wasn't an Internet freak.

'What did you do?' I asked.

'What do you mean?'

'How did you find this?'

'I was doing some stuff at school on terrorism, and I found it by accident.'

I wanted to throw up. We were busting our guts trying to catch criminals, and some lunatic in the USA provided the world with recipes on how to kill people.

'Jesus Christ!' I muttered, jumping from one foot to the other.

'Okay here we go,' he said, shifting from the chair. 'I found it.'

I looked over his shoulder and saw that he was right. 'Can you print this stuff?' I asked. In front of my eyes were clear instructions on how to steal money from telephone booths.

'Sure, hold on a sec.'

He did a COPY and PASTE command from the web side to Microsoft Word 6.0, followed by a simple lay-out, and printed the article.

In less than a minute I was holding the information in my hands.

How to Get Money out of Pay Phones
by Jolly Roger

I will now share with you my experiences with pay telephones. You will discover that it is possible to get money from a pay phone with a minimum of effort. Theory: Most pay phones use four wires for the transmission of data and codes to the central office. Two of them are used for voice (usually red and green), one is a ground, and the last is used with the others for the transmission of codes.

It is with this last wire that you will be working with. On the pay phone that I usually did this to, it was colored purple, but most likely will be another color.

What you will do is simply find a pay phone which has exposed wires, such that one of them can be disconnected and connected at ease without fear of discovery. You will discover that it is usually a good idea to have some electrical tape along with you and some tool for cutting this tape.

Through trial and error, you will disconnect one wire at a time starting with the wires different than green and red. You do want a dial tone during this operation.

What you want to disconnect is the wire supplying the codes to the telephone company so that the pay phone will not get the 'busy' or 'hang-up' command. Leave this wire disconnected when you discover it.

What will happen: Anytime that someone puts any amount of money into the pay phone, the deposit will not register with the phone company and it will be held in the 'temporary' chamber of the pay phone.

Then, (a day later or so) you just go back to the phone, reconnect the wire, and click the hook a few times and the phone will dump it all out the shute. (What is happening is that the 'hangup' code that the phone was not receiving due to the wire being disconnected suddenly gets the code and dumps its 'temporary' storage spot.)

You can make a nice amount of money this way, but remember that a repairman will stop by every few times it is reported broken and repair it, so check it at least once a day.

I had seen things which were of poor taste. But this kind of information really irritated me. Sure, I believed in freedom of speech, like most people, but I objected to instructions on how to break the law.

'You didn't go around and try this?' I asked Michael.

He gave me a sour look.

'I'm sorry,' I said. 'It's just that, I mean you found this information. So, I thought maybe you wanted to try it out.'

'And because I found it, it means I'm going to use it?'

'No, but you're a bit young.'

He sighed angrily and said, 'What would you know, anyway? You're never home to find out if I grow up or not.' Bitterness infested his tone.

I knew he was right, but I had to defend myself. Part of my nature was to argue. 'That's not fair, Michael. I'm trying to make the world a better place.'

'Well, how about starting here?'

Damn! I couldn't get used to how kids talked to their parents these days. Okay, I promised to myself I would never be mean to my children, but now I realised everything had a price.

'Michael, don't talk to me that way.'

'Forget it,' he said and left the study.

I flicked the computer off and threw the printed page in my in-tray.

Half an hour later, we were having dinner over the dining table. We seldom ate together, not since Michael was around eight years old. It felt kind of weird for the both of us.

Michael ate his oven fries, fish fingers and three vegies, avoiding eye contact. It hurt me like hell to think I was becoming the parent I swore I would never become. But there was never enough time in the day to do everything and to take care of someone else as well. God only knew how the other mothers managed.

And then, suddenly he announced that he would be away for the weekend. He'd be staying at a friend's place on Friday night and wouldn't be back until Sunday evening. I knew better than to ask him why. I just smiled and said, 'sure'.

After dinner, Michael left for his room, and I did the dishes.

Right on 7.00 p.m., I decided to go to Terry Bennetts' Gymnasium.

I was kind of surprised to see Ken there because he usually turned up at around ten o'clock. Now that the Wilson investigation was over, I felt at liberty to discuss the details with him.

Ken seemed particularly alert that day, as if those daily four hours of body building were finally paying off. I told him once that if he'd put as much effort on studying as he did on body building, he'd be a genius by now. But he replied he abhorred anything which involved mental activity. His reply surprised me because I found him so in touch with himself and the world around. For a man who never tried to go beyond his high school certificate, he possessed an amazing sense of self-awareness and understanding of the world around him. Working at the State Library obviously gave him a chance to dip into hundreds of books a year. And although he never saw it as intellectual stimulus, his general knowledge far surpassed many people I knew.

'I don't see anything wrong in visiting Teresa Wilson,' he said between two one-hundred-and-twenty-pound deadlifts. He wasn't wearing a top, and I felt a bit uncomfortable standing too close to him. Not that I expected to lose control and suddenly jump on him, but near-naked men made me feel in awe. I hadn't slept with anyone for a long time and began wondering if I'd end up like an old maid. Funny enough, I didn't feel a strong need for a sexual relationship, but some warm body contact, cuddles and love would have been welcomed. I guess I could have always used Frank for that purpose, but I wasn't that type of woman.

I watched Ken lift those weights the way I lift two shopping bags. 'I know there's nothing wrong in visiting her,' I said, 'but her husband just got his head cut off, and I don't know how I could handle a normal conversation without mentioning his name.'

Ken dropped the weights. I thought they were going to go straight through the first floor and down to the garage below. 'You don't need coaching to hold a conversation,' he said while walking to a cable-rowing machine. 'You're the only person I can talk to for hours without being bored to death.'

'Thanks,' I said, feeling myself blushing as I took a sip of water from my Coca-Cola drink bottle. I liked Ken because he got straight to the point. You knew where you were standing with him. I wished more people were like him.

I worked my chest, biceps, shoulders and abs.

By the time I finished, I was certain of two things. I was incapable of doing another sit-up, and I would go and visit Teresa Wilson the following day.

I had to give a lecture in Introduction to Crime Scene Investigation at Swinburne University of Technology on Wednesday afternoon, so I decided to visit Teresa Wilson at St

Patrick's Hospital in the morning.

On my way to the hospital, I worried about my afternoon lecture. I was poorly prepared and would have to improvise.

The Quality Management Branch at the VFSC designed the Diploma of Applied Science in Forensic Science in conjunction with Swinburne University of Technology and the Australian Federal Police (AFP) in Canberra. The only course previously available of its kind was an Associate Diploma in Applied Science in Forensic Investigation, which was only opened to Australian Federal Police crime scene examiners throughout Australia. Other crime-scene examiners had to be satisfied with on-the-job training only, and usually complemented their skills by doing training courses in areas considered to be associated with the duties of crime scene examiners, such as photography, fingerprinting and laboratory technician courses.

The university ran the Diploma of Applied Science in Forensic Science for the first time in June 1996. The first course of its kind offered to the general public anywhere in Australia. As a result, most of us weren't really sure what we were doing, or how effective and useful the course was going to be.

To be there at 2:30 p.m. every Wednesday, when I had a non-scheduled week, was extremely difficult. I could be called up any time to help solve a homicide and as a result would have to miss a class. This was cruel to my devoted students, but when caught in limbo, I could only play the cards I was dealt.

What was fascinating was the variety of people who were interested in forensic science. Some of our students included lawyers, medical doctors, a writer, and some people straight out of secondary college, half of them X-Files fanatics.

A few travelled hundreds of kilometers a week to attend the course. One of my students, a young woman by the name of Stacey, even moved all the way from New Zealand because no similar courses were available back home.

Most students would never work in forensics on completion of the course. Forensic investigation was a competitive field, and unless they were employed in a related field by the end of the first year of study, they would be excluded from the second year.

The information presented at these lectures, especially in the second year, where students could specialise in crime scene investigation or fingerprint techniques, contained extremely confidential material.

The AFP didn't want the course material to be distributed freely to the general public. Everyone who would be accepted in the second year of the course would have to undergo a police check.

A big bureaucratic problem tangled up the system. Too many egos floated around the AFP headquarters in Canberra. Once again, some big fat cats were protecting their positions by restricting information to the general public. After all, if everyone knew what they knew, there'd be no need to pay them exorbitant salaries, an office the size of Buckhingham Palace, and titles to match their egos.

I was half-hearted about the way the program was being conducted. I hadn't made up my mind if it was indeed a good idea to exclude people from the second year. As far as I was concerned, you could never tell who had the potential to make an outstanding forensic investigator. But I had the entire AFP going against my beliefs, and since I was only a consultant and not an employee, there was little I could say on the matter.

Still, I had discussed a vague idea of protest against the selection criteria with my students. I thought of using discrimination as the basis of that protest. Most students were keen to do the second year as means to gain valuable employment. I knew the whole thing would probably fall back on my head, and at the worst scenario, the AFP would terminate access to the first year of the course to everyone who wasn't a sworn member. I had to do some careful research before I made things worse than they were. Those people in Canberra had more power than the average citizens could ever imagine.

When I arrived at St Patrick's Hospital at 10.02 a.m., the sky was overcast, and I could have sworn it was the coldest day we had had this February. For a moment, I regretted not having taken a jacket with me. The white cotton dress and navy cardigan I was wearing seemed clearly out-of-season. But in Melbourne, everything was out-of-season within twenty-four hours.

I parked in a space reserved for doctors and emergency

staff only.

I went straight to Teresa Wilson's ward on the third floor.

The hospital smell didn't sit too well in my stomach in the morning. A faint nausea jolted my insides. And all those faces looking so miserable. And not just the patients. Nurses and doctors looked as if they required medical attention as well.

I couldn't figure out why in the world people would willingly spend all their lives in a hospital. I knew I could have never been a doctor or a nurse. My work might have been morbid, but with dead people, you knew it was over. When someone was injured and required medical attention, they proportionally caused themselves and everyone around them a great deal of stress. Not that I wished every patient in the hospital would die suddenly so that the rest of the world would be relieved from the burden of worrying.

I couldn't recall exactly where Teresa's room was, so I asked a nurse. She told me I was still on the second floor. I had to go up one floor and turn left into the West Wing.

You can imagine my surprise when I walked in Teresa's room and saw Frank sitting on the edge of her bed, holding Teresa's hand. My attention immediately shifted to twelve red roses elegantly arranged in a crystal-like vase on her side table. My body tensed up as I recalled roses were for lovers.

'What are you doing here?' I asked Frank when we made eye contact. He looked haggard and defeated. My tone of voice must have been accusing because he stared for a few seconds, as if I had just said a foul word.

'I just wanted to see how she was doing,' he whispered. Teresa was fully awake, and no one else was in the room, so I didn't know why he didn't speak out loud.

I wasn't sure if I was being paranoid, because it was normal for us to visit victims even after their ordeal was over. It helped them, but also helped us to cope with our post-traumatic stage.

And yet, we were both there at the same time, wondering what the hell the other was doing here.

I didn't notice straight away, but when I shifted my gaze in Teresa's direction, I was astounded to see how attractive she was. The bruising on her face had eased considerably, and her natural features were slowly coming back.

Teresa's blond hair had been washed, and I noticed for the first time that her eyes were emerald green. A child-like innocence painted an expression of tenderness on her face. Her cheekbones were high and her nose straight and narrow. She was one of the most beautiful women I had ever come across, in spite of her scratches and bruises.

The three of us made small talk, Frank and I obviously avoiding the subject of Jeremy by fear of not knowing if Teresa was ready to face reality.

I can't remember how the conversation turned that way, but suddenly Teresa was telling us why she thought Walter Dunn attacked them.

'He made a pass at me a while ago,' she muttered as she recalled the incident. 'But he didn't give up straight away. When Jeremy was away on business, Walter came and visited me.'

'Why didn't you tell him not to come?' I asked.

'I did, but there's only so much you can do when it's your husband's best friend.'

'Did you tell Jeremy?'

'No way. He wouldn't have believed me, anyway. Whenever he went away for a few days, he always told me to call Walter if I needed anything. Like it was his best friend. And even if he did believe me, God, I couldn't put him through this. Imagine, finding out that you're best friend's got his hands all over your wife. He wouldn't have believed me.'

I wondered what was the point of having a husband if he didn't believe you. If I ever married again, my husband would have to be my best friend and confident, or else I'd begin a serious relationship with a Teddy bear. I made the mistake once to marry someone for the sake of marrying, and regretted it ever since.

I moved closer to the bed.

Teresa went on, 'He tried to fondle me a few times, and I had to fight him off.'

'Did he hit you?' Frank asked, shifting uncomfortably on his corner of the bed.

'No, no. When I told him to stop, he stopped.'

'How did it end?' I asked.

'Surprisingly well. He stopped coming, and I thought, God,

he finally faced the fact that I wasn't interested.'

'Did he continue to see Jeremy?'

'Oh, yes. He still came to dinner now and then. But we never talked about his advances, not even when the two of us were left together for a few minutes. He just gave me those long, lustful stares filled with hate and bitterness. He couldn't handle rejection. And I knew it would mean trouble one day, but I'd never expected *that*.'

'And why do you think he attacked you?'

'I guess he wanted me so badly, and he knew it wouldn't happen, so he went for it anyway.'

'Yeah, but why all the beating?'

'Some kind of punishment. You know, it's not like I was submissive. He had to knock me around quite a bit before he raped me. And the squash ball, well, I guess that was his way of saying, "up yours bitch."'

I nodded, thinking her theory was as good as any, but surprised by her choice of words.

'And why do you think he killed Jeremy?'

'Jealousy, of course. Not only couldn't he have me, but Jeremy was starting to make some serious money with his work, while Walter just didn't have it in him.'

We chatted for a while longer, but she was beginning to repeat herself, and I had to make my way to Swinburne University for my lecture.

I ended up leaving Frank and Teresa by themselves.

For some reason I felt like the odd one out. Neither of them said anything about not wanting me there, but there was an uneasiness lurking in the air. My mind was filled with confusion and stress from the events of the past week.

But as I left the hospital, a small detail nagged me. I pictured in my mind's eye Teresa alone in that hospital room and her husband dead.

And then Frank holding her hand.

It just seemed so sudden.

So calculated.

Thoughts crossed my mind.

Silly thoughts.

Thoughts which made no sense.

For a while I thought Frank might have had something to do with the death of Jeremy.

But as I slid inside my car, I realised I was being completely out of character.

CHAPTER SEVEN

When I finished lecturing my class of Introductory Crime Scene Investigation at Swinburne University of Technology, the temperature had suddenly risen to the mid-twenties. I drove the Lancer with the sunroof open, letting the wind blow in my auburn hair, a change from my natural black hair.

Somehow, I did manage to give a worthwhile lecture in crime-scene contamination. Students seemed satisfied with what they'd been taught, and that was all which really mattered to me.

The traffic on Glenferrie Road was hectic, and other drivers seemed to be driving worse than usual. Maybe it was me who was becoming impatient with the world.

I got to my apartment forty-five minutes later. The red light on my answering machine flashed three times, indicating that there were three messages. Two were from Tim Simons, my *Herald-Sun* media contact, asking me to call back, and one from Frank.

I played Frank's message twice.

Hey, it's me. Just thought I'd call to see how you're doing. You didn't look too good this morning. Is anything wrong? You can call me if you want...oh, and by the way, I need you on Friday at 10 a.m. The director wants to talk to both of us regarding the other night. I did my best with the report, but we both knew he was going to raise questions. I just need you there for formalities. I'll do my best to get us off the hook. Just make sure you're there on time if I don't hear from you. The last thing we need right now is to make a bad impression.

The answering machine beeped twice at the end of the message.

I showered and wondered if I felt anything for Frank. If not, then why had I felt so odd that morning at the hospital? Jealousy? I tried to brush the thought aside, knowing there was no way I could fall in love with Frank Moore. He wasn't my type. On the other hand, I didn't know what my type was any more.

As I stepped out of the shower, I recalled I hadn't gone out with anyone for five years. This realisation frightened me. I couldn't see myself spending the rest of my life alone. And yet, I couldn't see myself spending the rest of my life with someone.

I married in 1982 to a young man I met at university while doing a Bachelor of Applied Science in Biology. I was twenty-one then and rushed from one thing to another. I wanted everything. A career, a family, a home and a life of my own. I was naive and thought I could change the world. It took me six years, a pregnancy and a divorce to understand that the world couldn't be changed. I had to change. I had to decide what I wanted from life.

After my divorce, I held a grudge against men for a few years. It seemed they had it easy. Their lives reeked with career opportunities. But I had to either chose a career or become a wife again, somebody's right hand. And since I had already been somebody's right hand for six years without much success, I decided a career was the way to go. But with Michael around, it had been rather difficult. He'd been shuffled from baby-sitter to baby-sitter since the divorce, and now I only had myself to blame if he was slowly turning away from me.

But that was eleven years ago, and now I doubted if I'd made the right decision. As the years went by, I felt increasingly lonely. If not deeply involved in a homicidal investigation, I spent a lot of time reading fiction and non-fiction alike.

For hours, sometimes days, I sat on the balcony of my apartment, overlooking St Kilda and the Port Phillip Bay, and wasted too much time drowning in my loneliness.

Now and then, I thought of placing an ad in *Single Life* magazine, but I felt uncomfortable with the idea. What man would want a self-righteous, assertive woman like me? And now that Michael was twelve years old, I also had to consider him. Bringing a new person into the family was a decision we both had to make. Michael would have to get on reasonably well with his new father. I'd be miserable if they were on each other's backs all the time. And anyway, I held this long-held belief that it was only desperate people who advertised for a relationship. Of course, deep down I knew this was untrue, and only an excuse for me to back out of any emotional commitment.

I had a friend a few years back who placed an ad in *Single Life*. She was a model, but also a single mother. She ended up marrying a psychiatrist who replied to the advertisement. The last time I saw them, she was pregnant with his child, and they were the happiest couple I had seen. She took a gamble and it paid of.

But I hated gambling because I never believed in chance.

I decided to wait for the right moment and the right person instead.

Maybe I would have to wait forever. Most people considered me ill-tempered, making it difficult for me to find a compatible partner. My childhood had been verbally and physically abusive, and because of it, I learned to become extremely defensive, to the point of coming across as arrogant.

With all these thoughts running through my head, I wondered if I was happy. But my mind had been in such turmoil during the last few days, I couldn't trust my own logic.

Michael came home at around 8.00 p.m. I tried my best to be nice to him, but I could sense that he knew I was up to something. I made him dinner, but he decided to eat it in his bedroom. When I requested that he has dinner with me, he asked me what was wrong. I gave up and let him get on with his life.

When I went to bed later that night, I stayed awake for hours. Flashes of Jeremy Wilson's decapitation kept coming to mind.

And then I thought about Teresa.

When I finally went to sleep, I woke up in a frenzy only minutes later. I had a nightmare in which I was Teresa. Walter Dunn came towards me, beating me with his hands, entering me savagely and finally inserting a squash ball up my anus. The pain was so terrible that when I woke up, I rubbed my backside thinking the dream had been reality.

Only the next morning I realised how badly I was dealing with the situation. Maybe I needed some counselling. But I was scared that if the VFSC and the CIB found out, they would find me inadequate to be contracted for their investigations.

Finally, over a cup of black coffee, scanning the headlines of the *Herald-Sun* and the *Age*, I concluded a holiday might be the answer. I hadn't had a real holiday for as long as I could remember. All my life had centred around my career. And although I was happy to have gone that far, I felt the need for some kind of break. I needed to stop for a while, reassess my priorities, figure out what I really wanted to do for the rest of my life. I needed to put it all behind me for a while.

At 9.32 a.m., I stepped into my car and decided to see Teresa one more time, just to get the load off my mind and help me to cope with reality.

When I arrived in Teresa's room at St Patrick's Hospital on Thursday morning, she looked healthier than the previous day. She even smiled. I was amazed at the speed of her recovery. The way she had been battered and raped, one would have thought she'd be staying in hospital for months.

'I'm surprised you came back,' she said, her lovely emerald green eyes sparkling as if she was glad to see me.

'I've been thinking about you a lot.'

'Why?' she asked, looking genuinely intrigued.

For a couple of seconds, I wondered what lie I was going to come up with. And then I decided the truth was as good as anything. The investigation was over, and there was no need for me to be one-dimensional. I felt a need to let my feelings show, to just be myself.

Slightly anxious, I locked my eyes into hers and said, 'To be honest with you, I don't think I'm coping with this too well. But don't go and tell Frank Moore, or it could be the end of my career.' I knew Frank would say nothing, but I abhorred gossip, especially if it landed on the wrong set of ears.

'He wouldn't tell anyone even if I'd told him. I don't think he's that way inclined.'

I was surprised at her confidence in Frank. After all, she'd only known him for a few days.

Then I noticed a bunch of red roses on her side table. I knew they were not the same ones that I'd seen the other day, because there were much more of them, and the others would have been dead by now.

'These are from friends, I gather?' I asked, pointing at the roses and feeling heat on my cheeks.

She glanced at the roses, looked at me suspiciously and said quietly, 'They're from Frank, actually. He came to visit this morning.'

I remained speechless for fifteen seconds. Goddamn it, maybe I hadn't imagined things the previous day, after all.

'Are you all right?' Teresa asked, a concerned look crossing her face. 'You seem drained. Would you like a glass of water or something?'

I held on to the edge of the bed. 'It's stuffy in here,' I lied, trying hard not to display the confusion which was boiling in my mind. Quickly, I changed conversation. 'So what do you do for a living?'

'I'm a set designer.'

'Really? What does that involve?'

'I design sets for theatres and plays. I was working at the National Theatre when the incident happened.'

'That's just down from where I live.'

'Well, there you go. Maybe we've even crossed each other in the street and didn't even know.'

We laughed lightly at the coincidence.

'So,' she muttered, 'what's going to happen from now on?'

I wasn't sure what she was getting at. 'What do you mean?'

'You know, with the investigation.'

'Oh, that. It's finished, of course. Well, almost. Just have to tie up a few ends. Paper work mostly.'

A concerned look crossed her face.

'Anything wrong?' I added.

'No, not at all. I just didn't expect everything to be all over so soon. It's just happened so fast.'

I smiled. 'Neither did I. It's better that way, I guess.' I took her hand in mine and squeezed it gently. 'You're a very brave woman, Teresa. I don't know if I could have survived what you've just gone through.' And I meant it.

'Thank you,' she whispered as tears came rolling down her cheeks.

I didn't know why I was being emotional about the whole thing. But seeing her there, putting on such a brave face after having lost her husband, being raped, and having her beautiful face scarred made me shiver.

As I held on to her hand, I wondered if my empathy was just an excuse because I was desperate for friendship. And Teresa was here at the right time, and looked as if she needed friendship as well. Was it so wrong?

I moved forward and kissed her on the forehead, wishing I could help her overcome the suffering she was going through. I wanted to hug her, but didn't want her to think it was more than friendship, although I was myself confused as to what I really was after.

Her tears brought tears to my eyes, and we ended up crying and laughing at the same time, like two teenagers sharing some forbidden secret friendship.

By the time I left the hospital, I felt much closer to Teresa. I would have loved to see her again, but I didn't think the timing nor the occasion was appropriate

And this thing with Frank was troubling me. I hoped he wasn't flirting with her. Really, it was probably none of my business, but it would look bad on his record. Well, at least that was the excuse I made to myself to rationalise my jealousy.

I stopped at McDonald's for lunch, and within half an hour I wished I didn't. Junk food caused an uneasiness in my stomach, but I was hungry and had to eat immediately.

I spent the rest of the day getting mentally prepared for the next morning's meeting at the VFSC, and wondered how I was going to track down the phone booth coin stealer. I hoped nobody was going to give me the third-degree at the VFSC because I was unprepared. Right now I felt extremely vulnerable, and it would have taken little to send me over the edge.

In the evening I went to the Astor Theatre, just a block

from where I lived, for a double-feature - 'The Brady Bunch Movie' and 'A Very Brady Sequel', both very forgetful.

I fell asleep at 1.10 a.m. on Friday over one of Garry Disher's Wyatt novels.

Frank and I were sitting on the other side of the mahogany desk, in Trevor Mitchell's office at the VFSC.

I glanced at the piles of paper work neatly stacked in the IN and OUT trays on top of the desk. My eyes circled the room and caught a framed, black and white photograph of a group of men lined up next to each other, all in business suits, smiling as if they'd just graduated from university. I recognised a younger Frank Moore, when he had more hair and no moustache. Trevor Mitchell was next to him, also looking a few years younger. I couldn't identify the rest of the men.

I'd been in Trevor Mitchell's office before, but I never noticed the photograph. My guess was that it had been put there recently.

I could feel tension in the air, and I clearly didn't want to be there.

Although Frank said nothing when I met him at the Liaison Office earlier on, I knew he'd rather be somewhere else as well. He fidgeted with his hands, and beads appeared on his forehead. I hoped he was well-prepared, because I felt devastated and not in a mood to argue.

The Director of the VFSC wore his usual dark suit and white shirt, with a yellow-and-white stripped tie, as if he meant business. His grey cropped hair made him look like an army officer. We were never called up to his office unless it was a serious matter.

And I hoped to God this morning wasn't going to be all that serious.

Trevor Mitchell retrieved a cream-coloured manilla folder from the top of his IN-tray.

'I've read the report on Walter Dunn, and I understand you were concerned about the safety of Mrs Teresa Wilson. However, you should both know better than breaching this department's regulations.' He stopped a few seconds so that we could absorb the full impact of his words. It sank in like the Titanic at the bottom of the Grand Banks of

82

Newfoundland.

He then turned to me. 'I understand you were self-appointed scene coordinator and were in control of the crime scene. I also understand that you've chosen to work with Frank. What I don't understand is how neither of you had the god-damn sense to call for backup or authorisation to proceed with this investigation. Investigating Jeremy Wilson's death beyond the duties you were assigned by this department is unacceptable.'

Frank leaned forward. 'Believe me,' he said in an assertive tone, 'it was all my doing. Dr Malina insisted we call for back up, but I told her I would take full responsibility for the outcome.'

I couldn't help feeling uneasy. What he had just said was true, but it made me look incapable of making decisions, which was why I was being paid in the first place.

Trevor Mitchell tilted his head back and forth and added, 'I really don't want to know the exact politics of who's been ordering who. The facts remain that your duties as forensic examiners for the VFSC are clearly assigned, and you've both been in the field long enough to know that.

'You have acted on personal values when making the decision to enter Walter Dunn's premises, regardless of whether you felt Teresa Wilson was in danger or not.

'You know very well that you should have called a detective or at least obtained authorisation to proceed into the suspect's home.' He waited a few seconds, enough time to make my stomach churn. 'And as for you, Dr Malina, you had been barred from this investigation. I thought that was made clear the other day.'

'I thought the Deputy Commissioner said until the end of this week,' I replied foolishly. 'And as I understand it, I've got rights under Section 462A of the *Crimes Act* to make a citizen's arrest in order to prevent a homicide by a person who was already suspected of killing someone. I don't need authorisation from anyone to exercise this right, and neither does Frank.'

He shook his head in disbelief. 'It's not your case, Dr Malina. Don't give me this hogwash with the *Crimes Act*. You've only been invited on probation at this stage. You're no longer an investigator in the Wilson's homicide. We all know you understood that clearly the other day. Don't make this more difficult than it is.'

I gave up. 'Yes, sir.'

Trevor Mitchell shifted in his swivel executive chair, smiled and went on, 'However, since you did find the killer, I guess I'll have to let this one go. But, and a big *but* here, my leniency towards this incident is not a green light for you to cross the line again in the future. Right now, the Deputy Commissioner of Police and the CIB are bitter about the way this whole thing has been handled. You knew Frank Goosh was opposed to the idea of having an unsworn contractor acting as an investigator in the first place. This is going to give him plenty of ammunition.'

'He certainly made it clear that he wanted me out of the job,' I said, unable to control my loose tongue.

Trevor Mitchell ignored my comment. 'We're having a hell of a time with the media. And thanks to the Shadow Minister for Police and Emergencies, every time we make a slip up, someone is jumping up and down. You do understand there will be an independent inquiry on this matter?'

We both nodded.

'You also understand I'll do my best to explain your actions but cannot guarantee heads won't roll.' He then turned to me. 'As for you, Dr Malina, I hope it won't come to the termination of your contract with the lab. I would be wasting words emphasising the vital role you've played in this department for the past five years.'

I lowered my eyes for a few seconds, wondering if I cared after all.

For obvious reasons, I felt as if I was back at secondary school, being called up to the principal's office for participating in some prank with a couple of girlfriends. We promised never to do it again and meant it while we were in god's office.

Standing beside Trevor Mitchell's desk brought back to mind the nauseous sensations of my teenage years when I felt more like committing homicides than solving them. I hated structured organisations, not so much because of what they did or didn't do, but because of the bureaucracy attached to them.

Every government department was a cobweb of fat cats and rules designed to serve those in power. From the day we went to school, we were talked down to, as if we knew nothing from right and wrong, as if we were incapable of deciding for ourselves. And now that I was a mature woman, I found things had changed little.

Sitting behind that desk, next to Frank, in front of Trevor Mitchell, made me want to pop a gasket.

But I knew better.

Although I hated the bureaucracy of the VFSC, I cared a lot about my work. My career was the only thing which kept me sane. The only reason why I wasn't locked up somewhere where they throw the key away forever because some damn relative decides you're not mentally fit to be let out in public.

Solving homicides made me sick but gave me a place in this world. And belonging somewhere was a basic human need, as basic as feeding and reproduction.

When people were isolated, psychotic and sociopathic behaviour settled in instead. Criminals were waste by-products of a civilised society, the unwanted, those who had no worth in the community, those who needed to be heard but were ignored instead.

As I stood up from my chair and smiled at the Director of the VFSC, I understood perfectly the criminal mind.

However, I knew I would never be able to do what they did as long as feelings of empathy were still attached to my brain. And I guess that was the main difference between us and *them*. We all had crazy thoughts of popping the guy at the traffic light because he stuck his middle finger up at us. But that was as far as it went. We obeyed our own imaginary, do-not-cross, white line. Sociopaths obeyed a broken, white line.

They could cross it now and then.

When Trevor Mitchell finished with us, Frank and I went for a coffee at the VFSC staff room.

The room was filled with people from various departments having their ten-minute break or early lunch. Students and police personnel who attended courses offered by the VFSC were also present.

We both bought a coffee and sat quietly opposite each

other for a full minute, unable to discuss our present situation.

I broke the silence after my first sip of coffee, 'You haven't told me about Teresa Wilson.'

Frank looked up slowly, and I could tell he'd been taken by surprise.

'Told you what?'

'What you're doing with her?'

He shook his head from left to right. 'What are you, the thought-police or something?' He was still worked up from the meeting in Trevor Mitchell's office.

'I just don't want you to get hurt.'

'Thanks for the concern. But you're not my mother, and I think I'm old enough to make my own decisions. And anyway, I don't know what the hell you're talking about.'

I leaned forward, spilling some of my coffee on the white Formica table. 'Don't jerk me around, Frank. I saw the flowers in her room this morning.'

'So?'

'So, she told me,' I lied, hoping to God I was on the right track.

He froze for a few seconds and then stood up, sending his chair flying a metre behind him.

All eyes in the room turned to us, and I felt redness on my face.

'Fuck you, Malina. I don't have to put up with this shit.'

'You don't have to be so —'

'Yeah, whatever,' he interrupted. He turned to all the eyes in the room. 'All right, the show is over. Do you mind?' And then back to me. 'The last time I checked with you, you were not interested. So what's all the concern now? You think I can't hold my dick straight or something? Is that what it's all about?' He jabbed his finger in the air, right in front of my face. 'Let me tell you something, Malina. People are starting to talk around here. They think you're losing it. You're cracking up. All these years of homicide investigations are finally playing with your head. And you know what I think?'

I stared at him, shocked and puzzled by his personal attack.

'I'm beginning to think they might be right. Because right now, what I do know is that my private life is none of your business. Have we got that clear?'

I maintained my composure in spite of feeling deeply hurt. I glanced around, but everyone in the room pretended not to pay attention.

Frank and I had been friends for a very long time, and he never spoke to me that way. I might have got a bit personal, but was that a reason to judge my whole career? And what about this rumour going around? Were people really talking about me that way? I knew I needed a holiday, but was it so obvious?

'I'm sorry,' I muttered. 'You're right. It's none of my business. I won't interfere in the future.'

'Yeah, well, you better not,' he commanded as he left the table, his coffee virtually untouched.

CHAPTER EIGHT

When I got home later in the evening, I drank half a bottle of Southern Comfort. Just as well Michael had gone to his friend's place for the weekend.

A dark night filled my evening and my soul. I felt as if I'd reached the end of all meaning. No matter how I turned everything in my head, I knew I was heading for a disaster. The VFSC and the CIB were on my back, and I had just turned Frank into an enemy. For a brief moment, while the alcohol simmered in my brain, I wondered what it'd be like to lecture full time at university. The pay would certainly be better.

I should have gone to the gym to release my frustration. I seldom touched alcohol, and this binge wasn't going down well.

First I cried myself dry, cursing my parents, my childhood, my world, Frank Moore, Teresa Wilson, Trevor Mitchell, everyone at the VFSC and the CIB, and later myself.

Then the lounge room spun in my head, sending chairs and tables and everything in sight around the ceiling, across the room, in and out of my brain.

My nerves were raw, and I was a total mess. I couldn't remember feeling so low, ever.

I tried to sleep it off on the couch, but it was impossible. Round and round it went, until I truly believed my heart was going to burst out of my chest. I swore out loud that if I ever got back to normal again, I would love trees, birds, traffic,

Frank, and everything else I took for granted.

I crawled down from the couch and into the bathroom.

I just wanted my life back, but instead I was hunched over the toilet bowl, emptying the contents of my stomach, feeling useless, miserable and stupid.

I wanted to call Frank and tell him what he had done to me. I wanted him to feel guilty, to understand what a complete jerk he'd been. But I couldn't do it because, in spite of being off my head, I knew I was the one who'd been a jerk.

I walked up to my study, threw open the top drawer of my filing cabinet and removed the Jeremy Wilson file. I flicked through the photos I took at the crime scene, and the only good that did was send me back with my head down the toilet bowl, looking at the world at angles I had never experienced before.

I lay on the couch in the lounge room for the next twelve hours, and I swear to God, I really thought they were my last twelve hours.

Late Saturday morning, I was level-headed enough to open the balcony of my apartment and take in some fresh air. The sky was overcast, and I wished it would rain. It seemed the most beautiful day in my life, in spite of feeling as crook as a dog. I loved this city, the trams down Chapel Street, people arguing, pigeons responding to their calls of nature on my car.

I stood on the balcony for a good hour, gently experiencing flashbacks of soberness. I knew I would never again be able to touch a drop of Southern Comfort. Just the smell would send me into a violent fit of near-hysteria.

I took a shower, letting the hot water sooth my cranium, feeling my raw nerves slowly coming back to their natural function.

After a cup of black coffee, no sugar, I strolled past the study and noticed the mess I made the previous day. The Jeremy Wilson file was open, and photographs were thrown all over the floor, the desk and the filing cabinet. I didn't remember my act of terrorism, but since there was no one else who lived in the place, it had to be me.

I collected various photographs from the floor, realising I should really have handed over the entire file to the VFSC for their records. And frankly I'd had a gut-full of this investigation. They could have the entire damn case, for all I cared.

As I randomly collected the photographs from the floor and threw them back in the file, something caught my eye.

I sat in the chair behind my desk and looked closely at a crime-scene photo taken at the Wilson's apartment. I studied it for a full minute, like only drunks can, trying to recall the chain of events which led to Jeremy Wilson's death. Something in the photograph intrigued me. Being half sober, I lacked confidence in my forensic analysis, but even if I had been sober, I still needed a second opinion.

I picked up the telephone and punched John Darcy's mobile number.

John was a forensic biologist at the VFSC.

John Darcy was kind enough to see me at lunchtime in his home. When I got a hold of him on the phone, he was with his son at footy practice.

John only lived twenty minutes away from me in Mt Waverley.

When I needed straight answers without all the bureaucracy, I dealt directly with John, especially if the information I required had nothing to do with laboratory analysis and more with another expert's opinion.

When I arrived at the suburban two-storey brick-veneer house, a thick manilla folder tucked under my arm, John was watering the front yard. It looked as if it was about to rain any second, but I wasn't going to question his motive. Some people watered the garden every weekend out of habit, not necessity.

John looked younger than his fifty-two with his blond locks and sparkling blue eyes. Like me, he hated office bureaucracy and was also willing to help a fellow scientist whenever the need arose.

We made small talk in the front yard before he led me inside his home.

Mrs Darcy was making lunch for their three children, a nine year-old boy with the same hair and eyes as his father, and two three-year-old girls, who were miraculously born two days apart.

My eyes circled the lounge room to observe the inside of a typical suburban home. Family portraits hanging on the walls, a large television; a few never-read novels, ceramic figures and other useless items scattered on a wall unit; women's magazines spread on the coffee table. The furniture was cheap-looking, but with three kids and only one person working, they were probably doing the best they could.

Mrs Darcy, whose first name I had never asked, invited me for some lunch. I politely declined, feeling like an intruder invading a family weekend.

Instead, I followed John down a dark hallway and into his study.

His study looked like a miniature little laboratory. On one side of the room, he had his own lab bench, complete with water and gas taps, microscopes, beakers, burettes and pipettes. It looked as if I had stepped inside a VFSC-4-KIDS made with IKEA-assemble-it-yourself furniture. He confessed that he bought most of the laboratory equipment from the *Mebourne Trading Post*, a classifieds-only newspaper, or from auctions.

Next to his desk was an amazing collection of forensic and biology books from the USA, which I gathered would have cost him a fortune with the exchange rate and freight cost added. Some of the titles, *Inside the Crime Lab* and *Crime and Science: the New Frontier in Criminology*, amongst others, were familiar to me, except that my copies were usually borrowed from university libraries.

'So, what have you got?' he asked, shifting comfortably into a gas-lift height adjustable chair, finished in a paprika synthetic cloth.

He loved giving his opinion, because, like everyone else I knew, he loved to believe he was important to this world.

And he was.

I briefed him quickly on the Jeremy Wilson's homicide.

Like ninety-five percent of Melburnians, he read the case coverage in the *Herald-Sun* and the *Age*. And since journalists could only write up what they were given, the Wilson's coverage was rather disjointed and incomplete, not to mention poor in forensic details. Only when the case would be fully closed, the media would be able to release a more accurate version of events. As a result, some journalist, thirsty for fame and recognition, would win an impressive award for writing up something based on other people's misery.

I pulled two postcard-sized, coloured photographs from the manilla folder I had brought with me. The shots were close-ups of blood droplets from Jeremy Wilson's body. The blood samples had already been analysed, compared with a blood sample taken from Jeremy's body, and confirmed to be his blood. Not that anyone had doubts in the first place, but if evidence had to be presented in a court of law in any homicidal case, the VFSC not only had to present the evidence as exhibits, but also prove its source and location.

'Take a look at those,' I said, as I handed over the photographs to John.

He looked at them rather quickly and commented, 'These are drops of blood. I gather they're from the victim.'

'That's right. But what else do you see in them?'

I knew what I was getting at, but I couldn't believe how anyone could have missed something so obvious. Blood droplets were good indicators of past events at a crime scene. And yet, caught up in the horror of Jeremy Wilson's decapitation, no one bothered examining the pattern of those droplets.

John rubbed his chin and said, 'These drops come from a static source about two or three feet high.' He pointed to the shape of the drops. 'You can tell by the neat circles.'   All the drops captured by the film were starburst in shape, but perfectly circular.

'Okay,' I said, 'that's what I observed when I looked at them this morning. But what if the source wasn't static? Would you get splashes and spurts?'

'Certainly. Splashes tend to be common when a bludgeoning instrument is swung. Droplets of blood hit the floor or wall at an angle, clearly indicating the direction they've travelled from. They look like exclamation marks. Spurts are more common when a major vein or artery is severed. A forceful outflow of blood is sprayed around the victim, and, more often than not, onto the killer.'

Hell! I knew I had been right.

'So the guy who got his head cut off,' I asked, 'couldn't have been hacked to death?'

He looked at the photographs once more and back at me. 'Absolutely not. Impossible.'

'How would you describe the decapitation?'

'Based on these pictures, the head has been cut slowly from the body. This was performed methodically.'

I felt a pain at the back of my skull. I wasn't sure if it was still the effect of the Southern Comfort, or what John had just told me.

I nodded for John to go on.

'So, what are you getting at?' he asked.

'Something really bothers me here.' I removed a typed report from the Jeremy Wilson file. 'Listen to this.' I scanned the report. 'According to this, Teresa Wilson, the wife of the guy who got his head cut off, said her husband was hacked to death. But according to those drops of blood, he wasn't.'

He gave me a blank look.

I went on, 'Something doesn't match.'

'Maybe she got confused. Wrong choice of words, I don't know.'

'This still puts the entire case under a new perspective.'

'I don't see how.'

'Well, if he wasn't hacked to death, how the hell did the killer cut his head off *methodically*? Did Jeremy Wilson just sit there and say, "Okay, here we go now, a bit more to the left, yes, it's going in, I can feel it." Surely, he would have been fighting for his life!'

John puzzled over my analysis. 'You know, you've got a good point. But still, this doesn't mean Jeremy Wilson's wife lied.'

'I'm not saying she did. In fact, I don't think she lied. I want to know why Jeremy Wilson didn't put up a fight.'

'Maybe he got knocked out before he was decapitated.'

'I thought about that, but I've never recorded any wounds or bruises anywhere on his head during the initial observation at the crime-scene.' I passed him my typed report, pointing out the section which described the condition of the body when I found it.

He glanced at the report and then stood up from his chair. 'What does it matter, anyway? You've caught the killer, didn't you?'

John was right, but I hated to leave loose ends.

'You know what I'm like,' I said, 'if something bothers me, I won't let it rest, or it's going to annoy me for years to come.'

He circled the desk and moved towards the laboratory bench. He began fiddling with his compound microscope 'You're overworked, Malina. Why don't you take it easy for a few days.' He turned to me, smiled and went on,' And if you don't mind me saying, you look awful. Did you have a late night or something?'

'I'll tell you about it some other day. I could do with a cup of coffee, though. Lukewarm if you don't mind.'

We walked to the kitchen where he made a strong sugarless black coffee in a mug. 'I think you're going over your head with this one,' he said while helping himself to a glass of lemonade.

'I know, maybe you're right. Sorry if I'd disturbed you.' I drank my coffee in one go, hoping it would help me stay alert for the rest of the day.

'Hey, don't be like that. I admire what you do. I'd be interested to find out what else you come up with. You know I'm only a phone call away. Just trust that instinct of yours. It's all you've got.'

John was one of the finest people I knew.

I said goodbye to his wife and kids and apologised for the intrusion of privacy.

John walked me to the door. 'And don't worry about what people think about you,' he added, 'You're perfect as you are.'

His comment really helped, because right now I felt as imperfect as humanly possible.

When I slid back in my Lancer, he picked up a garden hose and continued watering the front yard.

I waved goodbye and took off for the South Eastern Arterial.

As I drove back home, I wondered what had really happened at the Wilson's household that night. Why didn't Jeremy Wilson put up a fight? I knew such small abnormalities usually triggered a stream of inconsistencies.

I was certain everything in this case was not as black and white as was first assumed. As far as I was concerned, Jeremy Wilson's death wasn't just an open and shut case.

I got home in less than twenty minutes, going over the speed limit and burning a couple of red lights in the process. Tired of living by the rules, I decided to bend them a bit, just to suit my own egotistical mood.

The next logical thing to do would have been to contact Frank Moore and tell him about my little finding. That was had we not had that little war of words the other day at the VFSC canteen. We had been working on this case together since the beginning, and it was only fair to let him know what I had dug up.

But I wasn't going to.

To begin, I'd received a direct order from my superior to stop investigating the Wilson homicide. The fewer people knew what I was up to, the less likely I would be to get in trouble. And I felt like I'd had my share of trouble for one week.

Secondly, Frank was too far up to his neck with Teresa Wilson.

That being the case, I thought it impossible that he would be able to keep his eyes open for more than fifteen seconds. If I had to confront him with something, I wanted to make sure it was more substantial. John Darcy made it clear that right now I had nothing but my instinct to follow.

However, there was still one person I wanted to visit to clear my mind.

In less than one hour, I was back at St Patrick's Hospital and had parked my car in the space reserved for doctors and emergency staff.

The taste of Southern Comfort occasionally rose from my stomach, and I worried that if I got pulled over for a random breath test, I'd be way over the legal limit of .05. Of course I realised I was being absolutely irresponsible. Had I been a cop, I would have suspended my driver's license for at least six months. People like me were death on the road. I promised myself that if I ever got drunk again, which I swore would never happen, not on Southern Comfort as long as I was conscious, I'd be catching cabs for an entire week, until every drop of alcohol had evaporated from my body.

A chill rippled down my spine as I entered the hospital.

This place began to feel like a second home.

I paced right past the front desk and went straight to Teresa's ward. When I got there, I was rather surprised to find her bed deserted.

When I inquired with one of the nurses in a freshly ironed white uniform, I was told Teresa Wilson had been discharged two hours ago.

I swore under my breath and headed straight for Port Melbourne. Maybe she had gone home, but I doubted it.

As I had more or less expected, no-one was at the Wilson's household.

I drove back to St Kilda and decided to stop at the National Theatre, located approximately one hundred and fifty meters from St Kilda foreshore, Luna Park and the Palais Theatre, on the corner of Carlisle and Barkly Streets. I had a hell of a time finding a parking space. After driving around Irwell, Belford, Carlisle, and Barkly Streets, I ended up parking in Greaves Street, a walking distance from the theatre.

I assumed since Teresa had left the hospital, she might be back at work. Logic said she would probably take the rest of the year off to recover from the death of her husband, but I had nothing to lose by stopping there. I've known people who'd returned to work straight away after a major trauma to help them face reality or to escape from it. However, the last time I spoke to Teresa, she seemed well aware that her husband was dead.

I entered the theatre, surprised at the grandeur of the establishment, which I had never bothered to visit. I treated myself to a small tour of the foyers, grand staircase and the auditorium.

As anticipated, Teresa wasn't at work, but I managed a conversation with the cleaner, a tall, dandy, twenty-one year old, blond lad with three earings in each ear. His name was Louis.

He explained how the theatre was originally built in 1920 with a three-thousand seat capacity for the showing of films. But soon after the opening of the nearby Palais Theatre in the mid 1920s, the theatre was closed for extensive renovations, and the seating capacity was reduced to two-thousand-five-hundred, which still seemed a large number to me. But that was back then, and currently the theatre only held a seven-hundred-and-eighty-three seat capacity. He went on explaining how the original stalls had been converted to Drama, Opera and Ballet Studios.

He invited me for an entire tour of the theatre, but I suggested another time.

After our little introductory chit-chat, I told him the true reason of my visit.

'That was terrible,' Louis said, emphasising on the word *terrible*. And I knew straight away he was *that* way inclined.

'So you've got no idea where she might be?' I asked.

'No idea. I was really surprised to hear her friend Walter killed her husband.'

I kind of liked the way he moved his hands when he talked. Something reeked cuteness about him, and I guess if he had been straight, I might have considered someone fifteen years younger.

'Yes, so was I. They stopped being friends quite a while ago,' I commented.

He looked at me blankly. 'Not that long ago!'

And then it occurred to me Teresa never mentioned how long they had known Walter Dunn. 'What are we talking about here? One year? Five years?'

'Oh, no, nothing like that. Three months at the most. No one said anything at first. You know, the whole situation was kind of awkward in the first place. She was married after all.'

Now I was completely lost. I could feel my brow creasing.

'Oh, you didn't know,' he went on, one hand covering his mouth as if he had just pronounced that four-letter word.

'Louis,' I whispered, 'maybe this is not a good place to talk. Are you free for lunch?'

'Sure.'

'Bala's at twelve noon?'

'Twelve-thirty.'

I approved and walked out of the National Theatre feeling something was very wrong.

CHAPTER NINE

I ordered a Vegetable Stir Fry with Pepper, and Louis a Thai Green Curry Chicken, a delicious looking chicken dish in hot coconut cream and curry sauce with vegetables. We shared a large coconut rice.

Frankly I wasn't hungry at all, but the food tasted fantastic, so I didn't exactly force myself to eat it.

Bala's was located just opposite Luna Park, on Shakespeare Grove, close to the corner of Acland Street, next to the recently-constructed Post Office and the Commonwealth Employment Service (CES). Its mission, read the menu, was *to serve fresh & fast, a fabulous variety of delicious food prepared daily in a clean & friendly environment at affordable prices*. The cuisine was described as 'Modern Asian', but 'Heaven' would have done just fine.

The inside of the restaurant was extremely modest, with only enough wooden tables and chairs to seat around twenty people.

A tantalising aroma of fresh vegetable, coconut and spices filled the air, giving the distinct impression of being in an exotic country, away from the stress of everyday life.

But this would remain a fantasy, because my brain was buzzing with curiosity, and stress was flowing in my veins like acid.

'Walter used to see Teresa,' Louis said, matter-of-factly. He was now wearing a stunning-looking maroon, wool jacket I would have killed for.

'Go out with?' I asked, wondering if it was a serious relationship or just a friendship.

'Yes, but it wasn't official or anything.'

'What about Jeremy? Didn't he say anything?'

'Jeremy and Walter were best friends. Had been for a long time. I don't think he suspected anything. But everyone else knew. And besides, he was having an affair as well.'

I was stunned.

Louis stopped for a few seconds, acutely aware of my reaction.

I didn't know why I had presumed the Wilson's marriage was a perfect one. Taking a full spoon of coconut rice, I raised one eyebrow for Louis to continue.

'Jeremy began to see the secretary of one of his clients. Teresa told me. She liked confiding in people. You know what some women are like. He'd been seeing her for a few months, but by then, Teresa had been having an affair with Walter for at least a year.'

'Jesus Christ,' I heard myself say, almost choking on my coconut rice.

Louis tapped me on the shoulder. 'You okay?' he asked, filling a glass with water.

I took a sip from the glass he handed me and said, 'You got any idea why Walter killed Jeremy?'

A blank look crossed his face.

I went on, 'He didn't get in the way or anything?'

'Jeremy kept to himself. He and Walter were still friends, and Teresa knew about his affair because Walter reported everything back to her.'

I was trying to figure out why Walter snapped. 'Did he seem crazy to you?'

'Jeremy?'

'Walter.'

'Walter was a quiet guy. We use to walk to have a pizza at Chichio's on Friday night, me, Walter, Teresa and some friends from the theatre. Walter didn't seem to be the violent type. In fact, when I heard the news, it shook the hell out of me. I didn't think Walter was capable of doing something like that. And then kill himself. I don't know, I guess you never know what goes on inside people's minds.'

I had to agree with Louis on that one.

'How long have you known them?'

'Since she began working for the National Theatre. Well, she's self-employed really. But we always used her whenever a new production called for a set-designer with superior skills.'

'And how long was that?'

'Oh, I'd say about two years, two and a half years.'

I nodded as I emptied my glass of water.

We chatted about his life for a while. He had a boyfriend in Sydney, which made their relationship rather difficult. I asked him if he'd ever considered moving up there. After all, Sydney was well-known for its Mardi Gras and its high concentration of gay people. But it was more complex than that, he explained. His parents didn't even know he was gay. I thought they were either blind or plainly refused to accept what was merely a fact-of-life. He'd known he was gay since he was back at school. Everyone gave him a hard time, calling him a fag, and other derogatory terms. He was sick and tired of people treating him as if he had a disease that was curable.

'They expect you to do the impossible,' he explained.

'How's that?'

'You know. If you're a heterosexual, which I assume you are, and I ask you to become a homosexual overnight, you couldn't do it. I mean, it's not like you have a choice. You were born heterosexual. And no matter how much I'll tell you that being a heterosexual is wrong, you wouldn't suddenly change your sexual preference. So why the hell do some people think that with counselling, every homosexual on the planet can turn heterosexual overnight? And even if we could, we probably wouldn't. People have to understand one thing: we're not ashamed to be who we are. Being different makes us even stronger. The only thing we can do is keep our chin up and accept ourselves as we are. And we've done that. The rest of the word has yet to catch up.'

I totally agreed with him. It made me bitter how some people could be so narrow-minded. I knew if I'd been gay, I wouldn't take shit from any one.

He had to return to work, so I paid the tab and said, 'You don't mind if we meet sometime again in the future?'

'You're welcome, as long as you keep on buying me lunch,' he said, chuckling away.

'And if anything important comes to mind, don't hesitate to call me.' I handed over my business card and thanked him for his time.

Being a Sunday, there was no point calling into the VFSC. I didn't expect to get any help, and frankly I didn't want to come across Frank Moore or Trevor Mitchell. If I was going to jump up and down about the Jeremy Wilson murder, I had to accumulate more evidence. So far, all I had was a photograph with suspicious blood-spatter patterns and good gossip.

I lay in a long chair on my balcony with *K is For Killer*, a crime novel by Sue Grafton, an American author who lived in California and churned out one book a year using a different letter of the alphabet for each new title. I wondered what she would do once she reached *Z is For* Z-something-or-another. Use the Chinese alphabet?

The sky was overcast, but the air was warm and thick. I could smell rain in the distance, and it made me feel anew.

I loved those days when I was safe from sunburn and could still wear next to nothing while indulging in some serious reading on my balcony.

I sipped a Dr Pepper from a mug and wondered what *normal* people did with their time? According to the amplified noises coming from under my neighbours' doors, they watched television almost twenty-four hours a day. I had a television, but the only thing it was watching was me walking from the bedroom to the kitchen and vice-versa.

Next weekend the Grand Prix was on at Albert Park, a couple of kilometres from Chapel Street, and I hated to be here when it happened. To begin with, I cared little about car racing. Secondly, the traffic would be unbearable, not to mention the screaming of tyres going on for three days in a row.

In the past year, there had been an uproar about staging the Grand Prix in a public park. I saw both sides of the arguments, but never made up my mind as to whether the State Premier had been right or wrong in locating the international car race in the park. But, as with everything political, there was always a lot of cards being dealt under the table. No-one really knew the real agenda for relocating the Grand Prix from Adelaide, in South Australia, to Melbourne, in Victoria, unless they were involved in the process.

My mind was pre-occupied with Jeremy Wilson's death, and I knew something in this homicide was being covered up. How could Jeremy have been hacked to death without putting up a fight? Why was it that there were no traces of bruising around his head? If he had been assaulted before the decapitation, why didn't he have bruising on other parts of his body? This was especially intriguing since Teresa had told us she heard Jeremy screaming in the hallway. This clearly implied he must have been hit by Walter.

I stood from my chair, stretched my legs, and sat down again. Real life was becoming more intriguing than my Sue Grafton novel.

Why did Teresa conceal her affair with Walter?

Okay, so far I was certain of two things: Jeremy Wilson did not get hacked to death, and he wasn't conscious when he got decapitated. I tried hard to steer myself into another direction, but somehow my finger wanted badly to point at Teresa. Could she have been the one who killed him?

I closed my eyes and pictured Teresa. The bruising and cuts on her beautiful face. The squash ball inserted in her anus. The semen found in her vagina. The state of shock she was in when we found her. All physical evidence clearly pointed the other way. *Teresa isn't the killer.* And yet her account of what happened didn't match the forensic investigation so far. Then why in the world did she lie to us?

Then there was Walter Dunn. A piece of dark fabric, which Frank had found in the woodwork of the window frame at the crime scene, did match up with a suede jacket we found at Walter Dunn's home. The fact that he committed suicide was no coincidence. This clearly placed him at the scene of the crime. And yet, questions remained unanswered.

Was he the one who really killed Jeremy Wilson? Did he have an accomplice? If so, who was the accomplice, and why did they kill Jeremy? Why did Walter commit suicide? Remorse? Fear of retribution for his actions?

I couldn't make up my mind. Further investigation was needed.

At times like these, all I had to do was pick up the phone and ring Frank. He would usually come over, and we would discuss for hours on end the hundred possibilities of a homicide. Bit by bit, each piece of evidence would bring us closer to the truth, until, at some stage, only one scenario would be possible.

But as it was, I was on my own. Barred from further investigation on this case, if I got caught I would be charged with obstruction of justice, although I couldn't figure out why since my only aim was to find the truth and not obstruct it. But then, who is ever certain that justice is a quest for the truth?

At 3.34 p.m., I wondered how Michael was going with his long weekend away. I had hoped he would call me to let me know everything was going fine. As it was, he hadn't left me the phone number of his friend, so I had no chance to check on him.

I sat in my study and read the Jolly Roger article on stealing money from telephone booths. I wondered how many people in the City of Port Phillip had actually taped into the Jolly Roger website in the past three months, which was approximately the time span the coin stealer had been operating in the area. I knew there was no way to get the kind of information Jolly Roger had in his article in Australia from a book or magazine. The information could have only been obtained from the Internet or word-of-mouth. Logic told me that I needed a list of all the people in the area who downloaded Jolly Roger's information from the Internet. Could that be done? I'd have to contact all Internet providers in this country to find out. Time consuming stuff, but as long as the telephone company paid me my $150 an hour, I was willing.

By 6.00 p.m., I should have gone to the gym, but there was still a good percentage of Southern Comfort travelling in my veins, draining me of all energy, giving me the perfect excuse to curl up in bed and vegetate in front of the Sunday night movie. I defended my action as being the first time I turned on the damn box for at least a year. I was kind of surprised it still worked. Since Michael had his own television in his bedroom, no one ever used the 58cm colour Sony television.

I slouched on the floral couch in my living room, feeling

light-headed. I couldn't believe how long the effect of alcohol could stay in my body. Was it the same for everyone? I guess the fact that I rarely consumed alcohol, except when I was out for dinner or celebrating the festive season, explained why my brain cells were taking it so badly.

I turned the television off at the end of the late news, and pondered on my next move.

In spite of all the evidence stacked up against him, I began to doubt whether Walter Dunn had actually killed Jeremy Wilson. If he did, he'd probably had an accomplice. I was uncertain as to why I came to that conclusion, but when you'd worked homicides for as long as I had, you learned to trust your instinct.

The other reason why I doubted Walter Dunn killed Jeremy was because Teresa lied. She was obviously covering up for someone else.

The only way I was going to find out whether there was a third person involved was by conducting further unauthorised investigation into Walter's suicide.

CHAPTER TEN

It is impossible to determine an exact time of death by analysis of a dead body alone. All we can do is make an estimate, and hope that the result will bear some weight on the investigation.

Sometimes luck plays part in the evaluation of a dead body. For example, a watch might get broken during an assault, clearly indicating when the person died. This is especially true with arm movement timepieces which give, in addition to time, a date, and sometimes even the days of the week.

But for most homicides, the best a forensic investigator can do is make a few calculations based on several factors surrounding the body or part of body, and derive a time of death with an error factor of a few hours either way.

There are several indicators which can help to determine a time of death, and estimations can accurately fall within hours at the best. The best known methods are rigor mortis; lividity, also known as hypostasis; and body temperature. All of them are subject to several changing factors, such as ambient temperature, the physique of the person at the time of death, the amount of exercise the person was doing, and consumption of alcohol and drugs.

The date when Walter Dunn died was crucially important to me. This would establish whether there was a chance that he never killed Jeremy Wilson in the first place. Based on the evidence accumulated so far, he would have committed suicide on the 20th of February or thereafter. This was the day Jeremy Wilson got decapitated.

In my five years as a forensic investigator, I've heard of alternative ways of finding out the time of death of a victim. The most obvious one being finding a witness who heard or saw something. In this case, a witness was totally irrelevant. Neighbours of Walter Dunn had been interrogated, and no one had seen or heard anything. This left only two choices. Events associated to the death or postmortem changes to the body.

Frank and I discovered the body of Walter Dunn in the early hours of Monday the 24th of February, exactly four days from the time we found Jeremy Wilson's body.

Before going back and examining all the associated events to the suicide of Water Dunn, I decided it would be easier to go over the postmortem examinations. Tests had already been conducted, and it was only a matter of tying up loose ends, something which no-one had bothered doing since the killer of Jeremy Wilson had been found.

The duty of the VFSC was to provide assistance to any detective involved in solving a homicide or to accumulate evidence for court presentation. Jeremy's homicide had been solved as far the CIB was concerned, and there would be no trial, thus terminating the need for the VFSC to conduct further forensic tests. Of course, anyone with some authority and enough reasoning who worked for the VFSC could have easily challenged the CIB and continued with testing whatever he or she felt relevant to furthering an investigation, even if that investigation had been classified as solved by the police. But at this stage, I was the only person who had doubts over the conclusion of the Wilsons' investigation, and since I possessed no authority whatsoever at the VFSC, there was little I could officially do unless I involved a sworn member who was willing to go along with me.

At 9.03 a.m., on Monday 3rd March, I drove to the VFSC in Macleod, via Punt Road. I didn't want to deal with the city traffic, especially since Swanston Street, one of the two main roads leading to the city centre, had been turned into the Swanston Walk thoroughfare a few years back. The Swanston Walk was a bit of a joke because trams, taxis, police and emergency vehicles were allowed to travel on it. To add to the absurdity, if people were caught walking anywhere, other than on the side-walks, they could be fined for jaywalking.

The traffic was horrific at that time of the morning. Bumper to bumper. Drivers abusing each other with hand-gestures. The blaring of horns. Cutting and changing lanes without warning. Burning red lights. Driving too slow or too fast. Tailgating every car in front. Trying hard to run over pedestrians. Getting cut off by rude bus drivers. I felt like jumping on a tram and getting lost in a good book. But I loved the way my car made me feel on the road. I was ten years younger.

It took me a good hour to get to Macleod.

I walked right pass the Liaison Officer after flashing my ID, hoping I wasn't going to come face to face with Frank Moore. After all, it was Monday morning, and he'd probably be in a foul mood like everyone else who had to rise early for the first time this week.

I went straight to the Biology Division where John Darcy was working.

He was in the lab when I walked in on him, and immediately I sensed he knew what I wanted to talk about.

'Be with you in a sec,' he said, acknowledging my presence before returning his attention to the ocular lens of a compound microscope and tens of labelled slide specimens lying neatly on a galvanised laboratory bench. He looked like a medical doctor with his white lab coat, and various coloured pens sticking from his breast pocket. A pair of safety glasses hung around his neck.

I circled the room with my eyes, observing with interest the hundred-thousand-dollar scientific equipment, including serology, liquid and gas chromatographers; mass spectrometers; four or five compound microscopes with a wide range of power; laboratory ovens; and various other optical and analytical instruments. Galvanised benches were hugging the walls around the room. Near a sink, glassware was waiting to be washed. Tens of hexagonal, yellow containers made of cardboard, approximately thirty centimetres tall, and labelled with a biological-waste-hazard symbol, were scattered around the benches. The ceiling was a multitude of fluorescent tubes.

I waited for about five minutes, my ankles aching from

standing still. This place was closing in on me, and I wondered how someone could spend an entire day working with no one in sight but machines and scientific equipment.

Finally, just as I was considering getting a cup of coffee from the staffroom, fifty meters from the Liaison Office, John Darcy finished scribbling observations in a notebook and said, 'Okay, let's go.'

Without a word, I followed him to a tiny room in one corner of the lab, which he referred to as his office, although it was the size of a cupboard.

While he sat at his desk, I shut the door behind me.

The office was tidy but lacked warmth and individuality.

A Bachelor of Science Degree and various post-graduate diplomas decorated the back wall of John's desk. Two oak-coloured multi-task utility cabinets, made from scratch-resistant melamine finish, stood in one corner. A house plant, which was barely surviving in the confined environment of the three-by-two-metre office, looked at odds with the rest of the office furniture.

'It's about the Jeremy Wilson case, isn't it?' he asked, re-arranging bits and pieces on his desk.

I took a seat and said, 'I need some information.'

He looked at me thoughtfully. 'I heard you got told off last Thursday.' His blue eyes locked into mine.

'You know what it's like. You're trying to do the right thing, and then...'

'I understand. But now they're watching you. Take a look over your shoulder before you cross the line.'

I was thankful for John's concern, but at the same time I wondered what business it was to him. He certainly seemed colder than when I saw him at his place on Saturday. I reassured myself that it was Monday morning after all, and everyone was in a grouchy mood.

He went on, 'So, what can I do for you?'

'I need the autopsy report on Walter Dunn.'

'For what?'

'I told you something was fishy. I have to check when he actually died. It could make a hell of a difference to this case.'

John creased his eyes. 'And why do you ask me? Why not ask the forensic pathologist at the mortuary?'

John was right. Copies of autopsy reports were routinely sent to the deceased's GP and family members. Although I wasn't a family member or Walter's family doctor, I probably could have secured a copy with relative ease, But if I asked for an official copy of the autopsy, Frank Moore would more than likely find out. He maintained good relations with Dr Charles W. Main, Director of the Victorian Institute of Forensic Medicine (VIFM) and head of the Forensic Pathology Department. The Director also held strong liaison with the Clinical Forensic Medicine, Forensic Toxicology and associated Forensic Scientific Services, which occupied the same building in Kavanagh Street, Southbank, only a kilometre away from Melbourne's famous Art Centre tower.

'You know I'm in no position to ask for the autopsy report,' I said. 'I've been barred from this investigation.'

'That's right,' he said, an oblong smile on his face, 'and you know just the person to ask.'

I smiled back. That was the John Darcy I knew, all smiles and ready to help.

'How long will it take?' I queried.

'Give me a couple of days.'

'Why so long?'

A look crossed his face. 'Malina, I'm doing the best I can. Usually, you wouldn't even get close to obtaining a copy of the autopsy. I'm doing you a personal favour here. And you should be grateful since everyone is watching your every move at the moment.'

John was right.

Although I was disappointed by the time delay, I didn't want to linger on with my nagging. He was already going out of his way to help me, and hassling him was not an intelligent move.

On Wednesday evening, Frank gave me a call at home. I was sitting on the balcony of my apartment, reading my forensic book by David Ranson, when the call came through. The sky was overcast, and I could smell the ocean sweeping north. I could hear the television from Michael's room.

I stood from my long chair and took the call from the kitchen.

'You're not still angry with me?' Frank asked, making an

effort to ease our damaged friendship.

'I'm not angry at you, Frank. I never was. You took things the wrong way.'

He obviously didn't want to argue with me, so he immediately changed the topic. 'The inquiry is not going too well. The Deputy Commissioner wants our arses badly. He claims we've breached our own code of practice, you know, as if they ever followed everything by the book.'

As much as I hated to admit it, Frank Goosh was right, of course. As members of the Australian and New Zealand Forensic Science Society, Frank and I had to obey a Code of Ethics implemented in 1990. The organisation was increasingly regulating and setting standards for its members' conduct. I had no doubt the Deputy Commissioner of Police would report our miscarriage of duty to the Society.

But right now, I was uncertain what to tell Frank, because, frankly, I wondered where the hell my career was heading. As much as I loved forensic investigations, I was fed up with being told how to behave.

'Let them do what they want,' I said firmly. 'If they want to get rid of me, I won't lose much sleep over it.' And I meant it.

'Maybe you're right. Just let it be, eh?'

I was surprised by his response. I had expected him to argue how there was more at stake for him since he was an employee of the VFSC, not a consultant like me.

I knew the timing was lousy, but I couldn't help asking the next question. 'So, you've seen Teresa lately?'

The line went silent for a few seconds.

All I could hear was his breathing.

'Since you're asking,' he said, his tone suddenly firm and authoritative, 'she happens to be staying at my place for the next few days.'

I felt as if an ice pick had just been plunged into my heart. 'Teresa? At your place? Are you out of your mind?'

'I can explain.'

'Jesus, Frank, we've already got the Deputy Commissioner on our back, an internal inquiry under way, and you lodge a crime victim in your home? What is this? A leap forward in your career?' I was playing nervously with the telephone cord.

'Hold on a minute, Malina. You know me better than that.

Things are not all that simple. It's not the way you make it sound. You're only seeing things the way you want to.'

'How many ways are there to see what's going on?'

'Many, Malina. To begin, two. Yours and mine.'

'I can't believe this.' I was utterly shocked. 'For a moment I thought I was making things up, You're seeing her, *aren't you?*'

He must have sensed the tension in my voice because he wasn't getting angry at me. 'This is not the right time to talk about it.' He sounded apologetic, as if Teresa was in the room, listening to our conversation.

'Is she there?' I asked.

'No, she's not.'

'Where is she?'

'Out.'

'Where?'

'I don't know. Christ, what's come over you? I only rang to find out how you were, and I'm getting shit in return.'

'I'm only trying to do what's best.'

'This is my business, you understand. My business alone.'

I shifted from one foot to the other. 'Frank, why don't you come over, and we'll talk about it.'

'I don't want to come over, and I've got nothing to talk about. I'm old enough to make my own decisions.' He sounded furious, but I was more angry than him.

'Frank, if you don't come to my place within the next half hour, I'm going to come pounding on your door. And I'm sure you don't need that right now.'

More silence.

'All right, all right, I'm on my way.'

He hung up before I had time to add anything.

In less than half an hour, Frank turned up at my place.

'She's lying to you, Frank,' I said, throwing my hands up in the air.

Frank paced up and down the kitchen floor. Hastily, he tucked his red chequered shirt into his jeans, even though it was already tucked in as far as it would go. I couldn't figure out whether he was nervous or angry. His cranium was bathed in perspiration, and it was obvious he'd rather be home.

'Aren't you gonna say anything?' I asked, locking my eyes into his.

'What the fuck do you want me to say?' He snapped. 'You've been carrying on like some kind of jealous girlfriend from the beginning.'

I frowned, thinking about Michael in the bedroom, and said, 'Is that what you think?' I was disappointed that every time we had an argument, he turned it around into some kind of sexual inadequacy towards me.

'What do you want me to think?' he asked.

'Jesus, Frank, you're unbelievable.'

His jaw dropped. 'What?'

I circled the room and stopped in front of him. 'Listen to me. Something is going on, and you're too blind to see it. I've checked Teresa's statement. Her story is inconsistent with the evidence we collected at the crime scene.'

'How can you be sure?'

'I spoke to people. I checked the files again. I got a second opinion.'

He let out a heavy sigh. 'What do you think you're doing? I thought we were not supposed to investigate this homicide? Weren't you listening to Trevor Mitchell the other day?'

'You rang me to go and see her in hospital, remember? And you weren't supposed to be there either. You know damn well this has nothing to do with rules and regulations. This case is about to be filed away for good, and I'm telling you, things are not what they seem.'

'What about fingerprints? Did we get the results yet?'

'How would I know? Go ask the CIB. They've taken over the damn investigation. No one is telling me shit. I have to unveil the truth by myself.' I looked down at my feet, and back at him, trying hard to soften the expression on my face. 'We were a team once, Frank. We worked well together. I don't know what's happening. I don't know why we can't even stand the sight of each other. I'm hurting.'

I could feel emotions building up, but I held my tears back.

I went on, 'I'm hurting to see us end everything this way. I need you to get through this. I need you to help me. I've got no one else, and I'm so scared of losing control right now.'

He stared at me for a few seconds. The look on his face

told me he thought I was pathetic.

But I was dead serious.

Suddenly Michael appeared from his room. 'Is everything all right?' he asked solemnly.

Frank and I turned towards him, unable to say a word.

Finally, I muttered, 'Everything's okay, Michael. Just go back to your room. It's grown-up stuff.'

He glanced at both of us and said, 'Sure, whatever you say,' and left.

'All right, all right,' Frank finally said, dropping his shoulders. 'So, what's your version of events?'

'I don't think Walter Dunn killed Jeremy Wilson.'

'Who did?'

'I don't know. That's what I'm trying to figure out.'

'And you have no idea whatsoever?'

'All I know is that the killer is still out there. In fact, the truth is probably staring us in the face.'

He puzzled over my response, rubbing the bridge of his nose with his thumb and forefinger. He glared at me and said, 'Are you suggesting Teresa killed her husband?'

'That's not what I said.'

'But you're getting there.'

'It's always a possibility.'

Frank was clearly unimpressed. He threw his head back and forth, and gave me his best performance in five years. 'For Christ's sake, Malina, listen to what you're saying. Teresa trashed her apartment, decapitated her husband, killed Walter Dunn and made it look like a suicide. But wait. To make it even more convincing, she beat and scratched herself in every possible place, and even managed to insert Walter Dunn's semen in her vagina. But, if that's not convincing enough, why not go the extra mile and add a finishing touch? Why not insert a squash ball up her arse? Hell, why not?'

For the first time since he came through the door, I felt at a loss.

'But...' I muttered, stepping back a couple of metres. I knew he would never do it, but it felt as if he was going to hit me.

'*But* what? Don't you think if Teresa had wanted to kill her

113

husband, she would have simply shot him or run over him with a car? Or at least try to make it look like an accident? Or hire a hitman? Does this strike you as a common way to get rid of a spouse? Come on, Malina, give me a break!'

I felt heat on my cheeks. Being made into a fool wasn't my favourite pastime. Frank's logic was hard to deny. His argument stood ten feet tall, while mine could hardly reach my ankles. But I didn't tell him Teresa had been seeing Walter for nearly a year. For now, I thought the information would better be kept to myself.

I wiped the perspiration from my forehead with the back of my hand. 'I don't know any more,' I said, now truly confused and overworked. 'I'm only trying to do what's right.' I let tears, which I'd held back for the last five minutes, stream down my face.

He froze for a few seconds, not knowing how to react. He seemed embarrassed by my crying. But it wasn't what he said which made me cry. I'd felt extremely sensitive in the past few days, and his timing was bad. It would only have been a matter of time before something would have triggered my outburst.

After watching me for half a minute, he stepped forward and placed one hand on my cheek. 'Let it go, Malina,' he said tenderly, 'just let it go. It's all over.'

I looked up at him and forced a smile.

CHAPTER ELEVEN

At around 8.30 p.m. on Friday night, on my way back from Parkmore Shopping Centre, I got caught in torrential rain somewhere between Clayton South and East Bentleigh. With the rain and the darkness, visibility was virtually zero, so I pulled over to the side of the road, heading straight into a large pool of water. The engine flooded, and when I tried to start it over and over, I flattened the battery.

Because my car was standing on a forty-five degree angle in the middle of the left lane, other cars had to diverge slightly to the on-coming lane to get around me. I didn't want to stay in the car. As much as I loved my Lancer, with poor road visibility someone might have run up its back, sending me flying through the windscreen and onto the wet bitumen. Thank God, I had my mobile phone with me. I managed to call the Royal Automotive Club of Victoria (RACV) to my rescue. It took me a while to explain where the hell I was.

'It won't take long, Ms Malina,' the RACV operator said at the end of the line. 'One of our service vans will be there within the next hour.'

I must have got the extended version of one hour because I stood in the pouring rain for well over an hour and a half on Old Dandenong Road, in the middle of nowhere. The area was creepy and dark, sending shivers rippling down my back.

The battery on my mobile phone was low, and I was scared to damage it under the pouring rain. I tucked it under my jacket but couldn't protect it fully from the raging torrent.

My hair and clothes were stuck to my cold skin, and I swore that if I came out of this alive, I was going to catch the worst double-pneumonia ever. I dreaded having to spend the next few days in bed because, frankly, I hadn't the time, nor the desire. My life was currently switched to high gear, and any distractions would only confuse me more than I already was. And since I could feel myself slowly sinking into a depression, like someone trapped in quicksand, getting sick would assure a fast way to the bottom of the pit.

Now and then, a vehicle drove carefully around my car, avoiding the pool of water which trapped me in this purgatory in the first place. I wondered if anyone was going to stop and ask me if they could help.

But car after car drove past as if I was nothing more than a tree, perfectly happy to be soaking in all the water from heaven above.

What has the world come to?

On the other hand, maybe it was a good thing no one bothered with me. My mind had nothing better to do than imagine thousands of scenarios of how a lunatic out there would finally pull over, ask me if I was okay, pull a knife and cut me open like a pig.

But to my relief, the yellow RACV patrol car arrived at the top of the hill. By then, the rain had eased, and I could even see stars in the sky.

I was soaked from head to toe, convinced this incident was going to send my chest cold into a new level of complication.

'What's up,' he said as he come out of the car and moved towards me.

'Jesus, am I glad to see you.'

He was in his mid-thirties and well-built. His drenched, blue shirt stuck to his front and back. 'You wouldn't guess how many people have being telling me this for the past hour,' he said, wiping the excess water from his face.

He explained how many vehicles broke down in this weather. He'd been standing under the pouring rain longer than I had, his head buried under various bonnets, rescuing people from their misery, and in return, feeling miserable himself.

'I thought you guys were issued raincoats,' I commented, realising how cold he must have been with only his shirt on.

'They're part of our winter wardrobe. We haven't received them yet.'

I guessed it was bad luck during those spring and summer downpours.

Half an hour later, I was home, feeling unusually warm but exhausted.

When I stepped out of the shower and headed for the kitchen, I noticed the red light flashing on my answering machine.

One message, it told me.

John Darcy had some news.

'I've got a copy of the autopsy report you wanted on Walter Dunn. Give me a call when you can so we can make a time to discuss it, preferably after hours.'

I checked my watch; 11.04 p.m. I found it inappropriate to call him so late. Unlike Frank Moore, John Darcy had a family. I'd hate his wife to think I was the other woman.

I called him at 8.00 a.m. on Saturday instead.

We agreed to meet at his place for lunch.

Frank Moore and I had already performed a preliminary examination on Walter Dunn at the crime scene. The formal examination of the dead body took place during the autopsy at the Victorian Institute of Forensic Medicine, home of the city mortuary.

The autopsy of Walter Dunn involved not only an external examination, which we had partly conducted at the crime scene, but also an internal examination by means of a dissection. A DNA test had also been conducted for further reference if required.

As far as Frank and I had initially concluded, Walter Dunn did commit suicide. But further forensic examination and laboratory analysis might have showed otherwise.

I sat behind John Darcy's home office desk, a mug of black coffee in my right hand, waiting for him to flick through the autopsy report, a bunch of documents and photographs neatly packaged in a large yellow envelope.

Across the window of the study, the sky was covered in

clouds, and John's kids were playing tag in the backyard. They seemed happy and full of life. It made me wonder what happened as we got older, how everything suddenly became so serious, how we forgot to enjoy simple things, like running around, playing ball, and taking everything one day at a time. It also brought to mind flashes of my childhood. I had never been happy as a child.

I turned back to John.

He nodded to himself, as if he was having an internal conversation between the right and left side of his brain, while curling his blond beard with his thumb and forefinger.

'So,' I said impatiently, 'you're going to let me in on this?'

He jolted on his chair as if he had forgotten I was in the room.

'You were right,' he said, his voice dead-pan. 'Something is wrong with this case.'

I wanted to smile, but I saved it for myself. About time something went my way.

He handed me, over the desk, a few pages from the report and added, 'The gun shot wound to his temple is not typical of a suicide.'

That was what I had hoped for.

I read through the section describing the gun shot wound.

The wound on Walter's temple was from a distant shot, probably more than fifteen inches, making it virtually impossible for the victim to have killed himself. If Walter had shot himself, he would have done it at close range and therefore leave traces of gunpowder on his skin. The absence of gunpowder from the full metal jacketed bullet, designed to penetrate its target without expansion, and the angle of the wound indicated he was shot by someone standing a couple of metres to his side, at an angle of approximately thirty-five to forty-five degrees.

At the crime scene, I concluded the absence of gunpowder around the gun shot wound was due to the putrid skin condition, which had been ravaged by maggots, insects and rot.

On the other hand, Dr Charles W. Main, the pathologist who performed the autopsy at the mortuary, was convinced the reason I never recovered gunpowder on the skin was because there was none there in the first place.

The other evidence, which supported the non-suicide theory, was the lack of gunpowder on Walter's hand. This clearly indicated Walter did not fire the gun, even though he held it tightly in his hand when we found the body. And even if he did, his arm would have had to be made of rubber to be able to twist it at such an angle to match the gun shot wound.

I look up at John Darcy, who now seemed as surprised as I was.

'Murder,' I said, perspiration dripping down the small of my back.

The sound of my voice hung in the small study like a four-letter word.

Silence took over for a full minute.

John glanced at his forensic hardcover books next to his desk. He seemed to be puzzling over a possible explanation other than murder.

I knew he was wasting time.

I took another sip from my mug as I wondered who in the world killed Walter Dunn. One thing seemed certain. If someone killed him, there had to be a motive. Homicides never occurred without motive. People who killed did so for a reason. The most common reasons I had come across during my five years as a forensic investigator were greed, love, hate and jealousy. In addition, over eighty percent of homicides were committed by people known to their victims, usually friends, neighbours or family members. It made you want to hibernate for the rest of your life. I hadn't quite reached that point, but I was certainly selective about my friends. With friends, quality over quantity was definitely the way to go. As far as family and neighbours were concerned, unfortunately fate was largely in charge of the matter.

I emptied my mug of coffee in one go.

Whoever killed Walter tried to make it look like suicide, but it was a clumsy attempt. The scenario was right, but the forensic research non-existent. This had been a deliberate set-up to give us a different impression of what really happened. And in spite of its simplicity, it almost worked. Caught in the horror of the crime scene at the Wilson's apartment, no-one bothered going over the evidence. And why should they? After all, the killer shot himself, and there was nothing more to it.

I turned my gaze back to John and said, 'Do you think whoever killed Walter Dunn is the same person who killed Jeremy Wilson?'

He raised both hands above the desk and said, 'That or there was an accomplice. More than one person could have been involved. If this whole thing was a set up, it might have taken two brains to figure it out. Your guess is as good as mine.'

'Or one person who had plenty of time on his hands.'

He nodded, knowing absolutely anything was possible at this stage.

So far, Walter Dunn's autopsy was the best evidence we had that foul play had taken place. We all got sucked into the suicide theory. The CIB had virtually sealed the case and filed it away forever. I wondered if they'd even bothered reading the autopsy report.

Poor communication between a pathologist and the detective in charge of a homicide usually resulted in a case not being solved, or the wrong person being sent to jail. Keeping those communication channels open was so important, and yet, over and over, I could see the same mistakes being made. Overall, people were either too busy, too lazy, or had lost genuine interest in their profession.

I placed my empty coffee mug on a corner of John's desk and wondered how Frank would react to this finding.

'What I need to know now is when Walter Dunn died,' I said, looking back at John.

'It's somewhere here,' he said, as he sifted through more pages of the autopsy report. 'Three separate tests were conducted to estimate the time of death.' He handed over two pages of the report. 'According to this, Walter Dunn died between the 16th and the 17th of February, not a day more, not a day less.'

I took in the information and realised something was definitely wrong. If Jeremy and Teresa Wilson were attacked on the 20th February, how could Walter Dunn have committed the crime if he suicided forty-eight to thirty-six hours before the event?

I shifted uncomfortably in my chair.

One of the tests to determine Walter's time of death involved forensic entomology.

The study of insect activity on a dead body provided a very accurate method of finding the time of death in a homicide. Since I took the pictures of Walter's body at the scene of the crime, I clearly remembered insect activity had taken place, and fluid had leaked from various orifices in the body. I knew for a fact this would eventually led to establishing a time of death, but it seemed irrelevant back then since we'd caught who we thought was the killer.

The autopsy report indicated formation of gas inside the body from bacteria dissolving tissues. The gas formed various blisters, two to three inches in diameter, on various parts of the skin. Because the temperature in the room had been moderately cool when we found the body, decomposition had progressed at a slow rate. The author of the autopsy report had taken this into consideration when estimating time of death.

Walter's body had been lying in his home for a while, therefore his body temperature had dropped to room temperature, a good indication he had been dead for at least thirty hours.

But the best indicator of Walter's death was the stage of development of the maggots which had nested in the rotting body.

The instar, the form assumed by an insect during a particular stadium or growth-stage, of the maggots had reached third level, a clear indication Walter Dunn died seven to eight days from the moment we found him.

The concluding paragraph of the autopsy report placed Walter's death at the 16th or 17th of February, the date John had already indicated. Assuming an error rate of ±24 hours, this still meant Walter died two to three days before Jeremy Wilson got decapitated.

'What are you going to do?' John asked, a worried look crossing his face.

I gave him back the autopsy report and said, 'Officially, I'm not even meant to be investigating this homicide. Morally, I'd probably have to tell Frank Moore. Legally, I'm bound to tell Teresa Wilson at some stage that Walter Dunn was not the man who killed her husband. But what I want to do right now is dig a little further before someone finds out what I'm up to and puts a stop to it.'

He shifted in his chair and smoothed his beard with his right hand. 'But surely, the detective in charge of the investigation would look into the matter seriously. You can't just withhold information because of your own curiosity.'

'I'm not withholding information. They've got access to this autopsy report as much as I do. It's not my fault if they're not doing their job properly.'

'What about pointing it out to them.'

'What am I? A school teacher? They told me to keep away from this case. Suddenly I'm supposed to turn up and say, "Excuse me, but I decided to nose around a bit longer, and guess what I found?"'

'You're dramatising everything.'

'I'm the one who's got to deal with these people. Trust me, I'm doing the right thing. Until I find out more information, there's no reason to raise the alarm.'

He shook his head as if I was being unreasonable. But he wasn't the one sitting in my chair. If he knew the whole story, maybe he would have thought differently.

'There's more to it than that, John,' I said, locking my eyes in his. Although I had no desire to explain my actions to John, I felt obligated to do so for personal reasons. I was sick and tired of people thinking I acted irrationally. 'Frank is involved with Teresa Wilson. I shouldn't be telling you this, but she's currently staying at his place. How am I supposed to reveal what we've just discovered while she's still living under his roof? For all I know, she could be the one who killed her husband.'

His brow creased. 'Are you sure?'

'Yes, I'm sure she's at his place. No, I'm not sure she killed her husband. In fact, I doubt it. But I believe she's a contributing factor to his death.'

John stroked his beard and tilted his head. 'I'm glad I'm not in your shoes. But if I was you, I would pass on the information ASAP either way. You really should get a second opinion. This is getting way above your head.'

I stood from my chair and said, 'The last time I tried to get a second opinion, I was told to let it go. I think I'll handle this one by myself.'

He stepped out from behind his desk. 'I've got to hand it to you. You've got one hell of a nerve.'

'I've got nothing to lose, John. The Deputy Commissioner of Police is determined to end my contract. The detective in charge of the investigation is not going to give me a bear hug when he finds out what I'm up to. I've got no choice. Sometimes you just have to go against the grain and hope you're not going to rub someone the wrong way in the process.'

'It's your call.'

'It's my call, and I'm willing to take a chance.'

He nodded, but I was uncertain as to whether he really approved or was just tired of trying to make me change my mind. 'I hope you know what you're doing,' he said, handing me a photocopy of the autopsy report.

I tucked the photocopy under my arm and glanced through the window of the study, and across to the backyard.

John's kids were still playing, running and shouting, free from worries, as if tomorrow would never come. But they'll grow up one day and have to deal with being responsible, with having to answer to some higher authority. As I stood there in silence for the next thirty seconds, I wished they would never have to.

I left John with his family and headed back home to St Kilda.

CHAPTER TWELVE

From my balcony, I could hear the roaring Formula One engines of the Australian Grand Prix in Albert Park. The sound was faint from where I was sitting, but I could imagine the torture people living close to the circuit had to go through. Frankly, had I been living closer to Albert Park, I probably would have gone away for the long weekend. I did promise myself the previous week I would escape from the city during the car race. But life took a different turn, and now I was too obsessed with Walter Dunn's alleged suicide to disappear even for a few days.

I was lying on a long chair, my Sue Grafton novel in one hand, wondering what it would be like to have a husband again. As much as I longed to have someone to call my own, I was uncertain if I'd cope with the change. It suddenly occurred to me that I'd been single for so long, I'd be incapable of living with another human being, apart from Michael. Even then, we were not really living together, just two strangers enduring each other. Surely, we would get on each other's nerves after a while. I could hardly stand some of my habits at times, how in the world was I going to stand his?

I looked up to the sky. White clouds were hovering, but it didn't look as if it would rain. All in all, it was a nice day, and a lucky one for the organisers of the Grand Prix.

My friend Jolly Roger was on my mind.

I'd contacted various Internet providers the previous day,

but none were capable of helping with a list of people who might have tapped into the Jolly Roger website. To begin with, they felt that providing names and addresses of their customers was highly immoral and breached the basic fundamental trust between the company and its clients.

Secondly, what I was asking was impossible to track, unless the website provider had devised a tracking system which recorded the initiators of queries. In this case, the provider was Jolly Roger. Based on the type of information he provided his 'customers', I doubted he would be willing to participate in investigating a fraud which had probably originated from his advice.

Another idea came to mind, but I would have to consult with the telephone company first to see if it was willing to finance my little plan.

The following day was labour day in Victoria, ironically a holiday dedicated to working. I knew I would have little chance of getting any co-operation from the VFSC or the VIFM as both institutions would be operating on skeleton staff.

I stood up from my long chair and felt a weakness in my legs, probably from lack of sleep and the worries associated with the Jeremy Wilson homicide.

I entered the lounge room, crossed to the kitchen and opened the fridge.

My eye caught a pile of dishes in the sink, which I had been putting off forever. The lounge room was in the same state of chaos, and so was my bedroom and study. I knew I would have to gather my strength eventually, and get the apartment back into an acceptable living standard. I never had guests, so it would be for no one but myself. And since Michael was never home and lived on McDonald's food, he'd never notice.

Disorganisation depressed me, and I felt it was due time to stop feeling sorry for myself. The state of my home accurately reflected my state of mind. I knew that cleaning things up around me might help me to clear things up in my life.

As I poured myself Dr Pepper in a glass tumbler filled with ice, I puzzled over my deteriorating relationship with Frank Moore. I'd never thought I'd see the day when we couldn't even talk to each other without losing our temper. I valued Frank's friendship more than anyone else's because I knew that in spite of our on-going tug-of-war, we both had a deep respect for each other.

I took a sip from my glass, letting the cherry-cola-like flavour treat my taste bugs.

My biggest concern was to see Frank fall on his face, and me not doing anything about it. But in a way, Frank was right. He was old enough to make his own decisions. Who was I to tell him how to live his life.

I took another sip from my drink as I crossed the kitchen and headed back to the balcony.

My life was a total mess right now. My relationship with Frank was going downhill, my son Michael felt like I spent too much time on the outside world and not enough with him, and my career with the VFSC was tarnished. But somehow I thought I could put some order in other people's lives. I smiled at the irony. At least I still had a sense of humour.

As I lay back in my long chair with the cold drink in one hand, my mind was working out a plan of action. Now that I knew for a fact Walter Dunn never committed suicide and probably never killed Jeremy Wilson, the possibilities of who did what were limitless.

Although I had suspected Teresa to have killed her husband in the last few days, I didn't truly believe she did. I found it hard to imagine a woman could be capable of committing such atrocity.

In a way, my belief seemed naive, especially when I had spent so many years working in criminal investigation, and, after my fourteen-month stint at the FBI Academy in Quantico, USA, I learned women were just as capable of carrying out acts of cruelty as men. In fact, some of my fellow students at the Academy believed women were capable of committing more horrid crimes than men. To date, I'd never seen evidence to support this belief. Even though I had studied hundreds of cases involving women killers, the cruelty they'd inflicted on their victims did not compare with the evil men were capable of.

I had little doubt the death of Jeremy Wilson had been inflicted by a man. How his wife fitted into all this, I was unsure. But Teresa lied to us and, therefore, had to be involved.

Maybe it was because this unusually violent homicide had

taken place in Australia, and Australia wasn't America, that I refused to accept Teresa Wilson as a murderer. The wort crimes always seemed to be happening on the other side of the Atlantic.

By 4.30 p.m., white clouds had turned to grey. A gentle breeze was blowing from the ocean and entering the apartment. I was in my study and had just finished printing out a monthly invoice for my services to the VFSC. I also updated my file for the telephone company, adding to a progress report what I had done so far. I had only put in a few hours work, but at $150 an hour, the balance had already exceeded $500. I made a note in my diary to send them a progress payment invoice once I'd reached $1000 worth of billable hours, just to make sure I kept up with my loan repayment for the apartment.

Half an hour later, I was getting bored, so I decided to drive down to the National Theatre to see if Louis was there. I could have started washing the dishes, but my mind wasn't up to it. *Will it ever be?* I wondered as I slid into my car, turned on the engine and cracked the gears.

I parked at the Alliance Française car park, a well-hidden parking haven for those who knew its location and were members of the French association. The yearly membership to join the Alliance was worth its price in gold, just to be able to use its parking facilities, especially in St Kilda, where parking officers seemed more hungry and cunning than anywhere else in Melbourne.

Louis was glad to see me and had wondered if I would ever call on him again. He didn't say, but I knew he was excited to be helping in an investigation.

Most people whom I approached for help felt as if they were taking part in a cop show, no thanks to the imagination of over-zealous scriptwriters. Frankly, I didn't know what the big deal was. They were fools to think pursuing criminals was a neck-breaking, hormone-pumping adventure. My life was no Die Hard film. Like everyone else, the only time I saw Bruce Willis was at the cinema or on a poster at Planet Hollywood. Most of my time was spent worrying to death about my next move, or wondering how I was going to overcome the bureaucratic anarchy of the VFSC and the Deputy Commissioner of Police.

I wanted to have a chat about Jeremy Wilson's affair with his client's secretary, but Louis seemed uncomfortable engaging in a long discussion while at work.

'Doing anything this evening?' I asked, shifting from one foot to the other, feeling slightly embarrassed catching him off-guard.

'Love to.'

He seemed glad to oblige, so I relaxed.

We decided to meet at Sadies, a bar club in Coverlid Place, between Bourke and Little Bourke Street, just off Chinatown.

Parking in the City was hell because of the Grand Prix and Moomba, Melbourne's own celebration of itself, taking place at the same time. I ended up parking in a Grollo construction site, just behind the Peter McCallum Institute.

I walked all the way up Bourke Street, not far from Hungry Jack's. I hated the area around Parliament House at night time because of the dim lighting, and the nearly-deserted streets. The only people in the area were bums, and Melbourne was increasingly getting its share of them, like all the great cities of the world. The people blamed the State Government, who in turn blamed the Federal Government, who in turn blamed the unemployed, who in turn blamed industries, who in turn blamed the unions, who in turn blamed the State Government, who in turn blamed the people. The great circle of a civilised society.

At 8.00 p.m. exactly, I paced down Coverlid Place, a narrow, spooky lane, which I would have never walked alone had I not had a rendezvous. I believed in minimising my chances of getting knocked off. Being a woman walking a dark street at night was definitely a good way to end up as the main feature story on the evening news. Maybe it was because I had seen too much human cruelty that I felt anyone out there could be a loony on the loose.

The high heels of my brown, leather shoes clicked on the pavement as I glanced constantly over my shoulder to see if I was being hunted. At times like these, I wished I was allowed to carry a concealed handgun. I'd told myself for weeks my license to carry a weapon would be approved any day, but all I kept getting was the run-around. My application form was still in the system, I was told, whatever the hell that meant. Unbelievable. I was a homicide investigator, and yet it took months to get my gun license approved. What were these people doing up on St Kilda Road, famous boulevard of the Police headquarters? Pissing me off on purpose? I had no doubt this was some little doing by Frank Goosh and his entourage.

The night was mild, but not enough to wear a shirt only, so I took a beige summer jacket with me. This was one of the few times I was wearing a dress, a white cotton/wool blend, cut just above the knees. I felt extremely vulnerable and a bit foolish to have invited Louis down this end of the city.

Stars hung above my head like decorations from a Christmas tree. I filled my lungs with the smells of exhaust fumes and multicultural cooking

Sadies was fifty metres away, to my right. The front door leading to the foyer was almost concealed. For a spilt second, I wondered if I was in the right street. But as I got closer, the illuminated sign with the name of the club confirmed this was Coverlid Place.

I was greeted by a funky gentleman dressed in a long black leather jacket and wearing a golden earing and a pony tail. He asked me if I'd been here before. I smiled, told him yes and walked straight past him.

I climbed a flight of narrow wooden stairs to the first floor, where I was supposed to meet Louis.

The club had different rooms, each self-contained with their own bar, making it an ideal place for private functions.

I pushed a door and walked into one of the rooms.

The main room had an unsual Japanese-like architecture, with paper lights and chair-less sitting arrangements, set on a split level below the floor line. A smaller room with a bar and stools was attached to the main room. I'd been there six months ago for a friend's twenty-fifth birthday bash, who was completing a PhD in engineering at RMIT University

In spite of it being Saturday night, the club was virtually empty, making it pleasant for a *tête-à-tête* conversation.

Louis wasn't here yet, so I climbed on a wooden stool, and made small talk with the Greek barman while sipping a bourbon and Coke.

The lights were low, bathing the room in a warm, friendly atmosphere. A jazzy tune, which could have tamed a hyperactive elephant, hypnotised me into a relaxing frame of mind.

No one was smoking, but I smelled cigarettes, probably from earlier on.

I was half through my bourbon and Coke, deeply engaged in a debate over Michael Schumaker's right to express his less-than-complementary opinion of the Melbourne Grand Prix track, and in doing so attracting much negative publicity throughout the previous week in the *Herald-Sun* and most television stations, when Louis walked in the room, wearing a red Hawaiian shirt and green cord jeans, and showing off his belly button.

He smiled as he paced towards me. That's when I noticed he was even more handsome in low lights than during the daytime.

Two men in seventies fashion, standing in one corner of the main room, stared at him as he walked in a dandy-like way. I could feel the lustful stares zooming through the air like the jazzy tune.

Louis looked so cut and neat and up with everything, I almost wished I was a homosexual male. I had a fetish for men who seemed sensitive and in touch with their inner feelings. The macho type put me off, although I never turned a blind eye to a well-toned body. The best looking men were always gay, probably because they bothered looking after themselves. Blackheads and greasy hair didn't turn on many women. Men's idea of looking good was to step in and out of a shower with a cake of soap. Never mind that us women spent a great deal of time in the bathroom, working hard on looking our best. In a give-and-take situation, most men still had a lot to learn about giving.

I left the barman playing with his bottles and bought Louis his first strawberry daiquiri, hoping it would set his tongue free. But the drink wasn't necessary, because Louis was in the mood for gasbagging.

I asked him about Jeremy's mistress.

'Haven't seen her since he got killed,' he said, sipping his alcoholic, fruit beverage from an orange straw. 'I guess she doesn't want to get caught up in this whole mess.'

'She got a name?'

'Claire Kendall.'

I slipped a notebook out of my hand bag and added her name to my short list of suspects.

'That's with two Ls', he added.

'How old is she?'

'Twenty-something. Probably twenty-two or twenty-three.'

' Pretty?'

'Well, if I was that way inclined, I'd say she was ready to wear. Strawberry blonde hair, green eyes, about one-seventy tall, not an ounce of fat, kind of girlish looking, always wearing floral short dresses, lightly-applied make-up, and a hell of a sexy voice for a woman, if you know what I mean.'

No, I didn't know what he meant because even though I could tell when a woman was attractive, I wasn't sure what men considered a sexy voice in a woman.

'She worked-out at a local gym,' he added. 'She had this thing for muscular guys, which was kind of weird because Jerry wasn't the muscular type.'

'Nationality?'

'I'd say Australian or Irish descent.'

I was writing all the details down in the notebook, giving him eye-contact now and then, so he knew I was still listening. I shifted my buns on the wooden stool, as if something was crawling up my underpants. The excitement of finding a new lead revitalised my interest in this investigation.

'Was there any talk of breaking-up?' I asked.

'Between who and who?'

'Claire and Jeremy.'

'Not really. He and Teresa were going to go on a second honeymoon. But the last I heard, Jeremy wanted a divorce. He had decided to marry Claire instead.'

This conversion was getting more interesting by the second.

'Wow, hold on a sec. Jeremy was going to dump Teresa so he could marry Claire?'

'That's what I heard.'

'Who told you?'

'Teresa.'

'From Walter?'

'Yep. You're a fast learner.'

All I was learning was that everyone had been talking to each other, and nobody knew what the hell was going on.

I bought Louis a second strawberry daiquiri, and he drank it almost in one go.

'And you've got no idea where Claire is?'

'Nope.'

'She never said?'

'I never asked.'

'When was the last time you saw her?'

'A week or two before Jeremy got killed.'

'Alone?'

'With him, you know, like I told you the other day.' He seemed annoyed to have to repeat himself. 'We sometimes went to eat pizza or pasta after work.'

'Chichio's?'

'On Fitzroy Street, yeah, that's right, that's the one near the George Cinema.'

I wanted to ask more questions, but someone invisible changed the softly-weaved background music into heart-thumping disco inferno.

'Do you know anyone else who knows her?' I screamed in his ear.

But he signalled he couldn't understand a word.

The damn music was deafening.

I repeated myself, but when he made a hand gesture for me to try again, I gave up.

A pause subsided for half a minute. He began playing imaginary drums on the bar top, completely lost in his own world. That second strawberry daiquiri was probably one too many.

We ended up dancing together on the centre floor, shaking our buns, doing things with our bodies I hadn't done since my university years. Being out of the disco scene for more than a decade, I'd never heard any of the music.

Louis wanted me to stay longer, but we'd already danced for more than two hours, so I refused. I was tired, but he insisted.

I didn't get home until 3.25 a.m.

CHAPTER THIRTEEN

On Sunday the 9th of March, I woke up at 11.07 a.m. with a whopper of a headache and a sour taste of bourbon in my mouth.

The hot shower felt good, but my body was aching all over, from my ankles, to the back of my thighs, my buns and my lower back. I suddenly remembered why I'd given up nightclubbing years ago. The mind was willing, but the body slugged behind. And that was in spite of going to the gym three to four times a week.

I opened the windows of every room to let some fresh air into my brain.

The sky was grey, but the temperature was mild and pleasant.

Over a cup of black coffee and two Heron pain killers, I went over the notes I took the previous day at Sadies.

What I needed to do now was locate Claire Kendall. Maybe she'd be able to shed some light into the mysterious death of Jeremy Wilson. Mysterious to me, anyway.

On my way to the study the phone rang.

Tim Simons from the *Herald-Sun* sounded bright and cheerful. We greeted each other and then he began, 'I heard you think Walter Dunn's suicide is actually a homicide.'

I jumped on the spot, wondering who'd been feeding him information. 'I can't discuss anything now, Tim, but you'll be the first one to know.'

'What do you mean you can't discuss anything? The police are treating this as a suicide, which means you can talk all you want. There's not going to be any investigation. '

I swallowed. Jesus Christ, journalists should consider working in homicide. They had a nose for minding what was not their business. 'Trust me, this is not the right time.'

'I broke rules for you when you asked me to. You owe me more than one, Malina.'

He was right, of course, but since I wasn't supposed to investigate this homicide, the last thing I needed was my face splattered all over the paper with a quotation one-fourth the size of a tabloid page.

'If I tell you what I know, promise not to release anything until I give you the green light.'

'Promise.'

I should have known better than to trust a journalist, but I knew I would need Tim in the future for one reason or another. Many cases were solved from good, diplomatic co-operation from the police and the media. And Tim was the perfect connection. I hated to lose him. I also knew I had to learn to trust people to a degree. At some stage I had to put my faith in another person. If that other person betrayed me, he would just get crossed off my phone book.

'If you print any of this before I tell you to do so,' I went on, 'I'm going to have your neck.'

'You know I'd never do that.'

'No, I don't. That's why I'm begging you.'

'You keep your part of the deal, and I keep mine.'

I told him most of the stuff I knew, but left details of Claire Kendall out. After all, I didn't know where she was, so I hated the thought of implicating her unless I knew for sure she was involved one way or another.

Tim didn't make me repeat anything, so I gathered he was taping the conversation. Of course, he could have been writing in shorthand, but knowing Tim, his shorthand skills would be rather rusty.

I told him not to bother calling me back until I got in touch with him.

He thanked me and hung up.

Just then, Michael came out of his room, wearing an

expression typical of the morning after the night before.

He said g'day, and I asked him how his homework was going.

'Fine,' he replied, helping himself to a bowl of Coco Pops.

'How come you never show me any of your homework?'

'When would I do that?'

Good question, and I had no answer.

Then, suddenly, I said, 'Michael, are you happy here?'

He poured milk in his Coco Pops, puzzling over my question. I let him think for a while.

'I guess I am,' he finally said. 'Why do you ask?'

'Because you said the other day I don't spend enough time with you.'

'Oh, that was just talk,' he said. But I could tell by the tone of his voice he didn't mean that.

'I agree with you. I think we should spend more time together. How about if we went on a holiday somewhere. Just you and me.'

He gave me a cold stare, as if I was trying to make a fool of him. 'Mum, I know you're busy with your work. It's okay, I can take care of myself.'

It broke my heart the way he cast his eyes down at his breakfast cereal.

'Give me a chance. I'm trying to make it up to you.'

He took off for his bedroom and snapped. 'Bit late for that.'

I felt a lump in my throat and couldn't swallow the rest of my coffee.

I decided to use the Compact notebook in my study to find Claire Kendall's residential address. I knew of several ways to conduct a search, many of which have been used for years, legally and illegally, by debt collectors.

With the advance in digital technology, and the information superhighway being accessible by anyone equipped with a computer, a modem and a mouse, research had become a breeze in the last two years.

Unfortunately, technology also opened many new doors to crime, including opportunities for on-line paedophilia bulletin boards and child-pornography sites, with users actively seeking sex with minors; and recipes on how to make bombs, how to kill, and how to torture and rape women, as I had recently found out from Michael. If there ever was a university for scums of the earth, the Internet would provide all the core subjects.

Computer stalking was beginning to emerge as a serious problem in some western countries, despite government attempts to suppress information reporting the extent of the problem. Of course, the government had its own hidden agenda; using the superhighway to carry out its own stalking.

Criminal superhighway activities were extremely difficult to monitor because criminal law changed from country to country, and even from state to state. And because the Internet was such a recent thing, governments didn't know how to deal with it. Since there was no central database which monitored what was on the Internet, information was coming fast and furious from everywhere around the globe.

Of course, it was also extremely naive and paranoid to believe the superhighway's only purpose was to encourage criminal activities. The fact remained that most people who tapped into the Internet did so to communicate, educate or entertain themselves.

I sat at my pine desk in the small study, shifted some pens and papers around, and took a sip from my coffee mug. Time for me to do some stalking on behalf of the government, although they had withdrawn their consent for me to do so.

I wasn't a computer buff, but knew my way around the superhighway and learned how to hack into various company and government databases, including Vic Roads, the Australian Taxation Office, the Department of Social Security, Telecom Master Directories, the Education Department, the Electoral Roles records, the Australian Securities Commission, and the Rental Bond Board.

I turned the computer on and waited for it to boot up and do an automatic virus check. When a message prompted me to do so, I entered my secret password, which showed up as five stars on the LCD screen.

I went straight to the Telecom Master Directories because it was the obvious choice. My search was narrowed down since the Claire Kendall I was looking for was in the Melbourne area.

Only seven 'C Kendall' were listed in the Melbourne area. I chose the one with a Richmond address, the closest to the city. Logic told me Claire lived somewhere other than Heildelberg or Frankston, which would have taken her too long to drive up and see Jeremy. On the other hand, she did meet Jeremy on the job, so she could have lived anywhere for all I knew. But since I had to start somewhere, I followed my instinct, as I often did.

Because I had to make sure the address was in fact that of Claire Kendall, I cross-checked the information with Vic Roads. I found one Claire Kendall at the same Richmond address with a 3 February 1974 birthdate. A quick mental calculation confirmed this person was indeed twenty-three years old, approximately the same age given to me by Louis.

Next, I hacked into the Telecom Accounts Department and looked up Claire Kendall's telecommunication activity status. Interestingly enough, she never made a single telephone call since the 16th February, not even a local call.

This little finding began to jolt my mind. This date coincided exactly with the estimated time of death of Walter Dunn, a connection which made me shiver.

I shifted uncomfortably in my chair.

Either Claire Kendall had killed Jeremy Wilson and Walter Dunn, and was now far away in another state or country, or she had been the subject of another homicide which was yet to be discovered.

I emptied the content of my mug, letting the dark Jamaican coffee pump its way through my veins and into my nervous system.

Of course, if Claire Kendall had in fact killed Jeremy Wilson and Walter Dunn, this did not explain why Teresa told us Walter Dunn raped and savagely beat her up.

I switched my Compact powerbook off, and stared blankly at the window in front of me. A tram passed by, and I heard tyres scream.

One thing was certain now. Teresa Wilson had been lying.

Why?

I didn't know, but I was damn curious to find out.

When I arrived at Claire Kendall's unit on Hill Street at 3.32 p.m., her letter box was filled with junkmail, a clear indication she hadn't been home for a while.

Her brick veneer unit was set in a block of four, but was fully self-contained. Each unit was totally separate from the others. The setting was no different from a retirement home.

I spotted Claire's unit straight away. In contrast to the others, the front garden had been completely neglected. Weeds had taken over every bit of dirt and began to make their way to the edge of the lower window panes.

I feared the worst as I got closer to her front door, clearly labelled with a large, gold number 2. With the past weeks' trail of bodies, I wasn't sure if I was ready to stomach another corpse, especially when I still had a slight hangover from my night clubbing with Louis.

I knew there would be no point knocking at Claire Kendall's door, but I did it anyway, just to give me enough time to come to terms with what I was about to do. I glanced around to see if anyone was watching me.

As anticipated, no one answered the door. Scanning the other units, I wondered if I should break in. A perfectly illegal activity as far as my job description and the law were concerned, but since I was already under scrutiny, I didn't give a damn.

I walked back to my car and removed a lockpicking kit from my glove box.

Part of my stint at the FBI Academy included decoying security systems, and breaking and entering virtually every type of premises.

Claire Kendall's door was fitted with a pin tumbler lock, that is one fitted with a series of small pins. The tumblers were in fact held together by other pins called drivers, which in turn were held by a series of springs. When inserting a key, the tumblers were driven to a specific point. At this stage, the door became unlocked.

I could have just kicked the door in, since the lock was cheap and the door made from two layers of plywood with air sandwiched in between. But it would become obvious someone broke in, something I had to avoid in case Claire Kendall was on vacation by sheer coincidence.

Lockpicking is much harder to perform than it appears on television and in the movies. To be competent at opening locks, one must have a certain degree of dexterity, which, as I had found out during my training with the FBI, I possessed.

My lockpicking kit consisted of a pick and a tension tool made from spring steel. I used the tension tool to control the pressure on the lock. I inserted the pick in the keyhole. After a few seconds of manipulation, I raised the pins to their opening point. The tension tool, placed directly under the pick, kept pressure on the pins while rotating. The pins were held in their open position by the pressure applied from the tension tool. With my fingers, I could feel the vibration of the pins. I listened patiently for a distinctive click, and then pushed the door open.

I shut the door behind me.

Cautiously, I stepped forward into the hallway.

The two-bedroom unit was well illuminated, but as I entered the living room, a film of dust covered a small coffee table, a television, a boom box, a bookshelf filled with romance fiction, a sofa and a pair of matching armchairs.

In one corner, near a window, a large plant was dying from dehydration.

I stood still, listening for any noise and sniffing the air at the same time.

I smelled nothing was rotting in the apartment, only a mild odour of garbage coming from the kitchen.

I didn't know if I was relieved or disappointed. On one hand, I had built myself up thinking I would find Claire Kendall's decomposing body being eaten by a wide variety of insects. On the other, I was glad I didn't have to call Frank Moore and explain what I was doing in an apartment with another dead body.

I circled the apartment rather quickly. Not a soul in sight.

Quietly, I sifted through Claire's belongings. I began in the kitchen, where unpaid and expired bills were stuck to the fridge by means of advertising magnets. The name and addresses on all the bills were hers. She wasn't running away from anyone or trying to hide her identity.

In my experience, people with different names on their utility bills tended to hide from the past. Maybe a lover from a relationship gone wrong. Or a brush with the law. Or thousands of dollars in unpaid parking tickets with an outstanding warrant rotting in the bottom of an in-tray at the Sheriff's office.

I opened the fridge, and a bad smell smacked me in the face. Lifting a carton of milk with my thumb and forefinger, I noticed the expiry date read '20Feb1997'. If Claire Kendall had gone on holidays, surely she would have emptied the fridge of perishables.

Fruits and vegetables had gone green and pulpy at the bottom of the fridge, where a brown stream of rot was making its way onto the tiled floor. I pinched my nostrils and shut the door.

I turned my attention to the kitchen sink where I filled tap water in a glass. I crossed the kitchen, and entered the living room, and emptied the content of the glass in the dirt of the sorry-looking plant. It broke my heart to see it dying, and I almost wanted to take it away with me.

Next, I continued my illegal search to the bathroom and the bedroom.

Claire Kendall's red toothbrush and other cosmetic belongings were still in the bathroom cabinet. This prompted me to conclude she'd never gone on holiday after all, unless she bought a new set of everything, which seemed very unlikely.

A tap in the bathtub was leaking, causing a green line of copper to appear from one end of the bathtub to the other. Reddish mould had begun to form under the shower head. A yellow rubber duck with sad eyes longed for its owner to come back home.

In the bedroom, I found fresh underwear, a collection of short floral dresses - Louis had a good memory - and a mountain of *Australian Women's Forum* neatly stacked under the double bed. They were in mint condition.

I flicked through the pages of one of the women's soft-porn magazines, admiring men's biceps, pectorals, and other body parts, which I'm not at liberty to describe.

I felt a sense of guilt as heat rose to my cheeks.

Embarrassing myself, feeling God must be watching from somewhere above, disapproving of my actions, I slipped the magazine back with the others.

To my disappointment, I found nothing which led me to where Claire might have been. No notes, no signs of struggle, no plane tickets or copies of travelling documents, no answering machine with vital messages on it. And the only person who would have known her whereabouts was at the mortuary with his head savagely severed from his body.

When I left the unit, I concluded Claire Kendall had disappeared suddenly with no intention of being away for more than a couple of hours, a couple of days at the most.

I would probably never get to meet her.

CHAPTER FOURTEEN

I got home agitated and needed to burn some energy. With everything trotting in my head, I knew I'd never be able to get a good night's sleep if I didn't burn some calories. Plus I had to make up for the drinking binge the previous night.

At 9.35 p.m., I parked the Lancer on High Street, fifty metres from the main entrance of Terry Bennetts' Gym. While climbing the dark, narrow stairs to the first floor, I could hear the clanking of workout machinery.

Ken was there, his hair freshly washed, and his abs looking more cut than usual. He had no shirt on, apparently a habit of his when he got too hot. He was referred to once as the naked librarian when someone spotted him at the State Library without a shirt on. He thought it was hilarious, especially when that someone happened to be a well-known writer, criticising him in one of her non-fiction books.

We greeted each other, and he said matter-of-factly, 'You look like shit.'

'Thanks, that's exactly what I need to hear.' His observation decreased my self-confidence by a couple of notches. But as I looked into the full length mirror behind him, I realised what he meant. My posture was sluggish, and I had heavy bags under my eyes. I looked like a pale-skinned vampire who hadn't seen the light of day for over five hundred years.

'Did you have a late night or something?' he asked, his arms across his chest.

'A late night *with* something,' I joked, knowing he understood I had too much to drink.

'This is not becoming a routine thing, is it?'

Although I should have kept it to myself, I told him everything I knew about the Wilson's homicide. He wasn't a journalist, and certainly not the kind of person who would go and tell everyone. And I needed to share my findings with someone, other than cops and scientists, just to get a down-to-earth, no-bullshit opinion.

My head was boiling over with information overload and uncertainty. Or was it alcohol, caffeine, and fear of the future? I knew much more than anyone else in this case, and yet I knew so little. But with no one around to share my burden, stress was beginning to take its toll.

Delivering my monologue to Ken did something strange to my mind. I felt light-headed, as if someone had pumped my stomach out after an overdose.

'Go and see Frank and tell him everything you know,' he commanded, while doing a second set of barbell-seated-preacher curls.

'It's not that easy.' I began my warm-up with stretches, standing on one leg and bending the other backwards until the heel touched my buttocks. The muscle on my thigh was warming up gently, but feeling a bit stiff.

'No one said it was. All I know is that if you're right, then Frank could be in danger.'

'But we don't know if Teresa was involved directly in her husband's death.'

He lost concentration and dropped the weights back on the machine. 'Malina,' he said, glaring directly into my eyes, 'I know you care about Frank, and I know you don't want him dead. From everything you've told me, we both know Teresa has been lying about the death of her husband. Like you, I don't know if she killed her husband or not. It would be very unlikely because of the beating she received herself. The fact remains she's lying and can't be trusted.'

'You're right, I guess.'

I stood on my other leg, and stretched the first one.

At the back of my mind, I had come to the conclusion that Teresa was untrustworthy, but I needed to hear my judgement from someone else's mouth. Acting irrationally under pressure would have been too easy. And lately, I felt as if I was under more pressure than I could handle. Working on a homicide was hard enough, but when your whole career was on the line because of it, then you have to be pretty level-headed to push through life with a clear mind.

I stretched my arms behind my back, feeling strain on my triceps.

I went on, 'Frank is going to get upset. I don't want to hurt him.'

'Frank is your friend. If Frank gets upset, let him get upset. If he's a true friend, he'll come back. And if he doesn't, at least you've done the best you can.'

'Have you got any friends, Ken?' I asked, trying to throw another obstacle in his way.

'What's that got to do with it?'

'Just answer the god-damn question,' I snapped, surprising both of us. 'Have you got any friends?'

'Of course I've got friends. You for starters. You may not consider me your friend because you only see me at the gym, but I consider you mine.'

I was touched, so I withdrew my attack. 'Forget it.'

'Go on.'

'Nah, forget it. I don't know what I'm talking about.'

He went back to his biceps exercise without forcing those demons out of me.

I drank half the content of my drink bottle, wishing life was as straight-forward as he made it sound. Maybe it was, but embroidered in the mess I was in, I found it hard to see beyond my own reasoning.

As I crossed the gym and made my way to the leg-extension machine, I decided to go ahead with Ken's advice. I would talk to Frank and hope he would take it well. I'd already lost him as far as I was concerned, so anything that happened between us from now on could only improve our relationship.

I worked my legs, calves, chest, triceps and abs, but kept the sets down to two of each because of tiredness and lack of motivation.

When I left the gym one hour later, Ken was doing squats with what looked liked two hundred and fifty pounds.

I was so exhausted on my way up to my apartment, I thought I was going to pass out.

Next time, I'd invite Louis for a workout instead of a drink.

Monday was Labour Day in Victoria, and most shops were closed. Public holidays didn't agree with me because they were unproductive. Even though I could have done with a break, hanging around, waiting for the minutes and hours to tick by depressed me.

I stayed in bed half an hour longer than usual.

Autumn had crept upon Melbourne already, but outside my bedroom window the sky was clear, and the world seemed inviting. A left over piece of summer had come down on the city, pushing the mercury to twenty-five degrees. It brought a smile to my face as I realised it didn't have to be a rotten day after all.

I showered quickly, gulped a mug of black coffee, and went to do some shopping on Acland Street with Michael.

I was glad to live in a city which was defined as touristy. Acland Street shops were open seven days a week, every day of the year. European-styled cake shops and cafés occupied the top end of the street, giving an excuse for tourists and locals to add a few kilos to their diets. Apart from Safeway, most shops sold items which I could do without. Bric-a-brac, discounted goods, electronics, designer-street clothes, books and take-away food.

'Did you work out this thing with the telephone?' Michael asked, while we were queuing up at a cash register at Safeway.

'I've looked into it. No breakthrough, though.'

He grabbed a Mars bar and tossed it in the trolley. 'Any plans?'

What a smoothy, I thought, but decided to let it go. 'I've got something in mind which is going to pin the culprit down. But I'll have to discuss it with the telephone company first.'

'What?'

'Can't tell you yet. It's confidential.'

He jabbed me with his elbow. 'I'm *your son*!'

I explained for the fifth hundred time that being my son didn't mean I could discuss unsolved cases with him. 'I'm still working on this, Michael. There are some procedures which

I'd like to follow by the book, if you don't mind.'

'Sure, whatever,' he said, and sulked for the rest of the morning.

Within an hour, the crowd bothered me, so I bought a large plant pot and rushed back to my apartment. I was thinking of heading to Claire Kendall's unit and saving the poor creature in the corner of her living room from dying. The more I thought about it, the more I was convinced I would never get to meet Claire Kendall. Her plant would probably get tossed away with her belongings. My life consisted of dealing with the dead. Somehow it made me feel good to think I could save a life, even if it was only a plant.

Early afternoon, I felt unusually tired and grumpy, so I stayed home. Despite my protest, Michael left with his skateboard to see his friend Chris. I decided to use my time wisely and review all the information I had accumulated so far on the Wilson's homicide.

Ken had been right about Teresa Wilson. She was untrustworthy since she clearly lied to me and Frank Moore. I had no doubt whatsoever Walter Dunn didn't kill Jeremy Wilson. Forensic evidence from Walter's autopsy report supported the hypothesis that he died before Jeremy Wilson, making it impossible for him to be the killer. The scientific facts were undisputable. Teresa's unchronological version of events was now very weak.

I sat on my balcony, soaking up the sun, my Sue Grafton novel stuck on page 176, wondering if I should call Frank and arrange an unofficial rendezvous before the working week began on Tuesday. As much as I wanted to get him on my side, my mind was unprepared for another major confrontation. I was uncertain of how involved he was with Teresa. Were they having a sexual relationship? This would have been unlikely since she was still covered in cuts and bruises, and her sexual organs would have been as raw as sushi.

It took me a while longer to make my mind up.

I read some of my novel, and dozed in and out of consciousness throughout the afternoon.

Finally, towards 5.00 p.m., I knew I had little choice. I feared continuing to investigate a homicide which was clearly out of my jurisdiction and authority. In addition, if I kept my mouth shut, I'd deliberately place Frank's life in danger.

I tossed my novel aside, climbed out of my long chair, and made my way to the kitchen.

My heart thumping like a kettle drum, I punched Frank's phone number on the keypad. My hands were clammy as I felt I was breaking some kind of unwritten rule.

She picked up the receiver.

'Is Frank there?' I asked, not bothering to ask whom I was talking to.

'Hold on.'

Nauseous, I almost hung up when I heard Frank's voice.

'Hello?'

'Frank, it's me. I need to talk to you,' I said in a tone of voice that meant business.

A pause, and then he retorted, 'If it's about Teresa, I've got nothing to discuss with you.'

'Give me a chance. I really need to talk to you. This has something to do with Jeremy Wilson's death. I have a legal obligation to inform you of what I've uncovered.'

'I'm not in charge of this investigation, and neither are you.'

'Well, you were involved, so you have to know.' My argument was weak.

'I thought *we* made it clear you were not to investigate this homicide.'

I took a deep breath. The sonofabitch was playing me against them. 'Frank,' I belted out, 'I don't have time to argue with you. I need to talk to you, so be at my place in one hour. If you don't, I'll be going straight to Trevor Mitchell to tell him everything I know. I'm sure he'll be impressed when he finds out you're screwing the wife of a guy who got his head chopped off less than a month ago.'

Silence, and then he said, 'You're making this hard for both of us. Why are you doing this?' His tone was apologetic.

I wanted to strangle him with the telephone cord, even though he was out of reach. 'I'll see you in one hour.'

I hung up.

Heat on my cheeks, I crossed the length of the kitchen floor back and forth. Why did he have to make me feel like such a jerk? I was only trying to help him. I was only trying to do the right thing. How did I end up being the bad person?

All my life, I'd always felt like the odd one out. When I first met Frank, he felt that way too. And together we'd built up a special friendship, a trust, a knowledge we would always be there for one another. But now, it seemed I was letting him down. It was my fault again. The same way I'd let my mother down when I told the counsellor at school about dad. She couldn't cope with it. She said I destroyed the family, that I lied because I wanted to get some attention. That I caused trouble because I couldn't face reality.

But it wasn't true.

All I wanted was for my father to stop what he was doing to me. In return I got punished.

My mother died two days before my sixteenth birthday from a Megadon overdose. She was the one who never faced reality.

My father was convicted on six counts of sexual penetration of a minor.

I was made ward of the State.

For years, I was angry, frightened, and hungry for justice. I swore to myself I would do everything in my power to stop people hurting others. I swore I would try to find some kind of justice for those who couldn't get it. Because I felt like I never got my justice. Even as a grown-up, I still ached from years of sexual abuse, for having had my childhood torn in half, for being punished by losing my mother when all I did was try to protect myself.

And now that I was losing Frank, I felt bitter against the world. But I knew with or without Frank, I would never lose sight of my quest for justice. I would never back down and run away. Because in my heart, I was still a little girl who cried in pain, who tried to get back the mother she'd lost a long time ago, who never understood why the people who were supposed to love and protect her could be so cruel.

I made myself a cup of black coffee as I wondered if there would ever be a way to end the hurting inside. I learned to live with it a long time ago, but now and then, when I felt unloved and unwanted, I didn't cope too well.

And it made my heart bleed that I wasn't getting on with Michael as well as I wanted.

I smiled to myself, wondering if I was just a big baby who

needed to grow up.

Tears came streaming down my face.

CHAPTER FIFTEEN

When Frank rang the door bell, I jumped from the sofa in the lounge room as if I was in cardiac arrest. In spite of having just emptied two mugs of black coffee, I somehow managed to fall asleep in less than ten minutes. I knew it was due to my irregular sleeping habits, worries about the Wilson's homicide, and, whether I'd like to admit it or not, the anxiety of not knowing where I would be in the next six months. I also worried about the internal inquiry by the VFSC and the CIB, and the independent inquiry by the Deputy Commissioner of Police. And the realisation that my friendship with Frank was down-spiralling into a dark pit of nothingness.

When I crossed the hallway and reached for the front door knob, I tried hard to control my churning emotion. I hated to jump on Frank like a scavenging vulture. He needed to know I was level-headed about Jeremy Wilson's murder. I didn't go and investigate behind his back because I was jealous of his affair with Teresa, although I wondered at times if that was true.

As soon as I opened the door, he began shouting, not giving himself a chance to catch his breath, 'I'm getting sick and tired of your bullshit, Malina! What the hell has gotten into you? Why are you trying to ruin my life? For the first time ever, I've found someone I really care about. Teresa Wilson might not be your ideal woman, but she is to me. Is this some kind of jealousy?'

I was about to answer, but he went on, 'Because if it is, you better get some help. This case has gone to your head. I've got enough on my plate as it is, and I don't need more shit from you.'

He stopped abruptly, obviously waiting for me to come down on him like a ton of bricks.

But I remained silent and looked at him with compassionate eyes.

Obviously expecting some other form of reaction, he froze in the hallway, lost for words. He played with the sleeve buttons of his blue shirt, and then tucked his hands deep inside the pockets of his jeans.

'Would you like something to drink?' I said calmly, not reacting to his verbal abuse.

The muscles on his neck relaxed as he realised how tactlessly he had just acted.

'Give me glass of water,' he ordered, his tone down a couple of notches.

I paced along the hallway.

He followed, muttering to himself.

Once in the kitchen, I filled two tumblers with ice and Noble's purified water.

He stood there the entire time, not saying a word. He was obviously trying to figure out his next move. I had let my guard down, and he hadn't expected it.

'Let's go and talk in the lounge room,' I said, carrying a tray with the iced water.

He grabbed one glass and sat opposite me, across the coffee table.

'Let me begin by this,' I continued.

He interrupted, raising one hand in the air, as if he was redirecting invisible traffic. 'My relationship with Teresa Wilson is none of your business.'

I pursed my lips. 'Are you going to give me a chance to explain, or is this going to be an on-going monologue?'

'All right. Go ahead. I'm listening.' He sipped from his glass.

I locked my eyes into his. 'Frank,' I said, 'let's get something straight from the top. I agree your relationships are none of my business.'

He nodded in approval.

151

'And your affair with Teresa Wilson is no different.'

He nodded again.

'But, in this case, we're not talking just about an affair.'

This time, he rolled his eyes to the ceiling.

I went on, 'If you could just put out of your mind your relationship with Teresa for a minute, we might get somewhere. I want to talk strictly homicidal investigation here. I want to throw out all emotions, all personal interest, all biased opinions. I want you to listen to what I have to say, and I want you to let me finish. Then, I will give you the same courtesy, because right now, it feels like you're not giving me much of a chance at all.'

He fidgeted with his hands, obviously upset he was made to feel half responsible for the communication problem we were having.

I continued, 'This won't take long, but it's important to keep your mind open and bear with me for the next twenty minutes or so. Okay?'

'Right,' he said, in a tone which implied I gave him no choice either way.

I told him everything I knew so far, even how Teresa had been having an affair with Walter Dunn for over a year. I told him about Walter Dunn's autopsy, and how it clearly indicated murder was the reason for his death. To support my point, I rushed to my study, raced back to the lounge room, and handed him the copy of Walter Dunn's autopsy report, which John Darcy had so kindly made for me. The important sections were highlighted with a yellow Boss marker.

As he scanned through the autopsy report, blood drained from his face. He passed one hand over his receding hairline, as if to check if hair had suddenly grown in the last two minutes. He was not taking this too well, and it upset me. I had no intention of hurting Frank, but I had little choice in the matter.

'Where did you get this from?' he asked, avoiding eye-contact.

The letterhead of the VIFM was at the top, showing clearly where the document originated from. What he really wanted to know was who gave me a copy of it.

'It doesn't matter where I got it from. This autopsy report

is genuine, and everything I've told you is genuine as well. I need your help Frank. This is getting too hard for me to handle alone, especially when I feel like you're against me.'

He threw the copy of the report on the table and remained silent for a few minutes.

I was unsure what he was thinking now.

Grabbing his empty glass of water, I went back to the kitchen for a refill. I wanted to give him enough space for the bad news to sink in. Being in his shoes would have been a nightmare. But had he known the truth later rather than now, his life could have been shattered.

'All right,' he sighed, 'what do you want me to do?'

I crossed back to the lounge room, his glass refilled with ice and water. 'Get her out of your apartment until we find out what's going on.'

He shook his head. 'It's not that easy, Malina. What do I tell her? What reason do I give her.'

'Tell her you're confused, you don't think you love her or something. You made a mistake, you need more time, God, I don't know. Use your imagination.'

He stared at me blankly. 'Jesus, Malina, I care about the girl. I can't just treat her like shit. It's not like I made this whole thing up.'

I sat next to him and moved my head forward. 'I know you care about her, but you're not the only person in the world who's fallen in love.' I didn't believe he had, but who was I to say.

'What would you know about love?'

'Frank,' I protested, 'don't. You don't have to judge my life every time we're having a disagreement.'

He hesitated and said, 'Wouldn't it be better to leave her in my apartment? If what you told me is true, I've got a better chance of finding out the truth by being close to her.'

'No, Frank, because the truth is going to hurt you like nothing else in the world can.'

'I can take it.'

'No, you can't. You can't even take it now. You don't even know how to handle this. I don't want you to get hurt, Frank. I care a lot about you.' My hands reached for his. 'Don't do this to yourself. This is difficult for the both of us.' I reached out for him.

He remained with his head down for a little while, his hands tucked in mine.

Suddenly he looked up and said, 'Tell me something, but you've got to promise me an honest answer. Okay?'

I knew what was coming, and I was unsure if I was ready for it. 'Okay. What is it?'

'Do you love me, Malina?'

I swallowed and, without hesitation, said, 'No, I don't. I really care about you, but I'm not in love with you.'

I had known that for a long time, but hearing it out loud felt kind of strange. I'd never expressed it so firmly before, not to myself, nor to anyone else. I guessed he must have thought the same thing, because a look of despair crossed his face.

Clearly upset, he retrieved his hands from mine. 'I don't understand you, Malina. It's very difficult for me to make sense of what's going on. You know how I feel about you.'

'I know, and you don't have to say anything.'

'And now you make me wonder if Teresa is just an excuse because I can't have you.'

'Don't be so impatient. You don't know what the future holds.'

'Impatient? Christ, Malina, I've known you for five years. How patient am I supposed to be? Do you know how long five years is when you have to work with someone everyday? I make myself sick every night, wondering if you're suddenly going to find someone else, and then I'd lose you forever. I hope everyday might be the right day to tell you how I feel. I took it slowly for fear of losing you. I've never forced myself on you. Never.'

'I know you haven't, Frank. And I appreciate that.'

'I respect you, you know. That's why I never made a pass at you. I didn't want you to think I was *that* kind of man.'

'I know you're not,' I assured him, but I was uncertain what he meant. How many ways was there to let someone know you cared about them, apart from being obvious?

I'd known he liked me from the first time we met, but I never guessed he was in love with me, although it seemed pretty obvious now. Men had a bad habit of falling in love too easily. Did he really want to spend the rest of his life listening to me telling him how to dress, how to think, how to be careful every time he stepped outside?

I felt bad for him, but it was impossible to fall in love with a man I wasn't attracted to.

He emptied his glass of water and said, 'This is a hell of a lot of stuff to take in for one day. I'd like to spend some time on my own, if you don't mind.'

I understood how he felt, because I had been feeling like that for the past two weeks.

'It's okay, Frank. You go and do what you have to do. But don't you do anything silly now. You know I'm on your side, no matter what. Friends, remember?'

He nodded with an awkward smile. 'If I wanted friends, I'd go to summer camp.'

His reply hurt.

I walked him to the door and kissed him on the cheek.

I was restless on Monday night after Frank left. I made myself sick, worrying about how he was going to cope, how he was going to react to having Teresa under his roof now that he knew things she didn't know he knew.

Michael called me and asked if he could stay over at Chris's. I told him okay as long as he kept in touch now and then.

I got out of bed four or five times during the night and tried to read. My mind floated from one stream of thought to another, making it impossible to sleep or concentrate on my Sue Grafton novel.

I tried to watch television for a while, but it bored me.

I made myself a mug of hot milk, hoping it would send me to sleep.

But it was way past 5.00 a.m. when I finally closed my eyes and forgot about everything for a while.

At 10.34 a.m., the telephone woke me up. The time was glowing in bright red letters on my clock radio, next to my bed.

I turned to the window and noticed the sky was clear outside.

The answering machine in the kitchen took the call before I had a chance to answer it from the bedroom.

I stumbled out of bed and made my way to the kitchen.

'It's John Darcy from the lab,' the voice said at the end of the line.

'What's up?'

'I've found something interesting you might like to see.'

'What?'

'It'll be better if you come.'

'Give me an hour.'

I hung up and jumped in and out of the shower in ten minutes. I dressed in a yellow skirt with matching jacket and a white blouse.

Back in the kitchen I washed down a multivitamin with a cup of lukewarm coffee.

Rushing downstairs, I almost forgot my mobile phone.

As I wondered what John wanted to show me, I inserted the key into the ignition of my car but instead of the engine roaring, there was a click and nothing.

I tried again.

Damn, the battery is dead!

I opened the bonnet, fiddled with the cables connected to the battery, jumped back in the driver's seat and tried again.

Nothing.

The RACV would take too long to come, so I decided to catch a cab at the corner of Chapel Street and Dandenong Road instead.

My Indian taxi driver asked too many questions. I told him I had a headache and would appreciate if he kept to himself. He pursed his lips, as if I had just given him the finger. And in a way I had. Just because I hired his car, it didn't mean I hired him as a psychologist.

I arrived at the VFSC at 11.37 a.m., three minutes later than anticipated.

Anxious, I cleared my name with Liaison, and flew straight to the Department of Biology. I entered the lab by pressing my ID card against a black plate next to the door. The door unlocked automatically.

John Darcy was adjusting his compound microscope. He looked exhausted. His hair looked unkempt as if he had been playing with a nail and a power point. He reminded me of a mad scientist with his white lab coat and surgical gloves.

He glanced up, and with a hand gesture told me to get closer. 'Check this out,' he said.

I crossed the laboratory and stood next to him, leaning on a galvanised work bench, lined with tens of yellow biological hazard containers.

'How long have you been here?' I asked.

'Seven a.m.'

He explained how he had a fight with his wife and needed to escape for a while.

God, relationships really began to scare me.

John shifted his swivel chair in front of a comparison microscope, a magnifying instrument with a relatively low range, 5 to 35x, making it possible to view two samples at once.

The comparison microscope worked by means of a double tube, whose separate images were combined together by a pair of mirrors and a pair of prisms into a comparison eyepiece. This instrument was mainly known to be used for comparison of bullet rifling and cartridge marks in ballistics. However, John had been using it to compare anything from hair, to fibres and tool marks.

'Look in there, and tell me what you see.'

I moved close to the eyepiece and viewed two dark samples of material placed on the stage. The one on the right was rugged and fibres were pulled out from the edge. The one on the left was perfectly cut.

'So?' I asked, wondering what he was getting at.

'One of those two samples is from the suede jacket we found at Walter Dunn's apartment.' I remembered Frank finding the jacket. 'The other is also from his jacket, but it's the one Frank collected from the window frame at the Wilson's apartment.'

'Which provided us with a point of exit,' I commented.

'Or so someone wanted to make us believe it was,' John corrected. 'The material collected from the Wilson's apartment is not the rugged sample, but the neatly cut one. If the killer had caught his jacket on the window frame, we would be looking at a tear, just like the sample on the right. But instead, the sample is perfectly straight, as if someone cut it with scissors.'

I looked at John and then back into the eyepiece.

'Okay,' I said, 'but we already knew Walter didn't kill Jeremy Wilson from the autopsy report.'

'Sure, but this indicates something else. Can't you see?'

I racked my brain for a few seconds and said, 'This was premeditated murder. Whoever killed Jeremy Wilson went through the whole trouble of cutting a piece from Walter's jacket and placing it on the window frame of the Wilson's apartment. And since we know that Walter was murdered and did not commit suicide, and he died a few days before Jeremy Wilson was killed, then whoever killed Jeremy planned this days ahead, maybe weeks, maybe months.'

He nodded with a smile.

I couldn't see what the funny part was.

'Jesus, John, we've got a real psychopath on our hands. The killer didn't just try to cover up his trail, but created an entire scenario of false evidence to send us in the wrong direction.'

'And you know what that means?'

I looked at him puzzled.

He jabbed his forefinger in front of my face. 'You'd better watch your arse. If the killer knows you're getting too close to the truth, you could be in for a nasty surprise.'

I swallowed as I felt my stomach churning. John was right. The killer was still out there and would probably do anything to protect himself.

'This could be someone clever,' he added. 'In fact, it could be someone who knows about police work. It could be someone we work with.'

I thought of Frank straight away, but he was too clever to make so many mistakes.

I knew I was dealing with someone intelligent, but not as intelligent as he thought himself to be. Someone cunning, cold-blooded, and capable of planning his killings well ahead of time. That person had a deep hatred of Jeremy Wilson and Walter Dunn. Especially Jeremy Wilson. The way he'd been butchered indicated revenge of the worst kind. Intruders killed fast and furious. Whoever had killed Jeremy Wilson took a hell of a lot of time to do it.

My mind did a juggling act, but came back to the same conclusion.

As much as I hated to admit it, I was almost certain I knew who that person was.

CHAPTER SIXTEEN

After lunch, I cancelled my afternoon class at the Police Academy in Glen Waverley. Instead, I called the RACV to put a new battery in my car.

Straight after the RACV patrolman left, I changed into a pair of Levis and a white T-shirt.

With its new battery, the Lancer was roaring with pleasure.

And so was I.

I raced straight to St Patrick's Hospital, making a nuisance of myself on the road, tailgating every car in sight, zigzagging between the traffic as if I was running in the Grand Prix. Cold wind blew in my hair, giving me the sensation of thousands of tiny fingers massaging my scalp.

No doubt, one day I would get pulled over.

I needed to talk to Dr Larousse, ask him if he had heard anything suspicious from his staff about Teresa Wilson. Since she'd been there for a few days, surely she must have spoken to someone. And if not, a nurse must have noticed something unusual, something which contradicted her version of the events of the 20th of February.

Dr Larousse wasn't expecting me, and when I walked into his office, unannounced, he seemed taken aback. I glanced at his fluorescent green tie, hidden under his white lab coat.

'Dr Malina, did we have an appointment?' he asked, pushing his rimless glasses up the bridge of his nose. He looked as tired as when I first met him. I wondered if there was anyone left in Melbourne who was getting enough sleep.

I stood in front of his desk and made eye contact. 'I'm sorry to interrupt you, but this couldn't wait. It's about Teresa Wilson.'

Dr Larousse stood up, circled the office, shut the door, and sat down again. 'Actually, I was meaning to talk to you about her. I never got around to calling you.' He almost whispered, as if he was about to reveal some great conspiracy. 'You know what it's like in a hospital. Always running around, shift after shift, and you keep on forgetting those really important phone calls you have to make.' He presented a brown vinyl chair on the other side of his desk. 'Please do take a seat.'

'Thank you,' I said, partly excited, partly anxious about what he had to tell me. Him wanting to talk to me just when I needed to talk to him was a great coincidence, something I rarely came across in my line of work.

He opened the top drawer of his desk and pulled out a cream-coloured manilla folder. A typed label with Teresa Wilson's name was on it. He opened the folder and pulled out two A4-size colour photographs.

I tried to analyse the pictures across the desk, but nothing made sense. A composite of fleshy-like tones.

'Take a look at those,' he finally said, handing over the photographs.

One picture showed Teresa Wilson's badly bruised and cut face. The other, obviously more recent, showed a reduction in wounds.

'The first photograph was taken at the preliminary examination. As you know, when Teresa Wilson first came to us, she was in a dreadful condition. This is clearly evident in the photograph you're holding. Our main concern at the time was to identify any life-threatening injuries, making sure the victim was breathing, stopping any major haemorrhage, looking for head and spinal cord damage, surface wounds, chest injuries and so on. Like I initially told you, it was obvious to anyone who attended Teresa Wilson's wounds that she had been cruelly battered and raped. But now, take a look at the second photograph.'

I placed the first picture alongside the second one.

Dr Larousse tilted his body forward and pointed to various

sections on the pictures.

'You see all the bruising and swelling on the photograph taken when she first came to us?'

I nodded.

'Okay,' he went on, sounding just as excited as when he first began, 'now look at this shot. The bruising has diminished dramatically in a small amount of time. This indicates the wounds were superficial in the first place. If you take a closer look at the lacerations on Teresa Wilson's face, it's much easier to identify them on the second photograph than on the first one.'

I noticed the scratches on Teresa's face were unusually well-scattered.

Dr Larousse stopped for a few seconds, giving me time to absorb his comments. He pushed his glasses back on his nose again and continued, 'When someone gets assaulted, the scratches are random. But on Teresa's face, most of them seem to concentrate on the left side of her face, something which I had never picked initially in the original photos we took, no thanks to the amount of bruising and blood smear. Also notice how the scratches have somehow missed every sensitive area on her face, including the eyes, the nostrils, the lips and the ears. Do you see what I'm getting at?'

I opened my mouth to respond, but he went on, 'But wait, take a look at those.'

Dr Larousse removed another two A4-size colour photographs from the manilla folder, this time showing scratches on Teresa's arms.

'Look at the left arm,' he said, his voice filled with excitement, as if he had just discovered a vaccine for AIDS.

I looked at the pictures and noticed Teresa's left arm had ten times more scratches than her right one. All this had never been obvious at the crime scene since there was so much blood and chaos. I also never had the chance to examine Teresa Wilson because she had been whisked straight to the hospital.

'Okay,' he went on, 'when a person scratches herself deliberately, she tends to do it more on the side away from the leading hand. Since Teresa Wilson is right handed, the left arm is more scratched than the right one. Let me put it another way: left-handed people injure themselves more on the right side, and vice versa.'

I nodded as I stared at the pictures, not really surprised about what I was seeing. When I spoke to John Darcy that morning and concluded whoever killed Jeremy Wilson had *staged* his death, something triggered my mind. I suddenly recalled Teresa Wilson was a set designer. Her job was to make visual impressions. Only she never counted on the forensic evidence she would leave behind.

I looked at the pictures in front of me and wanted to throw-up, not because of the injuries on her body, but because I had felt so close to this woman for a little while. I'd been naive enough to believe only a man would do something so horrific. I'd never come across someone who had self-inflicted so many injuries just to make it look like she was beaten.

'What about the squash ball in her anus?' I asked, not because I needed more convincing, but because Dr Larousse seemed to be taking so much pride in his discovery. And also because I appreciated his extra research and good eye for observation.

'Ah, ha,' he said, 'now that's something you'd have to hear.' He pulled a typed page from the manilla folder. 'When surgery was performed on her anus, the surgeon who did the operation noticed that, and let me quote this, "the anus has slightly keratinised edges, and on close inspection, appeared to be chronically abraded". This woman was used to having things inserted in her anus. I'd say she was involved in passive anal intercourse.'

I knew keratin was a fibrous protein found in hard skin from my biology study at university. Unless Teresa Wilson had a serious constipation problem, Dr Larousse had to be right about her fetish for anal intercourse.

'So,' I said, 'you're convinced Teresa Wilson has inflicted all those injuries on herself?'

He looked me straight in the eye and said, 'Well, I'm not a medico-legal expert, and I certainly wouldn't want any of my comments to be used in a court of law, so officially, I'd have to get a second opinion for you from a forensic pathologist. A clinical pathologist just wouldn't serve the purpose. Problems in criminal investigation differ from problems in clinical work. You know as well as I do that writing up a report to be presented in court is not the same as writing a report for a medical colleague. The last thing you'd want is my testimony thrown out of court on the basis that I'm not qualified to comment. But between you and me, those injuries have got her signature all over it.'

'Do you think you could arrange a forensic pathologist's report for me?'

'Not a problem. You can nominate your own pathologist if you want, and I'll do the leg work. I can have a report for you within a week.'

'There's no way to speed up the process?'

He raised both eyebrows as if to say it's out of my hands. 'I'm doing the best I can. In fact, I've spent more time on this patient than can be justified. But after I heard you came back to visit Teresa Wilson a few times after our initial discussion, her case kept nagging me. Something didn't ring true. I knew I had to see you and talk this over.'

I thanked him for his time.

Just when I was about to leave his office, he said, 'Oh, and another thing. I got the opinion of a gynaecologist regarding the abrasions in Teresa Wilson's anus, and he didn't think it was the kind of marks a squash ball would leave. He said they were marks left by woman's fingernails.'

I turned around, surprised. 'How could he know it was woman's fingernails?'

'The cuts were short and steeply arched, just like the tips of a small manicured hand.'

When I got home, I took a long, hot shower to compose myself and remain level-headed.

I had suspected on and off that Teresa Wilson had killed her husband. But now, there was strong evidence to believe she did.

Or that she had deliberately dramatised the rape by inflicting excessive injuries on herself.

If Walter did rape Teresa, she obviously wanted the end result to look worse than what he did to her. Come to think of it, her actions were not as uncommon as I initially thought. When a rape victim felt the rapist hadn't left enough evidence on her body, she often highlighted the rape with creative evidence, such as self-inflicted scratches and wounds. This was common since so many rape cases never ended up in court because of lack of physical evidence. Rape victims failed to realise that wounds can also tell a story.

As I shampooed my hair, I realised I had to overcome two major problems. The first was to explain to Trevor Mitchell why I continued investigating the Wilson homicide when I'd been barred from it.

The second, a problem of a much graver nature, was telling Frank the full story. The thought of it made me sick. There he was, lodging a probable psychopath under his roof for the last two weeks or so and becoming infatuated by her when she was probably planning her next victim.

And more likely than not, it would be him.

I shivered at the realisation that I might find Frank in the same state as I had found the other bodies, all, I presumed, the artwork of Teresa Wilson.

I stepped out of the shower and dried myself with a white bath towel. The bathroom was filled with steam, so I opened the small window above the bathtub. The air was cool, but it cleared the moisture. I could see the sky outside, covered in white clouds.

As I slicked my hair back, my thoughts drifted to Claire Kendall, Jeremy's secret lover.

Surely if Walter Dunn was a good friend of Jeremy Wilson and the lover of Teresa, he must have told Teresa about Claire. By jealousy, Teresa killed Claire.

But why would she have killed Jeremy when she, herself, was cheating on her husband by having an affair with Walter? And why did she kill Walter?

The only consistency I had established so far was that Teresa killed the two men she slept with. And if that was anything to go by, I began to feel an all-consuming fear regarding the safety of Frank Moore.

I could have gone straight to the police and had her arrested. But to do so I needed a warrant. That would have taken a lot of explaining. In addition, the evidence I obtained to date might be inadmissible in a court of law because I had followed improper procedures. The defence would argue that since I was unauthorised to investigate the Wilson's case, then my findings would be worthless. This would earn a big cross over my name at the VFSC and the CIB. I would seriously have to consider a life as a private investigator instead.

But my main reason for refusing to get police participation was that I felt it might have been better to accumulate more evidence before Teresa got herself a lawyer. The amount of evidence was mounting up as I went along. This gave me faith to push a bit further. I knew if I persisted a bit longer, I would dig up many more secrets, enough to give her three life sentences. After all, in spite of how personally involved I felt to this case, my focus was to get her to court, not help her slip through the legal system. Once I'd found enough evidence, I'd pass it on to the detective in charge of the investigation, anonymously of course, and let him follow up my leads legally.

I knew I was pushing my luck by not getting police involvement immediately, but lawyers could be really cunning. We needed more than just suspicion. Someone out there would go over all the evidence we had accumulated since the beginning of this case with a fine tooth comb, and question the validity of every single test we'd done. Our legal system was increasingly becoming Americanised. You had to be involved in the system to realise what a bunch of losers some lawyers were. They were not interested in their clients guilt or innocence, but just how much money they could extract from them. A pretty lame way to provide justice in a country where seriously dangerous offenders, such as rapists and killers, were given lighter sentences than white collar criminals.

For a person to be found guilty of a criminal offence, the law required that the prosecution proved the matters alleged beyond reasonable doubt. If enough evidence was brought forward by Teresa's defense lawyer, the case would fall apart.

So far, I had accumulated enough circumstantial evidence, that is evidence which comprised details which pointed to the key fact proving a crime was committed.

At best I could prove Teresa Wilson lied. This could be backed-up by medical expert evidence regarding the injuries found on her body.

However, I had no direct evidence indicating she killed anyone.

And that was a stinker of a problem.

My best chance was to get it out of her through a

confession. To do so, I needed to be very tactful and diligent in my investigation.

I knew if I handed everything over to the police, they would arrest her immediately and botch up the investigation. Like myself, they would only be able to prove she'd self-inflicted her injuries, but would not be able to pin her with the murder of her husband and Walter Dunn.

I blow-dried my hair and stepped out of the bathroom in my bathrobe.

I crossed the hallway to the kitchen. While water was boiling, I scooped a spoon of instant coffee in a mug.

What I needed was an evidential glut, enough to have every intelligent lawyer refusing to even try mounting a proper defense. At this stage, the chance of losing my contract with the VFSC seemed completely irrelevant. I was going to nail the bitch even if it cost me my career. I had a deeper respect for the truth than for a job title.

And if Teresa did kill those two men, I also had a personal vendetta against her for humiliating me with her lies.

Fifteen minutes later, I was in my study with my mug of black coffee in one hand. I removed a copy of the original report from the crime scene of the morning of the 20th of February at the Wilson's place and looked for the name of the neighbour who called the police when he heard Teresa screaming.

Lionel Payne was a seventy-three year-old pensioner who had moved into the same block of units as the Wilsons two years prior.

I dressed in my Levis, a clean white tee and a wool sports jacket.

Within twenty minutes I was in Port Melbourne.

Like many people of his age, Lionel Payne was at home, looking out the window of his second-floor apartment, waiting for time to pass, for a friend to drop by, for family to visit, for his time to come.

I could tell he was glad to see me by the over-zealous smile on his face.

He had short, grey hair with a matching beard and seemed quite underweight for his height. His dark brown eyes sat deep inside his skull. A fine mist covered them, as if he was still looking in the past and was incapable of accepting reality. I could read thousands of stories in them, most of which he had lived through before I was even born. Lonely, old people scared me because I knew one day I would become one of them.

His five-dollar, K-Mart, chequered flannel shirt hung loosely on his body frame.

I sat at his kitchen table while he made coffee for two from an old aluminium saucepan. I was certain I would start convulsing if someone suddenly cut out my caffeine intake. More of the stuff ran through my veins than blood.

Two pigeons were making a nuisance of themselves on the window's ledge, which was covered in droppings. Because the window could only be pushed open from the inside, and we were on the second floor, it was impossible to wash the dropping infested glass panel. I had to drink my coffee while glancing through bird shit.

Disgusted, I circled the room with my eyes.

Three flying, ceramic ducks, the type I had seen thousands of times in other people's homes, in Copperart catalogues and in television commercials, hung on the opposite wall. Last I heard, these were worth a small fortune and sold as antiques.

It always amazed me how much rubbish from the sixties and seventies had suddenly become antiques or collector's items, and were sold for ten times the price they were originally bought for. It made me want to keep every tin, book, magazine, container, nail, overworn clothes and teddy bear, and pack-seal them until the year 2050. If I had been unwise with my savings, I'd be able to pay the mortgage off by selling collector's items in mint condition at the Sunday market.

The table I was sitting at was made of a pink, Formica-like surface, with metal legs, and a collection of stains from the last forty years.

An aroma of sweetness and recent cooking filled my nostrils.

I asked Lionel what he did all day.

His eyes lit up as he elaborated on his life.

Lionel Payne was the caretaker in the building. He swept the staircase, arranged the rubbish bins for collection, and

168

mowed the grass around the building. His other duties included minor plumbing repairs, changing burnt-out globes in the hallway, and maintaining harmony between neighbours.

'That was a terrible thing that happened next door,' he said, while opening a white tin of International Roast with the back of a spoon. 'How do you have yours?'

'Straight black. No sugar, no milk. Yes, it was quite horrific.'

He nodded as if he approved but was still shocked by the whole incident.

I wondered for a brief moment if anyone had offered counselling to the old man. 'How well did you know the Wilsons?' I asked as he poured water into two stained mugs.

'They kept to themselves. Well, sort of in a way. I never got to speak to them because they were so busy all the time. Busy bees, they were. In and out as if the world was about to end. I'm home most of the time, so I can see what's going on around me. And you could never keep up with them. Irregular hours. A crazy couple like all those young people out there. You never now whether they're coming or going. Too much violence on television. It's this world we live in. You watch the news, and you see all the violence. No wonder our children get affected. No respect for anyone. We never had crimes like that when I was young.'

Oh, yes, you did, I thought, but you never read about them.

'Is there anything you can tell me about the Wilsons?' I asked.

'Sure. They used to fight all the time. Terrible screams, throwing things at each other. Since they moved in, there wasn't a week that went past without her screaming her head off. She was a pretty girl, come to think of it. I'm sure I once heard her threaten to cut his thing off.'

'His what?'

'His *thing*, you know.' He blinked down where his zip was so I knew what he meant.

I smiled as he placed the two stained mugs of coffee on the table and went on, 'Of course, that's all talk. I mean, how many of us have made threats during our lifetime and never carried them out?'

I nodded as I took one sip from my mug, wondering if I was going to catch a disease. The coffee was too strong, but at least it would keep me on my toes.

I found it interesting that the Wilsons had been having violent arguments for so long.

'Do you know what they were arguing about?'

'I'm no snoop. Don't go around listening to other people's conversations. But I did hear them fighting over who could park the car in the garage.'

'They both have a car?'

'Oh, yes. She drives a Mercedez Benz, an older model, black, two doors, don't know the name. I was never really good with cars. Don't have a driver's license. Don't want one. What for? I don't go anywhere. He drives a BMW or a Volvo, one of those expensive cars, you know, yuppie cars. Yellow, I think it is. Yeah, that's right, just like a lemon.'

I swallowed half the content of my mug and said, 'Where's their garage?'

'Down the back. You mean you didn't know?'

I said no with my head.

He went on, 'I can show you if you want. I mean it's really none of my business, but... You're a cop or something, aren't you?'

'I work with the Victorian Forensic Science Centre. A bit like a cop,' I lied. I was a consultant and not a sworn member of the police.

'Okay, then, I'll show you around.' He grabbed a chocolate-brown cardigan from the back of his chair and keys from the kitchen bench. 'Just follow me.'

I gulped the rest of my coffee in one go.

CHAPTER SEVENTEEN

As soon as Lionel Payne opened the up-and-over Wilson's garage door, I recognised the smell. Being the caretaker, he had a key to every door in the building, which made my job easy. I didn't have to get the lockpicking kit from the car and play burglar in broad daylight.

'I think you better wait out here,' I ordered the old man.

He pursed his lips and played with his beard, obviously disappointed he would miss out on all the action. Then, ignoring my demand, he stepped forward.

'And I'm not kidding,' I added matter-of-factly.

He tucked his hands in the pocket of his brown slacks and glared at me coldly. I tried to avoid imagining what was running through his mind.

I entered the garage while he remained by the door.

A yellow BMW was parked right in the middle of the garage. The duco was shining like a polished fifty-cent piece. Jeremy Wilson loved that car once. He had had the final word on who was going to park their car in the garage. Was that why she killed him? For something as trivial as who would occupy the garage space?

Against the right wall was a workbench and a large variety of tools in good condition. A grinding and cut-off wheel, a unit drill, several types of cables and leads, and a cordless weed trimmer.

I glanced at the far end of the garage. I spotted garden

tools, including a hay fork, a cottage fork, two lawn racks and a trowel, neatly lined up against a wall, ready for some kind of military inspection.

Reluctantly, I moved closer to the bench where the smell was strongest.

'Anything in there?' I heard the old man yell out. 'Do you need some help?'

'No, thanks. Just stay where you are.'

He muttered foul language to himself.

Moving in.

Perspiration dripped down the small of my back.

I circled the car and noticed the black garbage bag at the end of the work bench. The stench was unbearable, but I knew that if I stayed another minute, my olfactory nerves would go numb, and I would no longer be able to smell the odour. If I went out in the fresh air, and came back in again, I would have to start all over.

I whined as I took in a deep breath, feeling a warm, unpleasant sensation in my tummy.

I made my hands into fists, not looking forward to having to open the bag. If I found what I knew I would find, I'd be restless for many nights to come. I was tough, but still human.

I had to be careful with fingerprints or any other forms of contamination. The last thing I wanted was to leave my body blueprint behind and have someone drag me in to a court for breaking a law I wasn't aware of.

At this stage I was undecided on what to do if the content of the black garbage bag was in fact the body of Claire Kendall. I'd seen so much horror in the last month, my mind was becoming desensitised. But I knew one night I would wake up, shaking all over, throwing up my dinner, taking in what I'd experienced months, sometimes years ago. Like many crime-scene investigators, who were exposed to so much horror over the years, I was a walking, psychological time-bomb.

On television they showed you these cops who poked at bodies, faced crime after crime, got beaten to a pulp, and yet, by the next episode, recovered as if they'd begun the life of a Born Again Christian.

But in reality, humans were far more sensitive. Television

never showed the weeks of numbness, sitting at home, knees clutched to the chest, suicidal thoughts drifting in and out of one's mind, the urgency of wanting to call Lifeline, just in case you lose the strength to carry on for one more day. Were we born to take so much violence in our daily lives? How much longer would it take before all the minds in the world would give up and lay to rest?

I removed a pair of Ansell disposable surgical gloves from my sports jacket and slipped them on. I must have looked like a dental technician who was about to perform backyard surgery.

Two steps forward, one step back.

Get a grip on yourself.

Reluctantly, but in a professional manner, I closed in on the black garbage bag.

I kept telling myself this was only part of the job, nothing more, nothing less.

Unwillingly, I undid the white plastic nylon strap that was keeping the bag secure.

The pungent odour coming from the inside of the bag was a mixture of rotten meat, urine, and methane-like-gases, all mixed into one. Not a single word could describe the horrible smell.

I pulled my head back and creased my brow.

The mug of black coffee I swallowed ten minutes ago felt like a hot iron in my stomach.

The odour filled my lungs as I wiped my forehead with the back of my sleeve.

Inside the bag was the body of a woman dressed in what was once a short floral dress. She was badly decomposed, and it was impossible to identify her by looking at her face. It had been heavily eaten by insects and maggots, and was now covered in blisters and puss.

I pushed her head back as something unusual caught my attention.

Her eyes had been pierced with yellow corn-cob skewers, and her mouth was packed with cotton wool.

Grey clouds hovered over Melbourne on Wednesday the 12th of March.

At 8.34 a.m., I was sitting at the kitchen table of my apartment, a mug of black coffee by my side. Michael had already left for school. While sipping my coffee, I scrutinized polaroids of Claire Kendall I'd taken the previous day.

I had never seen anything like it in my life. Claire hadn't just been killed, but mutilated. This was more than a crime of passion. I smelled revenge and hatred coming from a dark and murky corner of someone's soul.

The mutilation of the eyes with corn-cob skewers told me the killer might have felt remorseful, as if he hated the thought of Claire watching him even when she was dead. And   the cotton wool packed in her mouth could mean one of two things. He suffocated her, or he wanted her to remain quiet about his identity, even after he killed her.

I was having trouble picturing Teresa Wilson being the killer, and that was probably why I imagined the killer to be male. But at this stage, evidence pointed to her, even though my instinct told me it was far more complicated than that. I hated to dismiss the idea that someone else was involved in these murders.

I had to plan my next move carefully.

I took another sip from my mug, feeling a sharp pain at the back of my cranium. I'd been sleepless most of the night, kept awake by the ghost of Claire Kendall.

When I left the Wilson's garage the previous day, I ordered Lionel Payne to lock up and call the police. No one had to know I found the body. *Just tell them you smelled something, so you went to check it out.* He agreed without knowing why, probably because he thought it exciting to be a participant in one of this state's most horrific stream of homicides.

I got home almost hysterical, looking over my shoulder, checking that the door and all the windows of my apartment were properly locked.

I was surprised Frank never called me when the police found Clare Kendall's body. Surely, he would have seen it since the *Herald-Sun* took delight in running the story on the front page of this morning's edition. For a while, I feared he might be dead as well.

For the next few days, I decided to lay low. I feared anyone connecting me with the finding of Claire Kendall's body. I also had to get over my post-traumatic stage if I wanted to think clearly. But unfortunately, time was a luxury I couldn't afford. I was thinking of seeing a counsellor after all, just to help me get over this difficult moment. I'd pay cash and would refuse to give the counsellor my name. I had a name and number with me from a friend who had been happy with the treatment she'd received. His name was Dr Peter Freemann, and he was a qualified clinical psychiatrist.

Straight after lunch, I went to see my contact at the telephone company, Mr Trevor Wood. He listened while curling one end of his dark moustache around his forefinger. He was reasonably good looking, broad shoulders, a straight nose and strong chin, but a bit too nerdy for my taste. Maybe it was the way he insisted on parting his dark hair to one side with a truckload of gel.

We were sitting in his partitioned office, listening to everybody else's bit of conversation, while I explained my plan on how to catch the coin thief.

He loved the idea, and said he would get some technicians to work on it straight away.

'Who do I give this to?' I said, waving my invoice in front of his face. 'I was going to post it, but since I came by, I thought I might as well drop it in.'

'I'll take care of it,' he said, a broad smile on his face, as if he was doing me a huge favour.

I stood from my chair and shook his hand firmly.

He seemed to be checking out my fingers.

'Dr Malina,' he finally said. 'You wouldn't be free by any chance?'

I gave him an inquisitive stare.

The colour on his face changed to deep red. 'I don't mean to be rude,' he added. 'It's just that, you know, you're quite attractive. Maybe dinner next week.'

I thought about it for two seconds and said, 'Okay, give me a call.'

He had a great body, and I could always talk him out of the hair gel.

Late afternoon, I called in at Frank's home. My mind was all over the place. I knew I would never be able to see the light of day if Frank got killed.

I pulled into his driveway and hoped to God she was away. It would have been easier to ring first from my mobile, but I was scared she would answer the call. The worst would have been if he told her everything I told him.

He lived in Richmond, in a Victorian terrace, one of those long, narrow houses built at the beginning of the century. Its selling price was at least three times more than a house five times its size in an outer Melbourne suburb like Sunshine or Noble Park.

I rang the door bell and waited half a minute, staring at the dark green coat of paint on the front door. My stomach churned as I wondered who was going to answer it.

Footsteps came down the hallway.

Crisis time.

My hands were shaking, as I anticipated the worst.

Through the yellow, glass panel to my right, I recognised Frank's silhouette. A great sense of relief enveloped me when he pulled the door open.

'Malina,' he said, sounding almost apologetic, 'I was meant to call you. I've been flat out.' He didn't look as worn-out as I had expected. I noticed his freshly-trimmed moustache. He wore sand-coloured Haggar pants with a blue, oversized Country Road shirt. She'd already changed the way he dressed, and as much as I hated to admit it, it was a definite improvement. An aftershave I failed to recognise whisked past me.

I glanced over his shoulder and said, 'Is she in?'

He opened the door fully to invite me in. 'She's at the hospital for a check-up. I'm not expecting her until seven.'

I checked my watch: 5.02 p.m.

Plenty of time.

I followed him into the narrow, dark hallway, wondering why he was being so friendly and courteous.

'Have you heard?' I asked.

'Of course I've heard. Doesn't mean anything.'

I was staring at the back of his neck when he said that.

We went straight to the kitchen, where Frank filled two glasses with ice and water, not asking if I wanted one.

Dishes were piled up in the sink. The *Age* newspaper was wide open on the table, and an odour of dampness circled the room. Cleaning was obviously not one of their favourite pastimes.

He sat at the wooden table opposite me with both drinks. He pushed one glass in my direction.

I tried to make eye contact, but he kept his head lowered, stirring the ice cubes in his glass with his forefinger. 'I'm sorry, Malina,' he finally muttered, tilting his head forward, 'but I don't know how to handle this.'

I was unsure what he was getting at. 'What's wrong? You need to tell me something?'

He looked up. His eyes were red as if he was about to cry. 'I was called up at work yesterday. The Deputy Commissioner of Police was there with two detectives from the CIB, and they started probing and asking questions. This was straight after they found the body of Claire Kendall. They wanted some answers. We talked for a while, and a decision had to be made. They gave me no choice.'

I felt nauseous. 'What Frank? You had no choice about what?'

'Your contract with the VFSC and the CIB has been terminated as of yesterday.'

I felt a lump in my throat. His words cut through my mind like a giant circular saw. 'Jesus, what did you tell them?'

'I explained how you were trying to help, all you wanted to do was find out the truth, but they wouldn't have a bar of it. They said you were only on probation. This was only an experiment, you know, having someone working as an investigator as well as a crime-scene examiner. Well, they thought it wasn't working.'

It took me a full thirty seconds for the news to sink in.

I could tell from the look on his face he expected an outburst.

Finally, I shifted on my chair and snapped. 'Why wasn't I called in? No one spoke to me. I could have explained everything. I could have at least defended myself. When they made me sign the damn contract, everyone was being friendly and courteous, as if they had just crowned me Queen of England. What the hell happened in there? Did you really try,

Frank, or was it convenient for you to get rid of me?'

He pursed his lips as I wondered why I was taking it so badly since I knew I was going to lose my job eventually. It would only have been a matter of time before the axe fell on my head. But I took it badly. I could live with losing my job, but not the way I lost it. No hearing, no chance to explain myself. At this stage I was considering taking them to court for unfair dismissal.

A heated rage built up inside me. Even though lately things had been patchy between us, I believed Frank was my friend. I thought he would have fought like only a friend could to save my job. If our roles had been reversed, I would have done my utmost to make sure he kept his job.

I shook my head in disbelief.

He could have insisted on having me there. They could have never got rid of both of us in one go. No one out there could jump into both our seats, not immediately anyway.

'Fuck you, Frank,' I went on. 'I risked my neck for you. I'm doing this because I'm scared I'm going to find your naked body lying in bed and your head watching television.'

He glared at me strangely without a word. Motion in his cheekbones indicated grinding of teeth. 'Everything could have worked out,' he finally said, 'if you didn't probe so far. You could have told me what you were up to.'

I wondered what he was talking about. Confused, I threw him an inquisitive glance.

He continued, 'I know you found the body of Claire Kendall before the police did. They told me.'

I felt heat on my cheek. 'What?' My surprise was genuine.

'Come on, Malina, stop playing games with me. Lionel Payne told the police. I don't think he meant to, but he's old, and he made a slip of the tongue.'

I felt like a total fool. 'You mean everyone knows?'

He nodded and gave me that sorry puppy look. 'Trevor Mitchell wants you to hand over every single file on every case you've worked on for the VFSC. He's going to make sure you've got nothing more to do with the Wilson's homicide.'

The idea of suing for unfair dismissal suddenly seemed pointless.

He stared at me as if it was out of his hands, but we both

knew that was not the case. He could still do something if he wanted to. He could appeal to a higher authority.

I was thirty-nine and had to look for a new job. Forensic investigation units were not Coles supermarkets. If I wanted to continue working in this field, I had to go interstate or overseas. Even then, my resumé was now tarnished.

I couldn't take any more.

'Fuck the VFSC, Frank. And fuck you.'

I stood up, sending my chair flying behind me. It crashed loudly on the tiled floor, invigorating my anger.

I raced down the hallway.

'Hold on,' I heard him shout as I slammed the door in his face.

The following day, back from some grocery shopping at Safeway in Acland Street, I dialled the VFSC from my mobile phone and asked to speak to John Darcy.

'Malina, I'm sorry about your contract,' John said as soon as he heard my voice.

'Never mind that,' I said, pulling into my driveway. 'I need your help.'

He didn't respond.

'John?'

'Yes, well, it's not all that easy. You're not working for us any more.'

'So, you're not going to help me?'

'I didn't say that.'

'So, what's the problem? They got to you too, did they?'

'Malina, you make it sound like they're the Mafia or something. I'm willing to help to a degree, but these people are my superiors. I'm not like you. I've got a family to think about. I can't just take risks like that. If someone finds out I'm leaking information to you, I'm finished.'

I pulled the handbrake hard. 'I get the point. Thanks for your help.'

I terminated the call and killed the engine.

The bastards were going to make it impossible for me to do anything. I had no access to VFSC facilities, no one to advise me on forensic tests, and the police were probably going to monitor my every move.

I could only see one advantage in all this.

Why should I stop investigating since I had already lost everything?

CHAPTER EIGHTEEN

Saturday the 15th March was sunny but the temperature was in the low twenties. I was up early, trying to come to terms with my new life as a nobody.

By 6.45 a.m., I was jogging on St Kilda Beach, alongside the Esplanade. Seagulls were hovering above my head, crying in unison. The ocean was magnificent in the morning, like a gigantic grey blanket blending in with the clouds above. A taste of sea water hung in the air, giving the illusion of being on holidays, hundreds of kilometres away from the city life, stress, and the too-often meaningless daily routine. The perfect place to clear my mind and think about my future.

Although I managed to put enough money aside, I hated the thought of living out of thin air. The last thing I needed was to drain my savings, sell my car, my apartment and my belongings one at a time, just to make ends meet. And I hated the thought of applying to Social Security. Unemployment benefits had a purpose, but were designed for people who were looking for work. I knew if I really wanted to work, I could get something within a week. It would take more than that for my Social Security application to be processed. In addition, I'd find it unbearable to stand fortnightly in a queue and beg for a handout.

I got back home and took a long, hot shower.

My first mug of black coffee was replaced by freshly squeezed orange juice and sultana enriched cereal.

After breakfast, I slipped into comfortable jeans, a white T-shirt and a black leather jacket I bought at the South Melbourne Market for a bargain, less than a hundred dollars.

By 9.26 a.m., I tucked under my arm a manilla folder filled with photocopies of the entire Wilson's case, or as much as I managed to get my hands on since the beginning of this investigation.

Did they really expect me to give up so easily?

Finding a parking space in front of St Patrick's Hospital was hell as usual. The spaces reserved for medical staff only were filled, leaving me at the mercy of the streets like the rest of the world. Even though I loved driving my car, I seriously considered getting a motorcycle for those days when I couldn't be bothered with the traffic or fighting over the last remaining parking space in Melbourne.

I ended up parking around the corner from Barry Street and walking back to the hospital, hiding my eyes behind a pair of Ray Bans.

As I climbed the stairs of St Patrick's Hospital on my way to see Dr Larousse, I hoped no one had got to him yet. I still had the basic right to talk to anyone I wanted. After all, he wasn't a detective, nor a VFSC employee.

The previous day, I'd returned the original documents from the Wilson's case, and every other case I worked on, to the VFSC. Before hand, I photocopied every single page, graph and photograph from every file and locked them in the first two drawers of my filing cabinet at home. I knew this would be a temporary arrangement. Someone might decide to get a warrant and search my place if they thought I'd kept documents which I had no right to. Eventually, I'd transfer every document to a CD and store it in the middle of my classical music collection. It would be a day's work, but worth every minute. I might even leave a copy at a friend's place, just in case someone stole my three-hundred and twenty-eight compact discs.

I took the original documents to the VFSC in person. I didn't want to see Trevor Mitchell or anyone. I left two cardboard boxes filled with confidential material at the reception. When the receptionist said the director wanted to see me, I bluntly retorted, 'Well, I don't want to see him.'

Dr Larousse welcomed me in his office. He assured me no

one from the police spoke to him and seemed genuinely disappointed my contract with the VFSC had been terminated.

'I don't have a problem helping you,' he said. 'Your contract termination wasn't all over the papers, so as far as I'm concerned, you're still a forensic investigator.'

Thank God, there were still humans out there, not just bureaucratic idiots who followed everything by the book.

I told him I wanted to talk to the doctor who examined and did the preliminary report on Teresa Wilson. The name on the report said Dr. M. Shubbert.

'You're in luck,' Dr Larousse said, pushing his rimless glasses up the bridge of his nose. 'I think she's on shift this morning. Bear with me for a sec.'

He left the office for a few minutes. When he returned he informed me Dr Marie Shubbert would be tied up for the next half hour.

I agreed to wait near the front desk.

When she finally came to the front desk, my mind had gone numb from waiting an hour, looking through the Wilson's files for the hundredth time.

Dr Marie Shubbert was a tall woman with a horse-shaped face, and dark hair tied into a pony tail. She seemed annoyed as she swept one hand past my face and said, 'My office is this way,' pointing down the end of the corridor.

She paced in front of me and never glanced back to see if I was following.

I could tell this person was going to be defensive and non-committal. If I had predicted this encounter at home, I would have worn something more dynamic than denim and leather. My wear gave her the perfect opportunity to look down at me as if I was one of those rich, bored housewives from South Yarra, who had nothing better to do than cruise around in cool gear and try to pick up men half her age.

She led me into a tiny office with bare walls and not a single book in sight. The room was so clinically empty, it made me nauseous for half a minute.

'What can I do for you?' she asked, taking a seat behind a white desk, avoiding eye contact for as long as she could. Her high-back, executive, maroon chair contrasted with the room's white walls, white floors and white table.

I steered my rear-end into an injection-moulded, orange, plastic chair, the type we had back in high school. The leather of my jacket squeaked as if it was complaining. I squeezed the manilla folder in my hand, slightly lacking in confidence, ready for the judge to pass her sentence.

When I looked at her, I had to shift my gaze upwards. She was the queen and I was the pawn. She certainly worked her superiority complex out to the last detail.

'Have I come at a bad time?' I asked.

She glared at me coldly for the first time. 'Yes, you have. But since you're here, you might as well say what's on your mind.' She was hissing like a snake, and I knew this woman would never become my friend.

I threw a copy of Teresa's preliminary report on her desk, shifted uncomfortably in my chair and said, 'In Teresa Wilson's preliminary report, you've stated that you've found semen lodged in her vagina.'

She grabbed the report and flicked through the pages. 'I remember that one,' she commented. 'Battering and rape.' She stopped at a specific page and added, 'Raped before being assaulted. They got the culprit, didn't they?'

I nodded in agreement.

'So what's this all about?'

'Was there any other indication that she was raped?'

'Such as?'

'Well, was there engorgement of the labia, the clitoris, redness of the posterior vaginal opening?' She looked at me blankly, so I reached over the desk and pointed to a section in the report. 'Because none of it is in your report. I mean, if you had detected any other physical evidence of rape, you would have written them down, right?'

She locked her eyes into mine and said, 'Of course, that's what I'm being paid for.'

'But there's nothing else in the preliminary examination which suggests she's been raped. How do we *really* know she was raped?'

The muscles on her neck tensed up. 'Are you a doctor, Miss...?'

'Kristin Malina. Yes, I've got a doctorate, but I'm not a medical doctor. I've got a PhD in Criminal Justice. I specialise in homicides and cases like this.' Before she had time to change direction, and point out how clinical examination was not my line of expertise, I added, 'So, why did you conclude she was raped?'

She fidgeted with her hands. 'The semen in her vagina. The bruising on her body.'

'Yes, but she could have easily had normal sexual intercourse, or inserted the semen in her vagina through other means. And we've already established with Dr Larousse that the bruises, along with the lacerations, were self-inflicted.'

Dr Shubbert seemed annoyed, and I could understand why. She shifted nervously in her chair. I hated making personal attacks on the people who helped me, but since I'd been fried, I had to make the most of what I had. Arrogance was my last resort.

She glanced at the report and let her defences down. 'You have to understand this is only a preliminary report. Initial observations. The man obviously raped her. Men are like that.'

'Yes, I know. But I like to have things clear in my mind. What about pubic hair? Was any of Walter Dunn's pubic hair found on her body?'

'Not according to the report.'

'No tearing or bruising of the vagina?'

'Not according to the report.'

'No teeth or bite marks on the body?'

'Not according to the report.' Her voice was dead-pan, and it was obvious she was losing patience.

I glared into her dark, green eyes. 'So, according to this document, the only evidence we have that Teresa Wilson was raped is the recovery of semen from her vagina.'

'That would seem to be correct,' she said, in a tone of voice which implied she was going to add *do you have a problem with that?*

'But surely, if Mrs Wilson had been raped, semen would have been found in other parts of her body, other than the inside of her vagina? Either that, or the rapist was wearing a condom, in which case no semen would have been found at all.'

'That's an interesting point.'

'Okay, Dr Shubbert. I know you're not a forensic

pathologist, but would you go to court and testify Teresa Wilson was raped?'

'Not based on the preliminary report. Like you've said, the evidence is somewhat on the thin side. I would have to conduct further tests. But between you and me, we both know she got raped. Men do this kind of thing. Why are you trying to deny it? The bastard is dead anyway.'

I could see that she was now clearly upset. I was seconds away from being thrown out of her office.

A few weeks back, I would have agreed with Dr Shubbert. Men were responsible for over ninety percent of all crimes on this planet, and it would have been easy to let my prejudice get in the way.

'Don't take this personally, doctor. I'm just trying to find out what's going on. And since I've just lost my job with the VFSC, you're the only expert I can rely on.'

She gave me faint smile, obviously realising I was in a worse situation than her.

'I need another favour from you,' I said bluntly.

'You've got one hell of a nerve,' she replied, obviously feeling more at ease now that I was on the begging side. 'I don't know why I should help you, but go ahead, ask.'

'I need an analysis done on the semen extracted from Teresa's cervix.'

'What type of analysis?'

'A DNA sampling.'

'We don't offer that type of service at the hospital.'

'What about externally?'

'How soon do you need it?'

'As soon as possible. This is really important.'

'I'll see what I can do. Can't promise, but how does this afternoon sound?'

'Fantastic.'

I told her to fax the result from my apartment and left her office.

As I made my way downstairs of St Patrick's Hospital, I knew why Dr Marie Shubbert decided to give in. She knew if she didn't give me what I asked for, I would have filed a formal complaint to her superior that her preliminary report on Teresa Wilson was biased, incomplete and misleading.

And I gathered that even though she was as stiff as a stainless steel ruler, she was smart enough not to let that happen.

When I got back home, I worked on the 'Jolly Roger' investigation. I sat in my study, my laptop turned on, glancing at the traffic down Chapel Street while gathering my thoughts.

The idea was simple. Since the person who collected money from pay-phones had to disconnect the wire supplying codes to the telephone company, as detailed in the Jolly Roger article, all the telephone company had to do is modify the wiring system. Whenever the wire in question would be cut, a signal would be sent to the telephone company, alerting them that someone was tampering with one of their telephones. The signal would tell them where the telephone was located. And since I knew the culprit would come back to the same phone booths in the next few days to collect his money, all that was needed was a surveillance team until he turned up.

I wrote a two-page report, detailing every aspect of the plan, and faxed it to Garry Wood at the telephone company.

Within ten minutes he gave me a call.

'I think the idea is brilliant,' he said.

Did he really mean it, or was he being nice because he'd asked me out?

'Keep me posted on the outcome,' I said.

'Sure.' He paused for a few seconds. 'What about this dinner? Are you free on Monday night?'

'I'm really busy at the moment. But if you want to drop by my place, I'll make dinner.'

'Are you sure? I don't want this to be too much trouble.'

'Believe me, it isn't.'

We agreed to meet at 7.00 p.m.

Dr Shubbert kept her promise, and at 2.33 p.m. on Saturday, the DNA profiling from Teresa's semen sample came through my fax machine like a gift from heaven. A sheet with numbers and figures, which only made half sense to me, followed. I was sitting in my study with a glass of iced water, going through some notes on DNA testing I had downloaded from the

Internet.

It is a fact that eighty percent of people are secretors, that is specific blood group information from those individuals is passed on to other body fluids. A laboratory test can reveal whether a semen sample came from a secretor or non-secretor, whether it carries ABO antigens or one enzyme sub-group.

Since the introduction of DNA profiling in 1984, rapists have been convicted from their semen 'fingerprint' left at the scene of the crime. DNA profiling is the most convincing means of identifying the rapist of a victim. DNA typing is so specific that it can help identify one individual from a million others.

Every human cell contains information required to create a whole human body. The information is actually incoded in the nucleus of each cell in the form of deoxyribonucleic acid, otherwise known as DNA. The result can be visualised in print form from an x-ray film, making it relatively easy to compare with other DNA results.

In the Teresa Wilson case, I wasn't interested in framing the rapist. According to the police, he was dead anyway. I needed a DNA test to prove that semen found in Teresa's cervix was not that of Walter Dunn.

The copy of Teresa's DNA autoradiograph, from the semen found in her vagina, was similar to a pattern of bands from supermarket bar-codes, except much longer and spread all over a page in four neat columns, one centimetre wide. I knew for a fact, with the exception of genetically identical twins, every person had a unique DNA blue-print.

I pulled out the copy of Walter's autopsy report , which John Darcy had obtained for me from the Victorian Institute of Forensic Science, from my grey filing cabinet. I knew a DNA test had been conducted from a blood sample obtained during the autopsy.

I turned the page to the photocopy of Walter Dunn's DNA autoradiograph and compared it with the one faxed to me by Dr Shubbert. I compared the prints from the several different polymorphic sequences from both autoradiograph copies.

The bands of the DNA test in Walter's autopsy report were different from those of the semen sample taken from Teresa's body. The reference sample was a complete mismatch in several of the polymorphic sequences.

I dialled the hospital and asked for Dr Marie Shubbert.

It took less than a minute to get her on the line.

'Thanks for those tests,' I said.

'Not a problem.' Her tone was matter-of-fact.

'I'm going through the other pages you've sent me. It's kind of confusing. I'm trying to compare them with the DNA sample from Walter Dunn.'

'Oh, yes, hold on a sec.'

A few seconds of silence.

I heard her shuffling some papers, and she went on, 'Basically, I've ordered a variety of tests, just to be on the safe side.'

'And?'

'Turn to the second page.'

I flicked to page two and stared at the following:

SAMPLE	HLA-DQA1	D1S80	HUMTHO1
WILSON SWAB	2,3	18/24	6/9
FREQUENCY	0.0489	0.160	0.0809

'Okay,' I said, 'I'm listening.'

'Now, can you look at the result from Walter Dunn's DNA result?'

I flicked through to the same page on Dunn's DNA report.

SAMPLE	HLA-DQA1	D1S80	HUMTHO1
DUNN SWAB	2,4	24/29	6/7
FREQUENCY	0.0489	0.160	0.0809

'Okay, so what?' I asked.

'See the three different tests. That's the numbers at the top of the section: HLA-DQA1, D1S80, and HUMTHO1.'

'Yes?'

'The results below, that's the number next to where it says WILSON SWAB, should exactly match Walter Dunn's, that is if he's the guy who raped her.'

I didn't need two hours to figure out what she was on about.

I smiled to myself, satisfied I'd made a significant break-through.

The VFSC could say whatever they wanted.

I knew for a fact Walter Dunn never raped Teresa Wilson.

CHAPTER NINETEEN

On Monday the 17th of March, I rang the VFSC from my study to speak to Frank Moore. I'd made myself sick all night, wondering what he was up to. Now that I knew Walter Dunn never raped Teresa Wilson, there was little doubt in my mind she'd committed a triple murder. Still, I found myself in the awkward position of having been pulled off the investigation and, yet, without authorisation, having found out too much. I knew everyone would be angry at me, whether I'd dug up the truth or not. No one else but Frank would listen. I knew he'd probably believe I'd lost my mind, but I'd be able to show him the DNA autoradiographs.

My feet up on the desk, one hand fidgeting with the waist button of my jeans, I punched the numbers on the key pad. The phone rang twice before it was picked up.

I introduced myself and made my request.

'Frank Moore has taken the week off,' the receptionist at the VFSC informed me.

Frustrated, I hung up and tried his home number.

All I got was the answering machine with *her* voice on it!

I tried his mobile number, but the voice at the end of the line said, 'The Vodaphone you have called is switched off. Please try again later.'

Goddamn it!

I jumped from my chair, paced anxiously to the kitchen and poured myself a glass of iced water from the fridge. I gulped the content of my glass in one go and returned to the study.

I rang the VFSC again.

'Did he say where he would be going?' I asked the receptionist.

'He's on leave. Decided to take a week's holiday.'

She'd already told me that, but I remained polite. 'And he didn't mention whether he was going away or not?'

'We're not that close.'

'So, he said nothing?'

'Not to me. But maybe you'd like to talk to Trevor Mitchell. Frank might have mentioned something to him.'

'Is Trevor Mitchell in?'

'Yes, he is. Would you like me to put you through?'

I hesitated half a second and said, 'All right, I'd appreciate that.'

Before I had time to change my mind, Trevor Mitchell's voice rang clearly in my right ear. 'Kristin Malina?'

'I'm trying to track Frank down.'

'Malina,' he said, injecting concern in his voice. 'Where have you been? You haven't tried to contact me.'

'For what? You and the others have already made up your mind about what to do with me.'

'Oh, no, no, no. You're taking this all the wrong way. I told you a few weeks back that there would be an inquiry. I warned you heads would roll, and in the meantime, you get yourself into more trouble. What did you expect?'

'Look, Mr Mitchell, thanks for the concern, but I'm trying to locate Frank Moore. I understand he's on vacation for the week. He didn't happen to mention whether he'd be going away? Did he?'

'Did you try his home number?'

No, I rang you up first to get my ears blasted!

'Sir, I tried him at home and on his mobile phone, but he's out of reach.'

'Well, Malina, he never told me where he was going. He put in a request for a week off two days ago, and I approved it. He seemed stressed and looked as if he needed it.'

'Thank you for your time. I'll try his home again later.'

I was about to hang up when he added, 'Oh, Malina?'

'Yes?'

'Why don't you drop by the office? I need to tie up a few loose ends. You need to sign a termination of contract and hand over your pass.'

'Sure, I'll do that.'

'By the way, you're not still investigating this Wilson thing?'

I swallowed and tried my best to sound sarcastic. 'Now, why would that be, Mr Mitchell? I understand I've been barred from the investigation. Or is this an invitation to get me back in on it?'

'You better not be, Malina. If someone—'

I hung up on him. He was no longer my boss, and I cared little for his advice. To begin with, I found it increasingly insulting to be referred to by my first name when I had the courtesy to call him by his last name. And secondly, the computerised VFSC photo-ID card might still come in handy. It gave me access to the mortuary and various other restricted areas. Thank God for whoever had the wise idea of giving me total access to any place which would make my job as an investigator as easy as possible.

My hand was resting on the handset when the phone rang.

I knew it was Trevor Mitchell, so I bent over and pulled the plug from the wall.

For half an hour, I sat at my desk, staring out the window of my study, looking over Chapel Street. Trams, cars and pedestrians went by, but I paid little attention to the outside world. My mind was preoccupied with greater concerns.

I needed to talk to Frank, because I now truly believed he was in danger. An entire theory on what really happened on the night of the 20th of February at the Wilsons brewed in a dark corner of my mind. Everything I had seen, heard and observed since the beginning of this investigation began to cling together neatly, like the last pieces of an enigmatic puzzle.

I shifted in my chair, hands cupped under my chin, gazing at the emptiness in front of my eyes.

No one had broken into the Wilson's apartment. Someone directed a damn good puppet show, and everyone, including me, had had their strings pulled. She manipulated, controlled and orchestrated this entire scenario. Everyone had played their parts perfectly.

I was convinced the only reason Teresa hung around Frank Moore was to create the least amount of suspicion. Frank Moore could influence the investigation any way he wanted. If she managed to twist him around her finger, he'd do anything she asked. The prompt termination of my contract with the VFSC was no coincidence. I was certain I had been right when I accused Frank of doing little to save my job. It seemed clear now he had more to gain by letting me go. I was an obstructive element in his grand plan. Or was it hers?

It broke my heart to realise how little I meant to him. Because he loved me all those years, like he claimed he did, I never expected something like that was going to happen. But my main concern was that once the investigation would be filed away forever, she might decide to get rid of him. So far, her method of getting rid of people had proven not only effective, but extremely sadistic.

Since I couldn't get in touch with Frank, I decided to move ahead with my investigation. I had a clear idea in mind. Time to move on and stop counting the losses.

I put on my leather jacket, grabbed my car keys from the kitchen bench, and headed for the National Theatre.

Louis was cleaning the men's toilet when I walked into the National Theatre. He had a pair of white overalls on and reminded me of one of us, dressed in our crime-scene examiners clothing.

'I need your help,' I said, glancing at his blue suede shirt, under the overalls, and his three golden earings dangling from each ear.

'What's wrong?' he said. I must have looked dreadful because he dropped his jaw by half an inch. 'Did someone else die? God, I read about Claire Kendall. Did you find out who killed her? I wanted to call, but didn't want to intrude. You know, you looked as if you were busy enough as it was.'

I told him talking here was awkward, but I needed his help immediately

'I can't leave like that,' he protested. 'I'll lose my job.'

'Louis, I need you *now*.'

A look of concern crossed his face. He agreed to drop

everything and come with me.

I waited while he got rid of his mop, bucket and overall.

We drove down to the Victoria Institute of Forensic Medicine in Southbank via Kings Way.

As usual, I raced like a lunatic.

Louis kept on throwing his hands on the dashboard every time I got too close to the back of another car.

One hand on the steering wheel, I explained to him how I believed Teresa Wilson had committed a triple murder. I kept my explanation simple because I doubted he would have understood everything about DNA sampling, antigens and enzymes.

He sat silently for a few minutes, obviously mortified Teresa could have killed so many people.

'You okay?' I finally said, wondering if I had done the right thing by bringing him with me. But I knew no one else in close proximity I could trust.

'God, I was working with her. It could have been me. You know, if she thought whatever she thought about Jeremy, Walter and Claire about me, I'd be dead by now. Thank God I'm not straight!'

I found his remark kind of funny because it was so true. His manhood might have saved him from being one of Teresa's chosen few.

'Well you're not dead yet, so let's do something about it,' I ordered, as I took a turn into Kavanagh Street. Of course, I never believed he was in any danger, but I was desperate for his assistance.

Briefly, I explained what my plan was once we'd reach the mortuary.

'Are you crazy? We're going to get arrested!' he said, glaring at me as if I had lost all reasoning.

'All you have to do is distract them, that's all.'

'Jesus, I'm going to get my arse kicked.'

'Hey, watch the language,' I joked, and he blushed.

I parked fifty meters outside the VIFM, killed the engine and locked my eyes into his. 'Three people are dead, Louis. Someone else could die. We've got to do everything we can to get Teresa arrested. All I've got is circumstancial evidence. I don't want to drag Teresa to court and have the prosecution fall flat on their arse. I need to get my hands on Jeremy Wilson's autopsy report. I need it, and they won't let me get it. I don't know anyone else who can help me right now. The more time this takes, the more likely she'll get away with it. Is that what you want?'

'No, but—'

'But what? You want me to drive you back and do this by myself? I'm going to stuff it up, and she's going to get away with it. And if she finds out what I'm up to, my funeral could be the next one you'll be attending.'

He shifted uncomfortably on his seat and stared down at his hands. 'I don't think I'm cut out for this. This is not my kind of thing. I'm a thinking person, not a Rambo-type of guy.'

'Please, I need you to do this for me.'

'I'm not the right man.'

'Louis, look at me.' He looked up as if I was going to reveal the secret of eternal life. 'You're *more* than a man. You can do this.'

He analysed me for five seconds, flung open the passenger door and said, 'Okay, partner, let's nail the sucker.'

The VIFM was the statutory body in charge of Forensic Pathology, Clinical Forensic Medicine, Forensic Toxicology and other forensic scientific services in the State. Over 3000 postmortem examinations took place at the mortuary, the Coronial Services Centre, located in the same blue-grey South Melbourne complex. Other than autopsies, the centre incorporated histology, microbiology and molecular biology laboratories, all contributing to forensic investigations throughout Victoria.

The Institute was also responsible for education in forensic medicine, and thus incorporated the Department of Forensic Medicine at Monash University, delivering quality undergraduate and postgraduate courses for medical and legal students. The complex was also the home of the Coroner's Court.

Unfortunately, the security system at the VIFM was also second to none. If I didn't have my VFSC ID, I'd have no chance to even pass the front desk.

I heard Louis scream as I went through the autopsy reports in Dr Charles W. Main's office.

All the reports were neatly filed in a four-drawer beige filing cabinet, clearly labelled by date, name and job number.

I couldn't believe my luck. Thank God, Dr Charles W. Main was away from his office and left the door open. I did have my lockpicking kit with me in case things had turned out more complicated than I had anticipated. But now I feared he might be only seconds away. I had to hurry, or else I would find myself in the undesirable position of being charged with trespassing.

I was curious as to what Louis had done to attract the security guards' attention, as it gave me enough time to sneak past the front desk, down the empty, blue-carpeted hallways, and to enter the office area. To pass each section of the building, I had to place my ID pass against a black plate attached to the wall next to each door. The card was read by a computer and access was granted once the user was identified. Fortunately, my name hadn't been removed from Ingres 4GL, the central database, just yet, making my illegal wandering a breeze.

After three minutes of sifting through hundreds of green files, I finally found Jeremy Wilson's report. The white label on the manilla folder read 20 February, the day we found him dead.

Dr Charles W. Main wasted no time on that one. Normally twenty-four hours would elapse before an autopsy would be carried out. Exceptions were made when a homicide was involved.

I circled the room with my eyes, desperately seeking a photocopier.

Nothing but a large director's desk, a swivel chair, a Medical Degree from the University of Melbourne, certificates of merits and commendation, hanging like war medals on the wall behind the desk, and a 486DX computer, outdated by at least three years.

No time to sneak into the other offices and risk getting caught.

I tucked the report between my jeans and the small of my back, concealing it with my leather jacket.

I let out a sigh of relief, knowing I was now in possession of what I'd been seeking.

Just as I was about to leave the office, I heard someone opening the door down the end of the hallway.

I froze, listening attentively for anything. Because the floor was covered in blue carpet, I couldn't hear footsteps.

Louis was no longer screaming. They must have gagged him or dragged him outside the building.

I heard the door close.

Christ, don't let it be Dr Main.

'Who's there?' someone with a coarse, military voice shouted.

My pulse increased as I looked around the room for an alternative exit or a hiding place. But the office was small, and there was no where to go.

I stayed glued to the blue carpet, now truly believing I would be charged for trespassing and stealing government property, not to mention tampering with an investigation.

'Who's there?' the voice repeated with authority.

Someone knew I was here, but I was uncertain how they found out. I wondered if the security guards beat it out of Louis.

Or maybe someone spotted me on one of the security cameras I'd been too careless to notice.

I took a deep breath and walked out of Dr Charles W. Main's office, my head high, radiating confidence.

Forcing a broad smile, I paced towards the stranger as if I knew my business in this establishment.

A security guard in blue uniform glared into my eyes.

I glanced at his name tag, which read Jason. His hair was parted in the middle, and he had a strong neck and wide shoulders. His face was red from either anger or excessive drinking. Either way, he didn't look like the type of person anyone would want to mess with.

'Who are you, and what are you doing in Dr Main's office?' His tone suggested he was ready to pin me to the ground if I gave him the wrong answer.

'*Jason*, I'm a doctor working for the VFSC. Dr Main asked me to get him an autopsy report.'

He scrutinized me up and down, as I realised I'd made a mistake wearing denim and leather.

'I've never seen you here before,' he said. 'Why aren't you wearing a visitor's pass?'

'I've got identification,' I said, removing my VFSC ID.

'You should still be wearing a visitor's pass. Why aren't you wearing a pass?'

Nervous, I found no answer. I stepped forward, trying to get past him. I was losing my composure as fear wiped the smile off my face.

A strong hand grabbed my arm, blocking the circulation to my right hand.

'Hold on a sec.' He spoke in his walky-talky, 'Steve, do you copy?'

I took no time to think and kicked him hard in the shin with one of the fashionable leather, metal-caped safety shoes I bought on Chapel Street.

'Ah, fuck!' he muttered and lowered himself to the floor, loosening his grip on my arm. 'You *bitch*!'

That's what my husband called me when I told him I wanted to file for divorce more than a decade ago.

I ran as fast as I could, not looking back.

The Jeremy Wilson autopsy report was rubbing against my lower back, causing mild discomfort.

I placed my ID against the black panel at the end of the hallway, pulled the door open, and ran as fast as I could.

'Jesus, fuck!' I heard him swear as I vanished down the end of the corridor.

I slowed down as I approached the front desk.

Not a soul in sight.

Looking across the glass door of the VIFM, I saw four security guards in blue uniform and a man in a suit surrounding Louis. I recognised the suit to be Dr Charles W. Main. We met once at an international conference on criminology at Monash University in Clayton. I'd spoken to him for only a few minutes, so I'd never had a chance to establish a personal opinion towards him. Come to think of it, I did recall that he was rather attractive, but right now it seemed irrelevant.

I crossed the empty reception area as fast as I could while

maintaining a walking pace. I stepped out of the building, smiled at the security guards, who smiled back at me, and headed towards the Lancer.

'And what were you doing in the pathology room?' one of the guards said to Louis.

'I told you I made a mistake. I got the wrong place. I thought this was the Blood Bank,' Louis screamed back.

Clever, I thought, the Blood Bank was only a block away.

'You stupid fag,' another guard said. 'Nobody's gonna take blood from you. You probably got AIDS or some shit.'

Dr Charles W. Main broke in, 'Hey, come on now, there's no need to use that kind of language. The police will be here any minute.'

And sure enough, just as I slid behind the wheel of my car, a white police car raced down the street, siren screaming as if the world was coming to an end.

I hoped Louis was going to get out of this without much trouble. I could have gone back and tried to rescue him, but the police car was closing in towards the building.

If Jason, the security guard who bruised my right arm with his mortal grip, raised the alarm, I'd be getting a free ride in the police car.

I turned on the ignition, cracked the gears, and manoeuvred the car into a u-turn.

I owe you one, Louis

CHAPTER TWENTY

As soon as I got home, I removed the autopsy report from my jacket and threw it on the desk in my study.

I compared the DNA autoradiograph from Jeremy Wilson's blood sample in the report with the one Dr Shubbert faxed me.

The polymorphic sequences from both autoradiographs were identical.

A perfect match.

The semen found in Teresa's vagina never was Walter's like everybody initially assumed, but her husband's.

Teresa's rape was a hoax.

I decided to read the entire autopsy report on Jeremy Wilson.

From first glance, I could see that the pathologist performed the medico-legal autopsy thoroughly.

After the body had been identified and toe-tagged, Dr Charles W. Main took two twenty-four exposure colour films of the body fully dressed and in the nude. The body was then measured, weighed and x-rayed. This was slightly awkward since the head of Jeremy Wilson was separated from his shoulders.

This was followed by fingerprinting.

External examination was carefully performed according to the information I had in front of me. Clothing was thoroughly examined, including any fibre samples and stains. Scars, wounds, tattoos, moles and other identifying markers were also recorded. Fingernails, hair and skin were also examined, and the skin of arms and legs were checked for needle marks.

Dr Charles W. Main then proceeded with the internal examination. He performed the obligatory body-length Y-incision, also known as the thoracic-abdominal incision because it began across the chest from shoulder to shoulder and down over the breasts, then changed into a midline incision along the abdomen and down the pubis.

The heart and lungs were exposed through cutting the ribs and cartilage, and a blood sample was taken from the heart after opening the pericardial sac to determine Jeremy Wilson's blood type.

The upper organs were then removed, weighed and externally examined before being sliced up into sections for examination of internal structural damage. Fluid in the thoracic pleural cavity was removed for analysis. Microscopic slides for each organ were prepared for further testing.

Organ removal and examination was then carried out on the abdomen. Like the chest area, each separate organ was subject to visual and internal testing. The stomach's content was measured and samples sent for toxicology.

And this was where I stopped going through the report.

Something caught my eye.

A handwritten note had been made on the margin next to the stomach's content analysis. See toxicology report - high level of drug detected.

I flicked forward until I got to the toxicology results.

A high concentration of Valium had been found not only in the stomach's content, but also in the blood sample taken from the heart of the victim.

I dropped the autopsy report on my desk, and placed the palms of my hands against my temples. Another layer had just been added to the Wilson's case.

This crime had been so carefully premeditated that everyone had missed the obvious.

I looked out the window of my room and down to the street below. I hadn't even noticed that it had been raining. A green tram stopped and one of my neighbours, a drunk on an invalid pension, stepped off without looking. He nearly got run over by a car trying to overtake the tram from the left-hand side.

I went to the kitchen and made myself a cup of black coffee. Pain jabbed at the back of my neck, probably caffeine withdrawal symptoms.

I tried to make sense of everything I had read, and how it could fit with everything else I had discovered so far.

As I returned to my study and sat back behind my desk, I recalled how John Darcy had told me that Jeremy's decapitation had been performed *methodically*. This had been established from the formation of the blood droplets around Jeremy's body. And suddenly the answer as to why Jeremy never fought while getting his neck cut open became obvious. He had been so heavily sedated that he was still alive when she decapitated him.

I flicked back through the autopsy and found the section examining the quality of the cuts on Jeremy's neck. Dr Charles W. Main observed that the cutting was a series of quite deliberate pressure cuts and not slashes, which fitted perfectly with John Darcy's theory that Jeremy couldn't have been hacked to death.

I then turned to my log book, and looked back at my entry from the 20th of February. I was looking for the serial number of the knife Frank had found in the back alley behind the Wilson's apartment. I remembered clearly taking the number down when Frank presented the knife to me at the crime scene. This detail reminded me how vital it was for a forensic investigator to make careful notes of everything at the crime scene. Details, which sometimes seemed trivial at the time, often made the difference between making a substantial leap forward in an investigation or coming to a dead-end.

I copied the serial number of the knife, G-66923, along with its length, width and other details I had previously taken down, into a small spiral-bound notebook.

If I was going to prove she killed her husband, I needed to trace the knife back to its place of purchase.

Michael was home when Garry Wood came to dinner later that evening. I'd been busy with the Wilson investigation, and by 6.30 p.m., I panicked because I hadn't begun to make dinner. I wondered why the hell I talked myself into this.

'So, who's this guy?' Michael asked, shifting from one foot to the other, while I was slicing a butter lettuce into a large glass bowl.

'Someone who works for the telephone company.'

'And what's he coming over for?'

'Dinner.'

'Like a date kind-of-thing?'

'Yes, like a date kind-of-thing.'

He tried to make eye contact, but I avoided him. I'd never dated since my divorce, and having my son scrutinising me half an hour before my beau walked in was a rather uncomfortable and embarrassing situation.

'Do you want me to leave?' Michael asked.

'No.'

'You're saying that, but you'd rather if I left. What if you guys decided to bonk?'

An alarm rang in my head. Did I hear right. 'I beg your pardon?' I snapped, my eyes now digging right into his.

His face flushed and he said, 'You know what I mean. Jesus, I'm not ten years old.'

'That's not the point,' I said, branding my knife up in the air. 'I wish you'd have a little more respect and stop talking to me that way.'

'Oh, great,' he said, rolling his eyes to the ceiling. 'Fine, whatever, preach whenever it suits you.' And he left for his room.

I paced towards him, the knife in my hand. I stopped, walked back, placed the knife on the bench, and followed him to his room.

Before I got there, he slammed the door in my face.

'Michael!' I screamed, 'I'm not going to take any more of this shit!'

I sent the door flying open.

He was sitting on his bed in tears.

Surprised, I froze, unable to say a word. I muttered

something which made no sense to me, nor to Michael.

'What's going on?' I finally asked, as I knelt down close to him. 'I'm sorry. I didn't mean to upset you. Why are you crying?'

I'd never seen him crying before, not since he was half the size he was now.

'You don't get it, do you?' he whispered between sobs.

'What is it that I don't get?'

He kept his eyes to the floor.

I placed one hand under his chin and pushed his head up. 'What is it that I don't get, Michael? Tell me.' His tears were dripping in the cup of my hand.

'You know.'

'No, I don't know. If I knew, I'd try to do something about it. Did I do something to upset you?'

He paused and said, 'You're never here. It's that stupid job of yours.'

My face creased. 'I don't have any choice, Michael. I have to support the both of us.'

'Why can't you get a normal job like normal people? What do I have to do to get your attention?'

He'd lost me. 'You don't have to get my attention, Michael. Why are you saying that?'

'I took the money from the phone booths,' he retorted in a firm tone of voice.

'You what?' I was more shocked than angry.

'I took the money from the phone booths. I knew you were working with the telephone company. I thought that if I'd help you, we'd be spending more time together.'

My jaw dropped, but no words came out of it. I found it hard to believe what I was hearing. 'You stole the money from the phone booths?'

'Yes.'

'Then why did you show me the Jolly Roger website?'

'Because then you'd think I was really clever and want to work with me. Cause then you wouldn't think it was me, anyway.'

I pulled my head back. 'Jesus, Michael, I've been billing the phone company through the nose to find out who did it. And

205

now you're telling me it was you all along?'

'I'm sorry.'

I felt a lump in my throat.

I didn't know if I was more angry at him or at myself for letting our relationship deteriorate to such a degree that he thought he had to resort to crime to get us back together.

I placed one hand at the back of his neck and drew him closer.

'Okay,' I said. 'It's going to be all right. We'll work something out. Jesus, I wish you'd told me that earlier.'

He whimpered and said, 'I love you, mum.'

Michael stayed in his room while I was having dinner with Garry Wood. Frankly, I'd rather he hadn't come, but by the time I'd made up my mind, he was already at the door.

I knew I could never have a relationship with this man now. He worked for the telephone company my son had stolen from, which meant I'd never be completely honest with him.

He was dressed in a shirt and tie. Thank God he'd got rid of the hair gel. For some reason, he looked better after hours than at work. In fact, he was goddamn sexy.

We talked shop over the dinner table.

After we had coffee, I said, 'I don't mean to be rude, Garry, but I'm really tired, and I'd like to go to bed.'

'Wow,' he said, trying to cheer me up. 'Sure, bed sounds fine to me. Lead the way.'

I smiled, half ready to take up his invitation, having waited so long for someone to hold me and make love to me. But instead I replied, 'Not with you. Maybe some other time. I promise.'

'Hey, it's all right,' he said. 'Never kiss on the first date. My mother told me the same thing.'

The perfect answer.

I leaned over the table and said, 'Well, mine didn't.'

I kissed him red and hot, thought what the hell, and led him to my room.

On Tuesday morning I unsuccessfully looked up every knife shop in the Port Melbourne and St Kilda area.

The temperature was barely fourteen degrees when I left home, and it looked as if rain would follow soon. For the first time that year, I wore my winter clothes: calf length black laced-up leather boots, a beige woollen overcoat and a green scarf with matching gloves I'd bought down Acland Street two winters ago. I was extremely conscious of looking more like an Eskimo than a forensic investigator, but now that my chest cold was truly over, I wanted to avoid the risk of another one.

After lunch at McDonald's, at the corner of Glenhuntly Road and Nepean Highway, I decided to try shopping centres.

Chadstone Shopping Centre was only twenty minutes away.

By 2.00 p.m., I'd located the seller of the cook's knife used to sever Jeremy Wilson's head from his body. Monique, the sales person at King of Knifes, a shop located on the first floor of the shopping centre, close to Angus & Robertson Booksellers and a Newspower newsagency, was extremely friendly and helpful.

She identified the knife through immaculately kept records.

This entire investigation was starting to look like a bad joke. The knife had been bought on the 12th of February by credit card, one week prior to Jeremy's decapitation. Credit card number 9654 0901 0091 7290 was used to make the purchase. It was a VISA card in the name of Teresa V. Wilson and due to expire six months from now.

Of course, having bought the knife did not prove Teresa killed her husband. But with all the other circumstancial evidence I had accumulated so far, it wouldn't take much to convince a jury that she did in fact commit the murder.

I left Chadstone Shopping Centre with a chocolate éclair from Donut King and a head filled with confusion.

Crossing the car park, I knew what my next step would be.

What I wanted now was a confession, and the only way to get it would be to come face to face with her.

I ended up lecturing at Swinburne University on Wednesday afternoon because I felt guilty I'd missed the previous week's class. The timing was bad, because my heart was not in it. More important things were pressing my mind. But I knew some students in my class would one day solve important homicides, so I had to take my job as a trainer as seriously as I took my job as a forensic investigator.

Although I tried to pay attention to what I was teaching, the importance of collecting evidence and making carefully written observations at a crime scene, half my attention was wandering around the Wilson case.

I concluded if Teresa Wilson was dumb enough to buy a cook's knife with her own credit card, she had to be dumb enough to have bought a ton of Valium under her name as well.

This case began to look like Swiss cheese, and I knew it would only be a matter of time before everything would blow up in everybody's face like a time bomb.

As much as I was excited to have gone so far, I began to fear the outcome. If Teresa was such a cruel and heartless person, maybe John Darcy had been right when he told me to watch my back.

I shrugged off the fear, which had slowly crept upon me as the hours went by.

In spite of my wandering mind, I tried hard to concentrate on giving a memorable lecture to my students.

On my way back home, just at the corner of Princes Highway and Alma Road, I tried Frank's home number again on my mobile phone.

She picked up the call. Her voice sent a chill through my entire body.

'Is Frank in?'

'No, he's not. Who's this?'

I ground my teeth. It was vital that I sounded relaxed and non-suspicious.

'It's Dr Kristin Malina. I met you at the hospital.'

A few seconds silence, and then she said, 'Oh, hi, Malina. It's so nice to talk to you. When are you coming around to visit?'

'Well, actually, I was wondering if Frank was there, so the three of us could go out for dinner.'

'I'm afraid Frank is away for the week.'

'He didn't mention where he was going?'

'No. Is this some type of emergency?'

'Not really. It's just that he never said he'd be going anywhere.'

'Well, that shouldn't stop us from seeing each other. I really enjoyed your company at the hospital. Why don't you come over, and I'll cook something?'

My stomach churned. This was not what I had in mind. I wanted Frank with me in case she decided to insert corn-cob skewers in my eyes and cotton wool down my throat as part of her haute cuisine.

'I really don't want to be any trouble,' I said, my voice losing its confidence.

'It's no trouble at all. I don't mind. I wasn't doing anything tonight, anyway. We can watch a video afterwards.'

Damn, she was tempting me, but I knew it was a hell of a risk. I wanted to face her and get to the bottom of this. But not just yet. She took me by surprise. My mind was confused and unprepared.

'How about breakfast in the city tomorrow? I just remembered I've still got to go to the gym today.'

Silence, and she added abruptly, 'Sure. Breakfast sounds find. You have a good workout. Give me a call in the morning.'

After I hung up, crazy thoughts crossed my mind. To begin, I was uncertain why Teresa seemed so excited and willing to see me. And secondly, it felt extremely abnormal Frank told no one where he was going. Especially me. But then, the way we've been getting along lately, it wasn't all that surprising.

What if she'd already killed him?

I shivered at the thought.

I had to move on. My choices were few.

While parking behind my apartment, I decided to backtrack any Valium prescriptions she'd taken out in the last six months.

I knew of a long way and short way to find out what prescriptions Teresa Wilson had taken out in the past six months.

The long way was to go to every pharmacy in the area and ask the chemist, who would probably refuse to hand over information without me presenting a warrant of some sort. And I had no way of getting one since I was an unsworn investigator. Basically my powers of search were the same as those of the average citizen.

The other way was to use my laptop and tap into the easily accessible Medicare database. The database held all personal records in relation to anyone's medical history, including what doctors were attended and when they were attended, as well as the usual name, address and other personal identifying information.

I entered Teresa Wilson's name into the mainframe, and the computer spilled back her entire history since she acquired a Medicare card in 1981.

I jumped quickly to the last few entries and noted Teresa had attended four doctors in the Port Melbourne area the week prior to the 20th of February. Two weeks before that date, she'd visited four different doctors in the Malvern area in two days. Unfortunately, the Medicare database information was limited. It didn't tell me why she attended those doctors, and how many prescriptions had been written out for her.

I knew what I had to do next.

I printed a list of the eight doctors and was going to pay them a visit the following day, just after I had breakfast with Teresa.

While the records were being printed on my inkjet printer, something caught my eye. On Friday the 14th of March, Teresa Wilson had visited four doctors in the Richmond area, and on Saturday the 15th of March, four others in the Hawthorn area. My face creased with concern when I realised Frank lived in Richmond, only kilometres away, and she visited those doctors just when he began his week long holidays.

At first I tried to reason her action. I told myself that she'd probably needed something because of the pain she acquired from her wounds and scratches. But I knew this was nonsense. St Patrick's Hospital was following her progress, and there was no need for her to consult with doctors, especially eight different ones in two days.

I printed a list of all the doctors she had seen.

CHAPTER TWENTY-ONE

When I arrived at Terry Bennetts' Gymnasium on High Street at 9.46 p.m., Ken was doing one-hundred-and-twenty-pound deadlifts.

'You look shocking,' he said as soon as he saw me.

I had to admit he looked as good as ever. I gave him a run down on everything that was going on.

'I'm sorry to hear you've lost your job,' he said, 'but hell, you'll have no trouble finding something else. You're such an intelligent person.'

'I don't know if I want anything else. Right now, I just want to get my life back.'

'Nothing a good workout can't fix.'

Maybe that was true in his life as a librarian. But my life seemed more complicated than that.

I nodded and began my stretches.

No one else was in the gym, and although Ken had always been friendly to me, I was in no mood to hold a conversation. He must have sensed it because he avoided bothering me during my workout.

After doing forty-pound bench presses, I gulped half the water from my Coca-Cola drink bottle. The temperature in the gym was moderate, but for some reason I was as thirsty as hell.

I worked my biceps, triceps and abs.

At around 11.30 p.m., Ken left the gym.

Even though I was tired, I decided to stay on. Too much energy buzzed in my veins, be it from anger or fear. I kept thinking about the next day when I'd have breakfast with Teresa. God, how was I going to approach the subject?

'Don't be too harsh on yourself,' Ken shouted as he disappeared down the narrow concrete stairs.

Half an hour later, I finished a set of preacher curls, when suddenly I felt the urge to pass water. It must have been all this drinking. I had refilled the bottle twice already.

I went to the women's room, which happened to be right in the middle of the gymnasium. I guessed the gym was initially designed for men, but when women began pumping iron decades ago, the owner built a separate toilet. With the lack of room, the only place left was in the middle of the gym.

When I came out of the washroom, I nearly had a heart attack.

Teresa Wilson was standing in front of me, dressed in a grey flannel tracksuit with Nike runners and a sports bag by her side. She looked stunning, like one of those girls from the cover of a Cleo magazine.

I felt heat on my cheeks as I wondered what the hell she was doing here.

'Couldn't sleep,' she said casually. 'With Frank being away, I kept closing my eyes and having nightmares. Plus I needed the company.'

I nodded but was speechless.

'You okay?' she asked, obviously realising I was shocked to see her.

I forced a smile and said, 'Just tired. I've been working out for the last hour.'

'Don't mind if I join you?'

'Suit yourself, but I'll be finishing soon. How did you find this place, anyway?'

'Frank mentioned you went to the gym. When I asked him which one, he said Terry Bennetts'. I looked it up in the phone book.'

When she stepped under the light, I noticed her facial wounds and bruises had vanished completely with the help of make-up. One could not have guessed she'd been beaten and raped a month ago.

And that was because she never had been, I thought.

'Should you be doing exercises in the state you're in?' I asked.

'I'm easing back into it. Don't want to start in a year's time and find my body can't cope with it. You know what it's like. You stop working out for two weeks, and it's like starting from scratch again. I hate that feeling of having to readjust to a new life. You know, it's a bit like living without Jeremy. Such a shock.' She said that in a neutral tone, making me wonder if she was poking fun at me for some unknown reason.

I walked to the bench press and felt a cold sweat. What the hell was Teresa really doing here? I wasn't that great company.

'Hey, you gonna show me how to do these things?' Teresa asked, casually following me. 'You've got a great body. You come here often?'

I felt like she was trying to pick me up. 'Three to four times a week. It helps me sleep.'

I did a set of bench presses, and she said, 'My turn.'

I took a gulp of water from my Coca-Cola drink bottle and stood behind her while she lowered the forty-pound barbell to her chest twelve times.

'How's Frank doing?' I asked.

She pulled the bar up to the rack and said, 'He's fine. Never been better.'

'You guys really have something going, don't you?'

'I guess we do. Hey, you wouldn't be trying to take it away from me?'

I was taken back by her comment. 'What makes you say that?'

'Just that you were really close, that's all. I knew he had a crush on you. He told me.'

Great, I thought, now I'm the other woman.

After I finished my second set of bench presses, I felt exhausted. 'One more set and I'm going home,' I said. 'I'm buggered.'

'Sure,' she answered as she began her second set.

I swallowed the rest of my drink bottle.

When Teresa finished her set, I lay on the bench and placed my hands parallel on the barbell. I doubted I would be able to finish the set, but Teresa was watching me, and I hated her thinking I was a wimp.

I pushed the barbell up and lowered it to my chest.

Suddenly, my head began to spin. I pushed hard on the barbell, but it wasn't moving an inch.

'Give me a hand here,' I commanded to Teresa who was just standing behind me.

No response.

'Hey, lift the damn bar! It's getting heavy.'

I rolled my eyes back and saw her smiling. 'You're not such a tough little bitch after all,' she said, injecting her tone with sarcasm. 'What's the matter? Not enough iron in your diet?'

And then she laughed a crazy laugh, and I knew I had been right for the last few days. She was a textbook-case psychopath.

'Feeling a bit tired?' she went. 'Have another drink.'

And she laughed again.

My chest was hurting as I realised she'd spiked my water with Valium. I should have known. She must have spiked my drink bottle while I was in the washroom passing water. Now that I was laying on the bench, I did recall the water tasted kind of salty, but at the time I just shrugged it off.

'Get this fuckin' weight off me,' I screamed.

My eyes were getting heavier. The thirty-pound barbell began to feel like one-hundred pounds.

Teresa circled the bench and picked up a large circular weight from the floor. Casually she added it to the right side of the barbell, crushing my right breast.

'Christ, what are you doing?' I muttered.

She didn't say a word, but added another weight on the left side.

'You killed them, didn't you?' I asked, my chest crushing under the weight.

'Yes, I did,' she said, dryly. 'I killed them both.'

'Jesus,' I said, 'Why?'

'Because all men are bastards. You know that anyway. You told Frank when you left my apartment that night I killed Jeremy. You said men were responsible for all the mess in this world. And you were right.'

What was Frank doing? Screwing her or telling her every minute of his life?

'Why did you kill them?'

'Jeremy cheated on me.'

'And you cheated on him.'

'But he didn't know that. Walter told me Jeremy was going to divorce me and marry Claire.'

'So what? You didn't care about him anyway.' I struggled with the weights.

'That's right. But the bastard had been bleeding our savings and joint accounts to another account without telling me. He was going to dump and leave me penniless.'

'What about Walter?'

'He was going to dump me, anyway.'

I tried hard to push the weights up. 'Please, Teresa, take the bar off my chest. This has nothing to do with me.'

'I agree on that last point. But your actions don't reflect what you're telling me.' She circled the bench again and added more weights on the barbell. 'You're a sneaky little bitch. If you'd just dropped everything like you'd been told, all of this would have never happened. In fact we might even have become good friends. I meant it when I said I enjoyed talking to you at the hospital. Cross my heart, I really thought I'd found a friend.'

And so did I for a little while.

I felt contractions in my chest. I could hardly breath.

Teresa went on, 'Anyway, like I said, Walter was going to dump me. He didn't say anything, but I could tell by the look in his eyes. The bastards were going to leave me loveless and without a cent to my name. Walter took me to a restaurant one night and told me it was over. I felt miserable. I went to the doctor to get some Valium to O.D. myself.'

'You went to *eight* doctors,' I managed to say.

'You've done you're homework, I see. Well, you know, some doctors won't give you what you want on request. So I had to try a few of them until I got the amount of Valium I needed.'

She stood behind me and placed both hands on the barbell. 'Feeling a little chest congested? Don't worry, you'll be asleep any minute now. Won't feel a thing. Everybody'll think it was an accident. Dr Malina thought she was Arnold Schwarzenegger.'

'And how come you didn't go ahead with killing yourself?' I muttered, struggling for some air.

'I thought, fuck it, why should I die? They fucked me up, and I'm going to kill myself? Had a change of heart. I planned it two weeks ahead of time.'

'How could you do it?'

'I don't know. You know, sometimes you think about killing someone, like some jerk in the car next to you at the traffic light, but you never end up doing it. Well, it started like that, but I went one step further. They fucked me up, so I didn't have any choice. I killed Walter first. Easy as hell. I never knew it was so easy to kill someone. But you'd know about that. You'd see a lot of dead people in your line of work.'

I tried to answer, but no words came out of my mouth. I knew I wouldn't last another minute.

'Then I got Jeremy. Got him to fuck me first to make it look like a rape, spiked his hot chocolate with Valium, and when he tried to take his socks off, down he went to sleep for the last time.'

An image of Jeremy's decapitated body, wearing bloody socks, came back to mind.

Teresa went on, 'I messed up the place pretty badly, and it kind of broke my heart, cause I chose all the furniture and decor, being a set-designer, you know, I had an eye for this type of thing. And then I worked on myself. I know it looked really bad when you found me, but I had built myself up to it, and when I did it, it was almost pleasurable, a masochistic experience. And I thought the squash ball was a nice sadistic touch. Would make the whole thing much more credible.'

But you never thought about the forensic evidence, you little shit.

'You're right,' she said, as if she read my mind. 'I never thought about the forensic stuff. But I'm a set designer. What you see is what you get. I didn't give a shit whether I'd get caught or not. I just wanted to kill the three of them. Jeremy, Walter and that fuckin' little bitch, Claire Kendall. That was all

216

I ever wanted. Whatever happened after, I didn't give a shit.'

She pushed the bar down to my chest, and I felt one of my ribs crack.

The last thing I remembered before passing out was Ken appearing behind Teresa and whacking her on the head with a twenty-five pound dumbbell.

EPILOGUE

It's Easter Saturday morning, and I have been sleepless all night once again. My breasts are killing me. There's little traffic outside my bedroom because of the long weekend.

I stayed at St Patrick's Hospital for three days before being discharged with two fractured ribs and a bruised chest. Dr Larousse said my injuries would heal with time if I didn't strain myself. The only reason I go to the gym now is to talk to Ken and thank him over and over for saving my life. I hated not being able to workout. I feared becoming overweight and lazy, especially when I'd gotten used to going to the gym at least three times a week.

Ken passed Teresa on High Street on his way back from the gym the night she tried to kill me. When he saw her going inside the gym, he knew who she was.

'I'd never seen that person before, but I knew she wasn't a member. You and I are the only two people who workout between nine and twelve at night. I went back upstairs and listened to your conversation. I have to admit it took a bit of doing to walk up to her and hit her on the head with a dumbbell. I never hit anyone before, let alone a woman.'

Teresa pleaded guilty at her trial and seemed in no way overwhelmed by the three life sentences with no parole handed down by the Supreme Court. Teresa's defense made no application for an appeal.

Dr Charles W. Main wanted me charged for stealing

218

documents from his office, but Trevor Mitchell talked him out of it.

Frank had in fact gone on holiday for a week when I got assaulted. He'd been so confused about what I told him about Teresa that he left for Sydney by himself without telling anyone.

I've begun a relationship with Garry Wood.

Michael and I have booked each other a full day every week to make sure we wouldn't miss out on the more valuable parts of a mother-and-son relationship.

My contract with the VFSC and the CIB is re-instated, and they threw in a bonus as well. From now on I'm the only unsworn member of the VFSC who's not a police officer, but licensed to carry a weapon.

When Frank came to see me in hospital, he brought in twelve red roses and a brand new silver .380 semiautomatic pistol.

I'm now sitting at my kitchen table with a cup of black coffee. In one corner of the kitchen is Claire Kendall's plant, which I begged Frank to get for me. The plant is fully restored now and looks glad to be alive, just like I am.

This afternoon I will go and deliver it to Louis as an Easter present and a thank-you for all the trouble he went through for me.

I think about my future a lot and wonder if I want to continue working for the police or set myself up as a private investigator instead. It's a difficult choice either way.

I take a sip of coffee from my mug and think about people for a while. But Teresa's voice and laughter keeps ringing in my ears. I only saw her yesterday at the prison. She got away with an undisplaced skull fracture. We had a little chat. She seemed perfectly calm and aware of her situation and surroundings. For a moment, while talking to her, I forgot I was having a conversation with someone who tried to kill me. She was the same friendly Teresa I met weeks ago at the hospital.

When I was about to leave her in her tiny prison cell for the rest of her life, she said, 'If I had to do it again, I would do it again. I recommend it to other women out there. Get the bastards before they get you.'